Ruth Pirt
S0-AZC-215
Please return #403

Wolf River

Margaret Riddell

Copyright © 2013 by Margaret Riddell
First Edition – January 2013

ISBN
978-1-4602-1156-4 (Hardcover)
978-1-4602-1154-0 (Paperback)
978-1-4602-1155-7 (eBook)

All rights reserved.
This book is a work of fiction. Names, characters, places, and incidents are either the products of the author's imagination or are used fictitiously.

Picture credits:
Front Cover: Dust in the Wind, courtesy of Watercolourist Diane Murison, Gimli, Manitoba
Two Wolves, courtesy of Linda Picken, Linda Picken Art Studio, Bentonville, AR
Preface picture: The Swimming Hole, courtesy of Rhonda Rhodes, Rhonda Rhodes Dancing in the Rain Photography, Foreman, AR

No part of this publication may be reproduced in any form, or by any means, electronic or mechanical, including photocopying, recording, or any information browsing, storage, or retrieval system, without permission in writing from the publisher.

Produced by:

FriesenPress
Suite 300 – 852 Fort Street
Victoria, BC, Canada V8W 1H8

www.friesenpress.com

Distributed to the trade by The Ingram Book Company

Wolf River

Prologue

Wolf River meanders through the prairie and brush land of southern Manitoba, draining the higher lands to the north and west and eventually discharging its flow into the Red River. It is not a large river at all, except when it decides to flood; the rest of the time it is a dawdling stream nurturing small pike, northern crayfish, and white sucker. It is an old waterway, old enough to have changed direction many times, leaving empty disconnected oxbows and low remnants of banks where none should seem to be. Majestic river bottom forests of basswood, oak, elm, and cottonwood line the banks and are visible for many miles, rising from the big bluestem and Indian grass of the prairie like dark islands in a vast golden-green sea. Fragrant wolf willow and pink-blossomed buckbrush thrive in the transition between river and prairie. Wildlife abounds. Geese and ducks nest close to the steep shores, hidden by long overhangs of grass. White-tailed deer, beaver, rabbits, and raccoons share the riparian habitat with their predatory enemies: foxes, wolves, and the odd black bear.

It is late summer, 1905. Three children on horseback gallop full-out along the river trail. A wake of thick dust roils behind them. The grey powder spreads in the windless air and hangs in a choking haze above the trail.

There are two boys and a girl, ten or eleven years old. The tallest boy, the one with the wild red mop of curls, looks to be the eldest. The blond boy is smaller, wiry and thin, and the dark-haired girl is between them in size. The children veer close to the trees along the banks. They pull up for a moment by a stand of poplar to regroup before they continue the race. The rules are well-established. Ahead is a stretch of straight trail running alongside what is known as the long bend. At the far end of the straightaway a clump of white birch stands apart from the rest of the river bottom forest. Past the birch and out of sight around the curve of the river, an ancient burr oak towers over a grassy clearing. The first rider to circle both the birch and the oak before returning to the starting point is the winner. The smallest boy bleats a ragged whistle on a blade of grass and the horses are off.

The older boy and the girl lead by a few lengths. All three dig their bare heels into their horses' flanks and lean into the flying manes. They are excellent riders, fearless, in spite of their size. The thundering of hooves drowns out the raucous cawing of a family of crows. The rush of wind they create fills their ears and masks the beating tumble of wings when a large flock of prairie chickens catapults from the tall grass. The first two children reach the birch clump and lean into the turn, headed for the oak. They swing around its great trunk and head back into the dust. Once back on the straightaway, they realize the other boy has not followed. The haze of dust drifts aside and a riderless horse skitters along the trail by the poplars.

The girl giggles. *He's trying to fool us again.*

The boy sees a chance of a different game. He grins like a devil, his eyes dancing under his unruly shock of red hair. *Let's just go back around the bend and hide the horses in the trees. Then he'll have to look for us.*

The girl, in this trio, is the voice of reason. *But what if something really did happen?* Several minutes pass. *If this is just another joke…*

They ride back past the bend. The dust is sifting and falling into the tall grass. The riderless horse edges toward them, nervous, moving sideways like a cat confronting a large enemy. A huge lone crow wobbles onto a branch over the trail and perches nervously, uncharacteristically silent. The bird's black eyes dart back and forth intensely between the children and the horse. There is no sign of the fair-haired boy. Something is wrong.

The eldest boy gouges his heels into his horse's flanks. The girl wheels and follows.

The fall grass waves high around the pale poplar trunks and the children are almost on top of him by the time they see his strangely skewed legs poking out of the tall stems. The boy is silent, still. The girl falls from her horse in her hurry to be first at his side, her ten-year-old mind struggling to make sense of the distorted limbs—a wrist twisted sideways like a crooked branch, legs impossibly bent, his face red with blood. This will be an indelible moment in her mind. The grass sways in slow motion in her peripheral vision and she can feel the heat of the late afternoon sun on her back and the stickiness of sweat on her hands.

The red-headed boy pulls her away so he can get closer. He brushes his rusty curls from his eyes. He flattens a patch in the grass and he half lifts, half rolls his friend onto the smoothed circle. The girl is crying now, kneeling close to the ravaged face.

Stay close to him, the boy says. He throws himself on his horse and the girl registers the clattering of hoof beats dying away down the trail. Small thin moans, like dark injured birds, squeeze themselves from the boy's throat. Wind rises from the northwest, clawing at the long grass.

She moves sideways to get a closer look. A raw tangle of scrambled flesh and shards of oak bark covers his face. His pale hair is matted with blood and grass. She takes off her jacket and pulls it over the boy's upper body, finds the hand of his good arm and holds it tightly. He clenches cold fingers around hers. She is his only connection to the world.

The sun falls to the west and its heat dissipates in the wind. The girl shivers uncontrollably. Her jacket still covers the boy and she holds his hand, stroking it softly. The huge silent crow has stationed itself on a high branch above them. A chorus of hoof beats and rattling wagon and squeaking wheels rises in the distance. The discordance approaches and the girl can make out a rider—the older boy—followed by two men in the wagon.

One of the men is the doctor from town; the other is the injured boy's father. They leap from the wagon and the doctor kneels close to assess the damage. The men lift the boy, his broken limbs flopping grotesquely, into the wagon. The child makes no sound. Before the father has time to finish covering his son with a blanket the doctor has the wagon on the move. The boy and girl are left standing helplessly in a choking haze of dust.

Chapter 1

Winnipeg 1987

Tall fingers of smoke reach far above their brick chimneys into the purpling predawn sky. It is exceptionally cold for February, even in Winnipeg. The *Tribune* delivery boy trudges down Hampton Street, the hood of his parka tugged low over his forehead, his brown scarf pulled up to his eyes. He shifts the heavy canvas bag from one shoulder to the other, pulls out a folded newspaper with his clumsy mittened hand, and turns into the next house on his route.

Through the fuzzy slit between hood and scarf he makes out an anomalous dark shape on the verandah where he usually drops the paper. The boy leans in closer to see in the thinning darkness and bends toward the form. He jerks upright, trying to process what he sees.

He heaves the burdensome bag from his shoulder onto the front sidewalk and flounders in a wild panic through thigh-deep snow to the house next door. The windows are dark and there is no response to his frantic pounding. Just as the boy is making up his mind to go to the next house a yellow porch light comes on over his head, followed by a large unshaven man, bleary-eyed and angry at having his sleep disturbed. The man glares malevolently.

"What the hell do you want, kid?"

"Miss Christie is dead," the boy blurts out, his voice cracking. He points to the yellow bungalow next door. "She's dead…"

The man leans forward, adjusting his eyes to the early morning darkness. He can barely make out the curled figure on the veranda. He comes to life and barks to the boy, "You go and stay with her. I'll call for help. Jesus Christ."

The boy plows his way back to the veranda through the drifts. The surly neighbour's porch light now casts a slight glow on the scene. Laidie Christie huddles lifelessly on her veranda only a few feet from her front door, knees clutched to her chest under a thin blue and grey checked bathrobe. One threadbare brown slipper lies nearby. The skin of her face is bluish-white like skimmed-milk porcelain. Her wide-open eyes stare unblinkingly at the boy's feet. He struggles to escape the dead gaze, edging down and across the steps where he sits clutching his paper bag for protection.

The police and an ambulance arrive within minutes. The attendants position the frozen curled lump on a stretcher and siren away, as if there is still hope. The police remain to investigate and the paperboy lingers on the street to watch until he remembers his paper route, which is now nearly an hour late.

Blythe Wylie arrives home from her night shift at Winnipeg General. She puts a pot of coffee on to percolate, takes off her foam-soled institutional shoes, and detaches her white stockings from the garters on her girdle. She allows the stockings to sag down her thighs while she readies a footbath of hot water and Epsom salts. She pours herself a large mugful of coffee and dumps in six sugar cubes and enough cream to fill it to the brim. She sips the sweet mess down to a level that can be carried to the living room without spilling and settles comfortably into the armchair to watch the morning news.

She touches a toe to the fizzing water and eases both feet into the hot comfort. Perfect. She closes her eyes and leans back in the chair, her mind devoid of thought. An urgently loud knock at the front door shatters the silence. She can make out a red stripe on dark pants through the intricate forest of frost on the glass panes of the outside door. She pokes her steaming feet into her slippers.

"Blythe Wylie?" A serious-faced young police officer peers through the chain-guarded crack in the doorway. "I'm Constable Smithson with the Winnipeg Police Department. May I come inside for a moment?" He holds up some identification.

She nods, studying him warily. She slides open the chain and motions him into the entrance. Visions of her eighteen-year-old son Michael flash though her mind like an accelerated slide show. Car crash? Victim of violence? Detained somewhere against his will?

The officer respectfully removes his hat.

"Is Adelaide Christie your sister?"

She nods again, a new breed of dread growing in her mind.

The officer delivers the news professionally, unemotionally, but kindly. "I'm afraid I have bad news, Mrs. Wylie. She was found outside her home earlier this morning." He hesitates. Too long. "She froze to death. I'm very sorry."

Blythe turns her back on the officer and returns to the living room. He stands for a moment in the entrance, waiting for a response, a reaction.

"We need you to come and make a positive identification, just for the records. I could take you, if you like."

She tries to concentrate, but her thoughts scramble and collide. She tries to understand and manage what she has heard. The footbath steams and fizzes behind her. She pauses for a long time, trying to control her emotions.

"No, I'll come down by myself later."

He nods, somewhat disengaged from the situation. "Is there anything else we can do for you right now?" He opens the door slightly and stands with his hand on the doorknob, watching the cold air turn to fog as it seeps in around him.

"No. I'll be fine. Thank you."

He steps out and closes the door behind him, and his yellow stripes fade away.

"Fucking ridiculous," she says aloud. "I just thanked someone for telling me my sister froze to death. Fucking absurd."

Chapter 2

Millfield, 1914

In the fall of 1914 Millfield's first enlisted men gather at the train station to leave for the port of Halifax. A west wind slices cold rain into the young faces. They are boys, really, some of them only seventeen and eighteen, the rest in their early twenties. Ford and Ruby McCorrie and their son Colin stand in the brave-faced gathering of families and friends on the wet platform. The train chuffs softly, patiently, as if it knows the sadness its departure will bring.

The McCorries survey the group on the platform. Darwin and David, the skinny and pimply-faced McKenzie twins, fidget restlessly. Walter Cuthbert's wide, callused, farmer hand rests gently on his wife's pregnant belly. Widow Cowell sobs inconsolably at the imminent departure of her only son, Willie. Rusty O'Reilly pulls Saharah Fletcher close and meshes his fingers in her dark hair, whispering something in her ear. She laughs and tousles her fingers playfully in his unruly mop of red hair. He turns and shakes Colin's hand and rests his hand on his best friend's shoulder. They exchange a few quiet words. Les Linford, with feigned bravado and his trademark swagger, is first to board the train. The rest follow, laughing nervously and too loud.

Colin McCorrie will not be joining them. The recruiters who arrived in town when the call to arms came early in the war refused him enlistment because of his pronounced lopsided limp. While this is nothing more than a mild inconvenience to Colin, it is the basis of a firm denial by the recruiters. He fumes to think a childhood accident has the power to deprive him of the right to serve.

The train's whistle blasts and an explosion of white steam erupts and dissipates into the wet air. The people on the platform wave with spurious smiles and cheers. The train's windows, framing faces pressed to the hazy glass, slide past them, slowly at first and gaining speed as the slow grinding of iron wheels on iron rails transforms to a rumbling and purposeful cadence.

The boiler discharges another blast of steam and the train picks up its rhythmic tempo, heading east. Where the track curves just east of Millfield, the caboose follows the train into a froth of fog. The crowd, mostly quiet now, looks about, small-talking bravely among themselves, not certain what to do in this new context of life. The O'Reillys are first to disperse into the grey rain and within minutes the dripping platform is deserted. In the distance the train sounds one last mournful whistle.

Colin McCorrie's friends will sail across the Atlantic to engage in battle in places they have not yet heard of—Ypres, the Somme, Vimy Ridge, Passchendaele—names that will soon become all too well known.

Ford and Colin return to the affairs of farming. Haying and harvest long since complete, their attention turns to the livestock. The three milk cows that calved last spring and their offspring, now half grown, will spend the winter in the barn, feasting on hay still fragrant with the flowers of summer. Olga the sow has her pen at the back of the little barn, where she does nothing but eat and gestate since her rendezvous with O'Reilly's boar. Once a day the cattle and horses are let out to water at the wooden trough, and Gypsy, the Border collie, ensures they never deviate from their pathway to the well and back. Olga and the chickens have their water delivered by Ford in a large tin pail, which is usually half empty by the time it has sloshed its way to the barn. The only animals that continue to work through winter are the horses. They pull the wagon box, converted to sleigh runners for the winter, and they haul manure cleaned from the barn. Ford has trained them to walk slowly without reins while he forks the manure onto his fields where the snow cover allows. He stockpiles manure too and leaves it to decompose into dark rich compost for use on summer fallow or on Ruby's garden. The chickens huddle in their corner of the barn, refusing to lay all but the occasional rare egg. Ford mends harnesses and carries wood into the woodshed and takes cold ashes from the stove to the barn shed for the chickens to scratch in. Colin does all the snow shovelling, a never-ending task this winter. Ruby separates the cream from the milk much as she does in the summer, and in her spare time she is taken up with stitching utilitarian quilts and knitting heavy woollen afghans.

Spring dawns early on the land and Ford scrutinizes his fields daily for traces of black nudging into view from beneath the white snow. He and Colin inspect the plough and the grain seeder, where a colony of mice has evidently spent the winter. Colin's snow clearing evolves into carving sharp little gullies to carry melt water away from drifts in the yard. Ruby plants garden seeds in flat wooden boxes and puts them on top of the sideboard where the wide kitchen window faces full southern sun. The air smells sweetly of warming breezes and thawing manure and awakening earth.

Strong prevailing westerlies follow the quick melt. By the last week of April Ford is overcome by the spirit of agricultural optimism and can wait no longer. He harnesses the team of Old Jim and Custer to the plough and heads for the closest field. Ruby and Colin knowingly smile and exchange glances without comment. They watch Ford disappear down the trail followed at a distance by Gypsy the collie, who knows she is supposed to stay home but also seems to understand when she might be able to get away with something. Ford is uncharacteristically late for the noon meal, which they call dinner because it is the largest meal of the day. When Ruby at last sees him on the trail he is plodding along behind Old Jim and Custer, without the plough. Gypsy trots obediently at his side. The plough is bogged down in mud at the low end of the field. Ruby and Colin exchange a small, knowing glance.

When it's finally dry enough to work the land, Ford is past impatient, as are Old Jim and Custer. In the closest little field, they begin the furrowing. Although a few farmers have embraced tractors, Ford still uses a single blade plough, which requires him to guide from behind as he walks. The horses strain their powerful muscles against their yokes, literally dragging the plough through the soil. Ford's job is to counterbalance by pulling down on the plough to keep it in the ground. The work is mercilessly and unimaginably hard, toil that leaves the muscles in Ford's legs, back, and arms burning and the skin of his hands blistered and raw. When he feels his limbs begin to drain of strength, he uncouples the horses, climbs to Custer's back, and returns home, where he will spend the rest of the afternoon on chores and repairs. Colin has eaten and fed the animals and is waiting to take his turn. His limp, although not painful, makes him slightly slower than Ford, but the field is nevertheless finished by dark. This is the pattern of days, with variations in implements, fields, and weather, until the seed is all safely tucked into the rich loam.

By mid-June, waving lakes of young grain cover the prairie. Ruby's expansive garden thrives with potatoes, carrots, beans, and onions. A small digging close to the house is overflowing with sweet peas and daisies. The chickens, barred by Gypsy from entering the garden, scratch industriously for insects and small vegetation to supplement their daily feeding. Three new calves cavort in the pasture behind the house and Olga has given birth to eleven piglets. One of these is a sickly runt, which Olga eats.

All is well.

Chapter 3

Millfield, 1915

The day before Dominion Day, 1915, Ruby McCorrie complains to Ford of a sharp pain in her abdomen. This is enough to worry him. In all her thirty-nine years Ruby has never been sick, save for the occasional cold. She sailed through pregnancy and delivery without incident. She sprained her ankle once picking wild raspberries on the riverbank and suffered more from the inconvenience than the discomfort.

"Is there anything I can get for you? Anything I can do?"

Ruby immediately regrets telling Ford about the pain; the last thing she wants is to be fussed over. "Don't worry. You go and do the chores," she tells him. "I'll make some tea to settle my stomach. I'll be fine."

She begins peeling potatoes and scrubbing tiny new carrots for the mid-day meal. By noon the unremitting agony is nauseating. When Ford and Colin come in to wash up for dinner, Ruby is vomiting into the slop pail from under the sink. She cannot find words to explain the discomfort.

"It's hard to describe. It's terrible, and it doesn't let up." She doubles over. "I think it's getting worse."

Ford half leads, half carries her to the sofa. He feels the heat radiated from her skin. She curls on her side and draws her knees to her chest, whimpering with each breath. Ford sends Colin to fetch Dr. Millan. The doctor is away attending to a birth and by the time he pulls up in his black Model T just after two, Ruby is sleeping fitfully. The pain is greatly diminished.

"Best to just let her rest," he advises.

Within an hour she is again in great agony and even the smallest movement causes her to cry out. Dr. Millan returns to find her fiery with fever and nauseated, unable to bear the slightest touch on her abdomen.

"It's her appendix. I believe it's ruptured."

Ford and Colin stand helplessly. "When can you operate?" Ford asks.

"I can't, it's too late. I'll have to send her to Winnipeg," Millan says. "If you hurry, you'll just have time to get her on the train at four. There's no time to waste. I'll telegraph the Salvation Army Hospital and make arrangements for someone to get her from the train. I can't go with her, but you can make your way to the city tomorrow."

There are tears in Ford's eyes. "I'll go tonight," he says.

Colin hitches up the team of horses while Ford hurries to make a bed in the wagon bottom. He places the thick old buffalo robe on the bottom for comfort, then layers quilts and pillows on top. Ford carries Ruby to the wagon and covers her with a light blue quilt. The afternoon heat is parching and heavy but Ruby shivers violently. Ford stays with her and adds another quilt, pulling it up to her chin. Colin drives the team and they follow the doctor, shrouded in the hot grey haze of dust stirred up by the Model T. Ford carries her with great tenderness into the first passenger car and does all he can to settle her into her quilts and pillows with as much comfort as possible. Colin comes into the car just long enough to say goodbye.

"I love you, Ma. Everything will be fine." She opens her eyes and smiles through the pain, gripping his hand.

The next day, Dominion Day, is stiflingly hot by eight in the morning. Heat waves ripple the young fields under the gas-flame-blue sky. Colin finishes the farm chores and gets ready to go to town. He plans to spend the morning enjoying the holiday celebrations and will be there to meet the train when Ford returns before noon.

The Millfield Marching Band is in the street in front of the livery barn, getting ready to lead off the Dominion Day Parade. Colin stands with the lines of people gathered along the side of the street. A queue of shiny horses with riders costumed in red, white, and silver lines up in position behind the band. Behind them Colin can see the procession of brightly decorated floats, each pulled by a team of horses. The band strikes up "Rule Britannia".

Dr. Millan's car scuttles around the corner at that moment and the vehicle is still rolling when he jumps to the ground. He stumbles across the street in front of the emerging parade. He cannot speak by the time he reaches Colin.

Wheezing, stuttering, and pained, the doctor struggles to make words. "It's Ruby. They telegraphed a few minutes ago. Ruby… She…" He crumples against Colin, who yanks him away from the parade onlookers and over to the buggy.

"What?" A loaded silence. "What the hell are you saying?" Shock, disbelief. "Tell me, you bastard. What are you saying?"

Millan, leaning on the wagon, sobs a guttural male sound.

"It's my fault," he gasps. "I should have known. I've seen it before. I could have done something. I should have known…" He makes fists and pounds the top of the high rear wheel.

Colin bellows like a wounded bull and charges the doctor, knocking him to the ground. Someone pulls him back just as the band marches by. The four horse team prances as if in time to the music. The costumed riders wave Union Jacks at Colin and the doctor, and the horse-drawn floats roll around the corner towards them. The line of onlookers claps and cheers. Somewhere behind the floats, bagpipes wheeze joyfully.

Ruby and Ford come home on the train the next day, Ruby in a plain pine box smelling of fresh sap and shadowed forest. The sun, hotter than it has been all week, glints off the windows of the passenger cars. Colin watches the train, surreal and dreamlike, hissing to a stop in front of the platform. Sam Dunham the undertaker is there to meet Ford and Ruby as arranged by Dr. Millan. Ford steps from the first car, his face red-eyed, vacant, and uncomprehending. Colin hobbles forward with his lopsided limp to collapse against his father. The undertaker is speaking, but his words waft past Ford and Colin like a distant buzz. Ford's cousin Frank Osbert is there too, having brought Colin into town. He comes forward to shepherd Ford and Colin to his new Model-T while Dunham brings his horse-drawn hearse, its black curtains lowered, alongside the platform.

Two days later the sense of shock and bereavement permeates the packed gathering in the tiny Presbyterian Church in Millfield. Ford, silent and staring at his polished shoes, endures the funeral and interment, and Colin wills his own tears to delay their overflow. After the service Colin takes his father's elbow and guides him back to Frank Osbert's auto.

The next day neighbours and friends arrive in a constant stream bearing cakes, cold dinners, fresh bread, and garden bouquets, as is the custom. Ford sits on the back porch in the shade away from the visitors, staring across the farmyard and seeing nothing.

If Ruby McCorrie was well loved and respected in the community, the sentiment pales in comparison to her importance to Ford and Colin. Ruby was a strong, attractive woman, and the heartbeat of her family. The quiet and efficient management of her domain revolved around her love for her husband and son. This was Ruby: twice weekly baking of fat loaves of bread, pies of berries or apples in season, or cookies and biscuits; her knuckles worn red and cracked and raw from scrubbing lye soap into laundry on a ridged glass washboard, her clean laundry flapping and snapping like proud sails on the clothesline in the summer or frozen like fragrant wooden cut-outs in the winter; patiently ironing with her orderly row of flatirons on the woodstove while the clean scent of fresh starch steamed upward. This was Ruby: her wide garden with neatly weeded rows and staked tomatoes, her endless sewing and mending on her treadle machine, her mops and dust cloths shaking their grey gatherings outside the door. This was Ruby: separating cream from milk still warm and churning the thick liquid into pale butter, strewing feed for the chickens in wide arcs across the yard, poking the cranky hens aside with a stick to get to the eggs beneath, picking saskatoons and pincherries in the scruffy bush. This was Ruby, married to the love of her life and blessed with a son. This was Ruby, who loved her life.

Ford and Colin are thrust like unsuspecting children into a world operating in an alien language and with alien equipment. Ruby's kitchen, always an organized centre of good meals, warmth, and chatter, has morphed into a place of mystery, where fried eggs and black toast are the only items on the menu, except for some canning left from last fall and whatever benevolent neighbours provide when they have time. The garden rows fill with dandelion, thistle, and spreading portulaca, and peas and beans over-ripen. Wild turkeys eat the raspberries from the canes, seeming to know Ruby is no longer there to chase them away. Clean clothing quickly dwindles until only Sunday best is available, so they wear shirts and pants and underwear for days. Ford sleeps on the sofa in the living room to avoid his cold bed, where the scent of Ruby still clings to the pillows and sheets.

Generous neighbours continue to bring baked beans and meatloaves, cakes and bread, although the landslide of food has become a trickle. Mrs. Elliott stops by to drop off a saskatoon pie just as they are getting ready to sit down to another meal of eggs, black bacon, and green onions which Colin has managed to find in the jungle of weeds in the garden. She stands in the doorway, pie in hand covered by a white sugar-sack tea towel, and stares as politely as she can at the chaos. Dishes, caked with dried food, are piled high on the sideboard. A layer of dust dulls every visible surface. A pail of unwashed eggs sits by the door.

Finally she asks in a quietly controlled voice, "Is there anything you fellows need?"

Ford shakes head. "I don't think so, Ethel." He looks at Colin. "Can you think of anything?"

Colin can think of many things, but he cannot bring himself to ask for such enormous favours.

"Thank you, Mrs. Elliott," he manages. "We can let you know if we think of anything."

Ford nods agreeably to the pie with its high sugared crust. "Thank you for the pie."

Mrs. Elliott backs out of the doorway, swatting the flies away with her hand.

"All right, then." She peeks back through the screen on the door. "Maybe I'll call in again in a few days?"

The suggestion is not acknowledged, but she is satisfied she has planted a seed of thought.

True to her word, Ethel Elliott returns before the end of the week bearing four loaves of bread, this time just after supper, which tonight was eggs, canned tomatoes, and a slab of meatloaf that had been left on the kitchen table sometime during the day by someone unknown. Ethel's sixteen-year-old daughter Annie peeks shyly around her mother.

"Is it all right if we come in for a minute?" Ethel asks.

Colin nods, curious, and takes the box of still-warm bread and sets it on a chair. Ford is getting ready to do some chores outside, but motions Ethel and Annie to the living room. It is dim and gloomy in the shade of the drawn curtains.

Ethel and Annie take a seat on the sofa and Ford takes his place in his armchair, while Colin sits in Ruby's wooden rocker. Ethel is typically aggressive but today she struggles to find some delicacy with which to explain her suggestion.

"Ford," she begins carefully, "We think you might need some help. It just happens that Annie is looking to work away from home. She's good at housework and baking and laundry. You would have room for her. Would you think about it?"

Ford scratches at the four-day growth on his chin and shakes his head, not in refusal but in uncertainty. He has not had time since Ruby's death to even contemplate such an arrangement.

"I don't know, Ethel." He glances at Colin, who is trying to visualize Annie in Ruby's kitchen, Ruby's garden, and Ruby's henhouse. "I guess we'll think about it."

Ethel, unusually reticent, pushes her ample form up from the sofa and gestures in the direction of the door. Annie, eyes focused on the floor, follows her mother to the entrance.

"I'll come by tomorrow and you can let us know," says Ethel with a sympathetic smile.

Ford trails behind her to the door and follows them out on his way to the barn. Colin lingers in the murkiness of the living room for a few minutes, as if waiting for a verdict from Ruby. He can see the encroaching squalor as Ford will not and he knows Ethel is right. He remembers Annie from school. She was a quiet and simple girl, plain in appearance, working as hard as was possible for her capabilities, but it was clear she could not be taught more than the simplest concepts. Still, Annie helped the teacher with school chores like bringing in fresh water once a day from the pump, gathering and handing out papers, cleaning the blackboards and brushes, and wiping the desks of their melange of ink and glue and crumbs at the end of the day. But what would she be able to do for the McCorries?

Colin joins Ford at the barn to finish the evening chores.

Annie Elliott arrives to start work very early in the morning on Monday. Bill Elliott hands her over, along with her own wooden cot, a chest of drawers made from roughly planed wood, and two sugar sacks filled with clothing and her few personal items. Ford and Colin have moved things from a small bedroom at the back of the kitchen to make a place for her. Bill unloads everything from the wagon, has a short whispered conversation with Ford, and briefly hugs his daughter, whose pale panicked face looks as if she believes she has just been delivered to a slaughterhouse. Colin shows her to the space they have readied and she whispers a thin thank you as they bring her belongings to the door. The room is not much larger than a cubbyhole but somehow Annie manages to get everything arranged with breathing space to spare. The two men watch from the far end of the kitchen until Annie closes her narrow door. They sit in silence for a few minutes, not speaking but each contemplating this new female conundrum, so unlike Ruby but in her own way already mysterious.

The men arrive at suppertime and wash up outside in a basin of cold water from the pump. They hesitate at the door before entering to find the table properly set and three pots bubbling on the woodstove, which has converted the kitchen into a sweltering cave. The wooden floor has been swept and dishes drain on the sideboard. Head down, Annie delivers her achievements to the table with wordless apology and retreats to her room. Ford and Colin eat in silence. They marvel at the pork chops, potatoes, and fresh garden carrots found somehow in the weedy mess. Baking powder biscuits and a slab of chocolate cake sit waiting on the table, still warm.

As one of her first missions, Annie strips the beds of their sheets and quilts. She scrubs them outside on the washboard and hangs them in the sunshine to dry. In the days to come, the garden is once again presentable, the eggs gathered and washed, cream separated from fresh milk, and fresh bread sits in the cupboard. Clean laundry appears weekly on the foot of each bed. Although Annie does not appear to have a problem washing the men's clothing, she flatly refuses to put it away. Annie has been convinced to eat at the table with the men. Ford returns to his bedroom.

Chapter 4

Millfield, 1915

One by one, the men of war come back to Millfield as they left. Even those with absent limbs, blinded eyes, and horrific, unspeakable scars alight from the train with joy to be home. Some arrive in a different way, and the huddled families on the platform bear witness to their final sacrifice. These times, the train gives the impression of being sombre and slower than usual, chuffing patiently while railway employees unload the plain coffins onto the platform. Elmer Land, the postmaster's son. Darwin McKenzie, one of the pimply-faced twins. Annie Elliot's brother, Andy. Widow Cowell's only son Willie. Dunham the undertaker always stands inconspicuously off to one side, as if feeling guilty to be profiting from the tragedies of war.

It is early April, 1915, almost six months since the train pulled out with the community's first group of enlisted men. Rain fell then, and a chilled grey drizzle returns to Millfield today to settle silently upon the huddle of mourners. Colin brings Sahara Fletcher to Millfield to join the large O'Reilly family at the train station where they wait for their son and brother Rusty. The O'Reillys crowd together in a tight group. Two of the younger children duck out from time to time between adult legs, trying to comprehend the tangible grief on the platform. The whistle shrieks, its message concentrated and intense in the heavy wet air, and the O'Reillys turn outward and rearrange their cluster of misery closer to the track. They are oblivious to everyone on the platform, including Colin and Sahara, who stand side by side with arms around each other's waists. Undertaker Dunham receives Rusty O'Reilly's coffin, and the family, not noticing the grey mud clumping heavily on their shoes, follows him on foot to the funeral parlour.

The procession fades around the corner and a young man, a stranger with a pronounced limp much like Colin's, climbs down from the train. He bends under the weight of an army kitbag bursting at the seams. Everyone is gone from the platform except Colin and Saharah. The man approaches them, extending his hand.

"Mac Ward," he offers. "I'm wondering if you can direct me to the Land Titles Office?"

"It's right down Main Street," Colin points. "The last building on the right. You settling here?"

Mac Ward nods. "I'm supposed to have a quarter section west of town but I'm looking for a rooming house for right now. Is there one in Millfield?"

Colin points again. "See that blue three-storey over there? That's Mrs. Collins' house. I hear she runs a good place."

"All right, then. Thanks for your help. I hope I'll see you again sometime."

"Well, good luck with everything. By the way, I'm Colin McCorrie, and this is Sahara Fletcher."

"Pleased to meet you both." Mac Ward tips his hat and turns in the direction of Mrs. Collins' blue rooming house.

Late August is that short interlude between the heavy heat of summer and the frantic pace of reaping and storing, the last reprieve before school. Colin McCorrie and Rusty O'Reilly always met Saharah Fletcher by the tallest basswoods at the long bend of the river, equidistant from each of their farms. But on this day only Colin and Saharah—no longer children—trot their horses along the river trail. They dismount in a stand of soaring basswood and leave the horses free to graze. In the three and a half months since Rusty's funeral, this is the first chance they have found to spend time together. Both feel the need for a therapeutic connection.

Wolf River, the scene of endless meetings and childhood collaborations, catalyzed the bond between the three friends. Now they are two. The river exists as a spiritual entity; a fourth character. It is a carrier of memory, of closeness.

"Do you remember all the picnics we used to have down here by the saskatoon bushes?" Saharah asks. "I always had to steal food from our pantry because Mother wouldn't allow me to eat away from home. Not even for a picnic."

Colin brushes his blond hair from his eyes and chuckles. "And what about the time you brought that cold chicken she was saving for company? She never did find out where it went, did she?"

"I think that was the same time Rusty brought the lemonade he accidentally made with salt instead of sugar." They both shudder at the memory of the disgusting taste.

"And what about the wood ticks?" Saharah is giggling. "I used to be afraid of them and you and Rusty always made me check your heads to see if you had any. I always felt like an old monkey, picking through your hair."

Colin looks at the picture in his mind. "Well, at least you didn't eat them like monkeys do."

"Like the time you dared Rusty to eat that big water beetle. He just crunched it down like candy, like it was something he did all the time, and we weren't even finished laughing when he ran into the grass and threw it up." This memory provokes teary-eyed laughter. Colin leans back against the tree and rubs his side.

"But I think the swimming was best of all. It's a wonder we didn't kill ourselves on that shaky old diving board."

"You and Rusty got to be such fast swimmers, and I was always spitting mad because I couldn't keep up."

"Maybe that's because you always wore clothes."

Saharah blushes. All three of them swam naked until they were about twelve, when encroaching puberty caused Saharah to adopt old cut off overalls and a blouse with its sleeves torn away. She insisted the boys wear something too. Rusty and Colin didn't see the point, but they abided by the new rule—they had to if they wanted her company in the river.

"And what about the old canoe?" Ford had helped Colin dig out the centre of a large basswood log with his wood axe, one of the few times there was any parental involvement in matters riparian.

"We spent all summer making a pier for that canoe out of crooked fence posts and binder twine. It took us so long I don't think we ever got a chance to use it."

"Well, at least we got the rope bridge finished."

Saharah shakes her head. "That's another story altogether. I'll never know what kept it from falling into the water. I think Rusty spent more time fixing it than we did using it."

"You miss Rusty a lot, don't you?"

"I'll always miss Rusty." She watches a water beetle skim across the river, leaving fragile touches of movement in its wake. "I'll always love him."

"Me too."

The silence stretches like a piece of gossamer.

Saharah leans against the rough bark of the basswood. "And I'll always love you, Colin McCorrie." She studies a spreading ripple in the river where a surfacing muskrat cuts through the water. She concentrates on the smooth wake behind the animal, widening and dissipating. "I've loved you since the day of your accident."

Colin assimilates this news cautiously. "My God, Saharah, we were just little kids when that happened."

"What difference does that make? It doesn't change how I felt. How I feel."

"I always thought you and Rusty were… "

"No," she interrupts. "It was you." She lifts her hand to the ropy cicatrix covering his left cheek and jaw and runs her fingers over its roughness. "It was always you."

No one is surprised when Colin marries Saharah Fletcher on the last Saturday of July, 1916, just over a year after Rusty's death. They are twenty and nineteen.

"I love you, Saharah McCorrie," Colin whispers in her ear.

She giggles and touches her fingertips to his scarred face. "And I love you, Colin McCorrie."

Everyone is happy—except for Ivy Fletcher and Annie Elliott.

Ivy is furious at having no say in the matter of the wedding—not the date, not the small list of guests, not even in Saharah's choice of a flowing pink silk dress. *And to think they married in the McCorrie's garden and not in the church in town.* She fumes. *Our only daughter surely deserves better than a limping, scar-faced farmer.*

Annie's job at the McCorrie farm is now finished after a scant twelve months. Her confidence and self-esteem have flourished with her responsibilities and as much as she dreaded leaving home, she now dreads returning. Colin and Saharah walk with Annie to the Elliott wagon, which has arrived to take her home, and Sahara hugs her kindly. "I promise I'll get you to come back if I ever need some extra help."

Saharah knows that will be soon.

Chapter 5

Winnipeg, 1987

Blythe Wylie returns from the morgue. The paperwork is complete. She has collected the yellow plastic bag containing her sister's belongings (one checked bathrobe, one slipper, one silver ring, one set of upper dentures, eyeglasses, one folded envelope.) She now stands before the yellow bungalow on Hampton Street, at last ready to begin the task of dealing with Laidie's affairs. A small piece of used plywood covers a broken pane in the door, which had been locked the morning Laidie was discovered. Blythe is expecting an antiaura of darkness to be surrounding the house, but it looks exactly as she remembers; bright and homey. She sucks in a long breath of cold air and huffs it out in an icy fog.

The specter of Laidie's frozen body refuses to remove itself from the yellow verandah. Blythe understands all too well the physiology of freezing to death. Violent shivering and fear, the pain of the cold as it bites razor-sharp teeth into hands and feet. Apathy encroaching on action, dimming thought. Disorientation and, finally, senseless resignation as the body cools to a state of non-function. Freezing blood filling the extremities with hard blood-crystals, and perhaps, as some claim, a final sensation of comfort as the heart pumps warmth into an ever-decreasing space.

Blythe last saw Laidie only a week before her death, but it has been several years since she last visited in this house. They spoke almost daily by phone and Laidie usually came to Blythe's place for dinner a couple of times a month, because, she said, it was more convenient that way. Besides, Blythe was allergic to Ricky and Spiff, the two little spaniels that were Laidie's only companions. When Laidie came to visit she often brought bags of day-old bread from the bakery, or a box of chocolates, or sometimes little packages of meat ends from the deli. I don't ever have you over to my place, she would say, it's the least I can do.

Blythe pulls another deep icy breath into her lungs, squares her shoulders, and unlocks the deadbolt with the key the police found inside. She pushes the door open and eases inside like a trespassing cat burglar.

The eye-watering stench hits her like a sucker punch. The exact source is impossible to pinpoint, as no part of the floor can be seen under piles of clothing, papers, and garbage. Labyrinthine passages snake through the litter, leading to essential areas like the stove or sink or bathroom. Dishes, caked with old food and mold, litter the table and countertops. Soiled paper plates spill from garbage bags. A layer of greasy brown sludge coats the sink and stove. Tin cans are scattered everywhere, some with contents so ancient only hardened casts of once-food lie shrunken in their bottoms. When Blythe touches them, clouds of tiny winged insects rise up like puffs of smoke. Discarded skins of larder beetle larvae are scattered among the tins and the adults and other insects scuttle for cover when their hiding places are disturbed. The pantry is stacked floor to ceiling with empty cereal boxes, plastic containers, and hundreds of plastic and paper bags. Along the wall next to the refrigerator stands a line of milk cartons with contents in all stages of decay—some still hold sour liquid, others solid curd, but most contain hardened orange bricks of what used to be milk. The living room is no better. Trails angle through the debris. There are mouse droppings on the floor, crumpled tissues testifying mutely to colds and the odd nosebleed, stacks of old newspapers and magazines, and bagged garbage. There are dozens of cardboard boxes, bulging and sealed. Horrified, Blythe moves along as quickly as she can, her arms pressed tightly to her sides, cautious about where she plants her steps.

She pushes on the door to the basement. It's jammed on a clump of something grey and soggy, like a small sack of wet mud. With an extra heave the door squawks open on hinges stained with rust.

This is where the dogs lived. Bones and remnants of food garbage putrefy at the foot of the stairs where they had been tossed. The floor is covered with dog feces, some recent, some dessicated. Blythe realizes this is the underlying source of the nauseating stench that pervades the rest of the house. From halfway down the steps she can make out dark water in the uncovered sewer drain. She knows the police have already removed the two worm-infested spaniels. By the information in their report to her, the dogs were unable to walk and had to be euthanized. She cannot force herself to descend further and backs up the stairs as if ready to defend herself from some kind of entity that threatens to surge up from the filth.

Disbelief. *When the hell did all this happen? When was the last time I was in here? Was it just before the boys and I moved out?* Blythe cannot remember.

The stairway to the second floor is barely passable. Junk is littered on every step. The two tiny upstairs bedrooms hold only the skeletal furniture of the past. The air is dank and musty. *Nothing to see here.* Blythe goes downstairs again.

She is dreading the bathroom and bedroom and leaves them until last. Steeling herself, she pushes the closed bathroom door inward. She's astonished. It's a surreal enclave in the midst of chaos. The pale yellow tub and sink and toilet are all clean, their porcelain surfaces gleaming like paint on a new car. A row of toiletries stands guard along the back of the vanity—shampoos, lotions, and bath oils. The medicine cabinet above the sink is sparsely populated with a few prescription bottles: medication for high blood pressure, Tylenol with codeine, thyroid tablets, and a few over-the-counters like antacid tablets, laxatives, and Buckley's cough syrup. An unopened box of Band-Aids and four toothbrushes, still in their cellophane wraps, occupy the top shelf. An oversized blue towel is folded in thirds and draped over a bar near the tub. The tiled floor is spotless and shiny and smells of wax. Blythe sits on the edge of the yellow tub and contemplates the incongruity of the bathroom.

The door to Laidie's bedroom is also closed. Blythe pushes it open cautiously. A maze of trails snakes through piles of magazines and unreturned library books, used tissues and unwashed clothing, and cardboard boxes of all sizes taped shut with grey duct tape. In the cedar-lined closet, however, clean dresses and suits hang in clear plastic dry cleaners' bags, twist-tied shut. The bed is not made but the bedding has been straightened and appears fresh. The slightly open window lets in a hint of cold winter air. In spite of the litter on the floor, the bedroom smells of lavender potpourri. Blythe decides to start in this room, where there is already a passageway between the bed and the closet.

She sets out the plastic coated dresses and sweaters and blouses on the bed, estimating how many boxes she will need for packing. The shoes at the bottom of the closet are stored in their original boxes and stacked four high. There must be thirty pairs, she guesses. She leaves the shoes, Laidie's weakness, in the closet for now. She empties the dresser drawers of wide white cotton panties, sturdy bras with ample cups and wide straps, an overabundance of hose and pantyhose, and enough socks to outfit a small militia. Everything is clean, mended, and respectable.

In death as in life, Laidie is an enigma.

The next day Blythe will bring boxes and begin to pack what is salvageable. The trash and litter she will leave for a housecleaning business to deal with.

Blythe supervises the two men she has hired to remove the garbage and newspapers and mouldering food remains from Laidie's house. They will be charging double to clean up the disaster in the basement. When they have finished, the exterminator she has engaged will come to disinfect the basement and fumigate the main floor. Once she has a space in which to work, she will go through the cupboards and drawers and the brown cardboard boxes. In the meantime, she continues her exploration of the rest of the main floor.

There is little of value in the kitchen, but the dining room has guarded its treasures well, probably because Laidie used the area only for storage. Mhairi Christie's Spode dinner set and some silverware and lace table linens are preserved in the china cabinet behind glass doors dim with grime. Blythe thinks she will be able to refinish the cabinet, along with the oak table and chairs that followed her family from Ontario so long ago. She examines the delicate floral carvings on the legs of the table and the backs of the chairs, and can hear her father's voice telling whomever will listen about the superior craftsmanship of the eastern provinces.

Blythe returns to the bedroom. There is a second closet behind the door and she unloads the contents of the shelves onto the bed. Cartons of tiny jars, balls of string, carefully folded used gift wrap, a huge box of greeting cards dating back decades, bags of ragged nylon stockings, ancient bottles of decaying perfume (probably Mhairi's), box upon box of fancy notepaper with matching envelopes —all these Blythe places in black garbage bags and sets outside the door for the waste removal crew. Many of the boxes sealed with duct tape contain only newspapers and magazines. She doesn't even attempt to sort through these before putting them out to be included on the cleaners' truck.

Blythe has purposely left the cedar chest at the foot of Laidie's bed until last. She pushes the button-like opener and eases open the weighty lid. The nostalgic fragrance of cedar fills her nostrils. Mhairi and Orville gave the cedar chest to Laidie on her eighteenth birthday. When Blythe was very young she loved to be invited to see the treasures within. Laidie referred offhandedly to the piece of furniture as the "hope chest". Blythe was always acutely aware of the great significance of the chest to Mhairi, and of Laidie's indifference, which she did not understand.

It has been many years since Blythe has explored the contents of the chest, but she remembers the order in which things will be removed and replaced. The top pieces are embroidered linens wrapped in white tissue, followed by white towels with finely tatted lace edging done by Mhairi. A cardboard folder protects dozens of crocheted doilies and a pineapple patterned tablecloth, along with embroidered "luncheon cloths", as Mhairi called them. As Blythe places each layer in order on the bed, the articles become weightier. A creamy woollen blanket is the penultimate stratum, laid out to cover small boxes, cartons, and scrapbooks. Pencil sketches, dozens of them, are bundled and tied with string. A worn red velvet bag of antique jewelry fills a crack between boxes and a paper bag stuffed to bursting with old black-and-white photo albums, scrapbooks, and newspaper clippings lies at the bottom of the trove. She packs up the boxes and bags and scrapbooks into a laundry basket to take home where she will be free to spend as much time exploring them as she wishes. Later.

The last item is a polished wooden box fitted tightly into one end of the chest. Blythe knows it holds the handsome silverware she loved to admire. Inside the chest, each piece is carefully wrapped in a thin piece of cotton to protect it from tarnishing. She unwraps a silver coffee spoon and is shocked to see the dark gunmetal discolouration that covers it like a blackened skin. The next two pieces are the same. Blythe holds the three spoons in her hand. *They're just like the things and people we try to protect. Sooner or later, no matter how well we guard those we love, no matter how well we hide things of the past, no matter what we do to cover our steps, the time comes when everything is laid bare. Sooner or later the truth will overwhelm, dark and shiny and astonishing.*

Blythe leans in to take one more breath of the sweet cedar fragrance before she closes the lid. She stands to leave and as she does so, she makes out something tucked into the darkness of the other corner of the bottom compartment. She lifts it into the light. It is a small box handcrafted of smooth white birch bark. The corners are folded and tucked in and carefully glued and tiny bark hinges hold the lid to the box. There is a slightly uneven initial "L" carved from a pale wood and stuck to the hinged lid with yellowed glue, which has squeezed out around its edges. The tin clasp on the front is attached with fine wire and a tiny padlock secures it. There is no key. Blythe adds it to the basket of boxes and scrapbooks to take home.

Chapter 6

Millfield, 1915

This soft June rain, now into its second day, is a blessing to the farmers of the Wolf River community east of Millfield. Crops and pastures drink up the moisture and one can almost hear the daily growth of wheat and hay.

Mac Ward has worked with tireless passion since arriving here nearly three months ago. He is exhausted. The rain is a blessing to Mac too, but mostly in the sense that he is forced to rest. He lies on the thin mattress on his bed and listens to the raindrops' small clatter on his roof. This is one of the few times of late he has had a chance to do nothing but think. Mhairi comes to mind. Mac has not written to his sister since he arrived in Millfield, except to send her his address. Unlike Mac, Mhairi is a faithful correspondent. Her letters still arrive as regularly as they did during the war. She never questions why most of them go unanswered. Mac rises and goes to his kitchen table with paper and pen.

Millfield, Manitoba, 10th June, 1915

My dearest Mhairi,

Forgive me for not writing you sooner. The transition from soldier to farmer has been challenging, to say the least. I must admit, it bothered me a great deal at first to have been sent home in a disabled state, but my injured leg has now healed well enough to allow me to work and I am grateful for that. First of all, congratulations on your engagement. I have worried about you being alone since Ma and Pap died. I will have peace of mind knowing you have Orville to take care of you. I believe I only met him once, but it sounds like he is an upright citizen and will be a good provider. I wish I could be there for your wedding on January, New Years, but it will not be possible. The quarter section I bought here is good land, and I was able to afford to buy animals and equipment and have enough for buildings, which I plan to be a house and small barn. I have stayed at a Mrs. Collins' boarding house in Millfield, riding back and forth to my farm on one of my new horses, until I had a roof to cover me. As you must be able to imagine, the past three months have not allowed me any time except for work and sleep. Finally, with the help of my fine neighbours, I have a small but comfortable cabin and a little shelter for the two cows and a team of horses I bought at auction in Millfield. A man came from Massinon last week to witch a well for me. Even though a neighbour recommended him, I have to say I was more than a bit skeptical. He showed up with nothing but a Y shaped willow branch, stripped of its leaves. He held the branch by the y and put the pointed end out in front of himself and went off back and forth across my yard. I was trying not to laugh, as he looked so foolish, but all of a sudden he stopped dead in his tracks and the piece of willow started to shake as if it were trying to get out of his hands and then the end pulled down and pointed at a spot on the ground. There's your well, he said. He marked it with a stone and I paid him his two dollars and guess what? I started digging a hole right after he left and the next day I was only 8 feet down and the water started to gush up in the bottom. I almost hate to admit it, but the water is excellent and plentiful. I have managed to clear enough poplar and scrub brush to create a little field of about ten acres, and after burning out the stumps I plan to have it ready for a crop next year. Of course, I have very little money left and I hope to be able to afford to eat over the winter! Both my cows will have calves next spring, and then I will have milk. In the meantime, Mrs. McCorrie brings me skim milk once or twice a week. The McCorries, by the way, are my nearest neighbours. Their place is called Wolf River Acres and it is one of the best farms in the district. Ford and Ruby and their son Colin and are the kindest and most helpful people one could imagine. Once in a while Mrs. McCorrie sends Ford or Colin over with a pie or some stew and I must tell you it is a great treat after my efforts at bachelor cooking. It is a good thing I have six hens, as they keep me supplied with eggs. I have something in common with Colin, as he has some bad scars and a leg injury from a childhood mishap and was not allowed to go to war. I, perhaps better than anyone, can now imagine how he feels. When the time comes, I have promised to help the McCorries with fall work in exchange for all they have done for me. I shall write you again when all is finished and ready for winter, which by the way they tell me will be colder than anything I have known in Ontario. I believe they are just trying to frighten me.

I hope all is well with you, dear sister.

Love, Your Brother Mac

Millfield Manitoba 23rd July, 1915

Dearest Mhairi,

You will no doubt be surprised to receive word from me so soon after my last letter, but I feel a need to put my thoughts down on paper. You will remember my mentioning Mrs. Ruby McCorrie the last time I wrote you? Well, poor Mrs. McCorrie has met an untimely death from a ruptured appendix. Everyone around Millfield is still shocked and disbelieving at her passing, which occurred about three weeks ago on Dominion Day. She was becoming like a second mother to me, and a lovely lady. As I have become good friends with her son Colin I can see firsthand how the tragedy is breaking his heart. Truly though, it is her husband

Ford who is suffering most. No one has seen him since her funeral. 25th July – I am back, after two days! One never knows what might happen next around here! Three of the McCorries' cows got loose and Colin was knocking at mye door asking for my help to round them up. By the time we accomplished the task it was late and, truth be told, I forgot about my letter. At any rate, there is a small bit of better news. Ford and Colin have been persuaded to engage a hired girl. She is only sixteen and her name is Annie Elliott. Colin says she is a bit simple but apparently has been well trained to cook and clean. I doubt that she will be able to make pies and bread like Mrs. McCorrie, but at least the men will now not starve. I shall try to write again soon my dear sister.

Your loving brother, Mac

Millfield Manitoba July 31, 1916

My dearest sister and Orville,

I am terribly ashamed to have let time slide for so long without writing to you. It is raining today so this is a good time to take up my pen. It is difficult to explain how busy and demanding work on a prairie homestead can be. This time of the year I am always up with the sun and working until dark. Even the winter months have much to keep me busy, but I must admit I have become good friends with Colin McCorrie and over the winter he and I spent a good deal of time playing cards, checkers, and cribbage, as well as going to Millfield perhaps more often than need be for some social visiting with a few of his friends (that is, when he was not with his girlfriend Saharah Fletcher.) As you can probably figure out, I am leading up to other news. Colin confided in me about two weeks ago that Saharah is "in a family way," as it is described, and just this weekend they were married. I was more than honoured to be the best man, which was a totally new experience for me. The only person who is not happy about the wedding is Annie Elliott, as she no longer has a job, with Saharah wanting to take over the cooking and cleaning. Oh, and I understand Saharah's mother Ivy also is not happy with Saharah's choice of husband. But from what Colin tells me, Mrs. Fletcher isn't happy with most things. Saharah, by the way, is a fine little person and I can tell she loves Colin dearly, even with his scars and his limp. My cows both had calves this spring, a heifer and a little bull (I named them Bessie and Bifteck). I believe I will have the bull calf made into a steer and I will have him slaughtered (I hesitate to use that word, as he is such a playful little fellow) so in a year and a half I will be able to be part of the beef ring. I am certain that is not something you would have heard about. There is a lot of beef on one of these animals, and none of us have a way of keeping it from spoiling, so the farmers take turns butchering a steer and everyone comes to help on that day and divide up the meat to take home. That way there is always fresh meat. Of course it is not so much of a problem in winter as we can keep it frozen in a barrel outside. I have been buying my beef from the ring so far and that has worked well, but still I look forward to being able to be more a part of it. My little field of wheat is thriving, but we have had a good bit of rain and are all hoping for some hot dry weather soon to speed up ripening. There is a farmer on the other side of Millfield, Charlie Wilton, who has a new threshing machine and a steam powered tractor and he takes his outfit around the farms in the fall, as few farmers can afford a big machine like that. He has agreed to do my wheat. You will be surprised to hear I even have a garden this year. Most of it is potatoes with the rest planted to carrots and onions. I have dug a small root cellar right next to the back porch so I can access it from inside the porch. It has dirt walls and I have a wooden cover to put on once it gets cold enough to freeze, and then some straw to keep the frost out. I will let you know how it works. Please keep your letters coming, even if you don't hear from me.

Your loving brother, Mac

January, 1917

Mhairi Christie unfolds the white tissue covering the dried roses and baby's breath saved from her wedding bouquet a year ago. The color is still amazingly true: dark velvety red petals nestled in a creamy cloud of tiny stars. She arranges the flowers on a crocheted doily on a glass platter, being careful not to break the fragile petals. She lays a coil of pink ribbon around the arrangement before setting the platter in the centre of the table. Two tall white candles flank the roses.

Orville will be home in a few minutes, at ten to six. Everything will be ready to serve at six, as he prefers. Mhairi takes one last look around the kitchen before retreating to the bedroom to change her clothes. She puts on a deep blue dress, new, with narrow white lace around the neckline and sleeves. The pearls Orville gave her for a wedding present shine at her throat. He has not mentioned the anniversary. Mhairi wonders what he might have in store for her.

The kitchen breathes roast beef and gravy and cinnamon apple pie. Coffee gurgles in the heirloom glass percolator that belonged to her mother. White china gleams in the flickers of just-lit candles. Everything is perfect.

Orville appears right on time, brushes wordlessly past Mhairi on the way to his office. *That's just the way he is. I'm getting used to it. It doesn't mean he doesn't love me. It's just the way he is.* Mhairi sets the roast on a plate, mashes the potatoes, butters the carrots and turnips, and ladles out a dish of homemade horseradish. She gives the gravy a final stir to make sure there are no lumps, cuts the apple pie into sixths, fingers the pearls at her neck, and waits.

Orville, at precisely six o'clock, comes to the table. "What's all this fuss about? Are we having company?"

"Orville? It's our first anniversary. You didn't forget, did you?"

He takes in the flowers in their nest of pink ribbon, the candles, the immaculate table setting. "No, I didn't forget. To me, it's the wedding day that was important. Not a day a year later. Do you want me to carve that roast, or are you going to leave it sit on the sideboard?"

Suddenly the pearls are heavy and strangling around Mhairi's neck. She pulls in a thin breath past the rising tightness in her throat. "I'm sorry, Orville, I just thought…"

"Never mind. Let's eat. I've had a long day."

Furious tears burn Mhairi's eyes and she battles to contain them. Everything she has so lovingly prepared now seems dull and pathetic. Orville heaps his plate full; obviously everything looks good to him. He leans back and looks around the table to make sure he has not missed anything.

"Do you mean to tell me that you made roast beef and there's no Yorkshire Pudding to go with it?"

"I'm sorry, Orville. I didn't think of it, but..."

"Never mind. You'd better get busy on that plate of yours."

Every mouthful goes down like thick paste, sticking on the painful lump in her throat. She is determined not to let him know how badly he has crushed her. She finishes everything and gets up for the pie. She can feel him looking at her back.

"Where did you get that dress?"

"I ordered it from Eatons. For our anniversary."

"You should send it back. We can't afford to spend money on frivolous things." He pushes back from the table, picks his teeth with a fingernail, and smooths his hair, oily with brilliantine. "I'll be waiting for you in the bedroom when you're finished the dishes."

Mhairi clears the table and piles the dishes into the dishpan and fills it with hot water from the reservoir on the back of the stove. She sprinkles soap flakes on the surface of the water and plunges her hands into the steaming water. She does not feel the heat.

Finally, she spreads out the white tissue and lays the roses and baby's breath and pink ribbon in the centre. She rolls the tissue tightly around the flowers, lifts the lid of the woodstove, and shoves the bundle into the flames. Sparks shower up and land on her blue dress, marking it with pepper-like specks of black.

She goes into the bedroom and pulls the door shut behind her. White rivulets of wax make their slow way down the length of the two candles and spread in cold hardening pools on the tablecloth.

Millfield Manitoba *17th August, 1917*

Dear Mhairi

This will be a very short letter, Mhairi, as this is a busy time here. Colin is waiting for me in the field to stack hay, but as I must go to Millfield tonight for supplies I will be able to take this letter to the post office. I just want to let you and Orville know how delighted I am with your news! I can hardly wait until December to be an uncle. Colin and Saharah's little chap, Joey, is seven months old now and loved to death by everyone. Annie is especially happy, as she has been brought back to the household to help Sahara. It just occurred to me, your babe will be born in the same year as little Joey. It would be so wonderful if you and Orville could come for a visit when the baby is a little older. Again, my dear sister, my happiest congratulations. You will be a wonderful mother.

Much love,

Your brother Mac.

Chapter 7

Radford, Ontario, 1917

December 30, 1917. In the heat of the yellow kitchen, Mhairi's fair hair clings to her forehead and cheeks in damp strands. She wipes the limp tresses behind her ear and checks the stove and table one more time. A small roast of pork, dark gravy, yellow beans, and finely mashed potatoes rest on the back of the stove. The kettle steams and puffs, ready to make tea. Rice pudding waits on the sideboard in glass bowls, along with a jug of cream. A bowl of canned tomatoes sits exactly in the centre of the table. Everything is just the way Orville requires it. He will be home at ten to six and, exactly ten minutes later, sitting in his place at the head of the table, which is set with plain white china, teacups, and clear glasses filled with water.

Mhairi rubs her back awkwardly. It aches more than usual and her swollen abdomen is stretched and tight. She moves her hands back and forth over the baby in its internal nest and sits on a chair to ease her bulging feet out of her black shoes. It feels good to rotate her ankles and wiggle her toes. She tilts her head forward on her chest and closes her eyes, squeezing them shut against the heavy hot air of the kitchen.

The porch door slams shut and Mhairi jolts awake. A blast of cold air follows Orville into the kitchen. He tracks snow across the floor to the small room he calls his office. On his way past her he says, "Put your shoes on, Mhairi. You aren't a peasant."

She looks at the snow on the floor, already beginning to melt and pool in the warmth of the kitchen. Her puffy feet refuse to fit back into the shoes. She hurries to the bedroom for her slippers before Orville comes back to the kitchen. She scoops beans, gravy, and potatoes into the serving bowls, which have been lined up in the warming oven of the stove, and sets them on the table. She sets out two small separate dishes, one for each of them, for the tomatoes. She arranges the roast on a small platter and places it just to the left of Orville's place at the table, along with a carving knife. The kettle huffs its steam into the space above the stove. Orville returns to the kitchen and takes his place without a word.

Mhairi eases into her chair. She passes everything to Orville first and waits for each bowl to return to her. She has no appetite but takes a little of everything. Orville clears his throat.

"There are lumps in the gravy. And get me another carving knife. This one is dull."

She hoists her front-heavy body from the chair and finds another knife. Orville carves slowly and meticulously, each slice a perfectly uniform thickness. He sets the platter in front of himself, and Mhairi, in a lapse of thought, reaches across the table.

"Where are your manners?" he demands. He pulls the platter from her hand, nearly spilling the meat onto the table.

"I'm sorry, Orville. Would you please pass the meat?"

He ignores her. "Is the tea ready?"

Mhairi has forgotten to make the tea. She leaves her already cooling dinner and pours the boiling water over the loose tealeaves. She brings the teapot to the table along with the rice puddings and the small pitcher of cream. Mhairi doesn't ask for the meat again. The sight of it gives her heartburn anyway.

Orville finishes his meal in silence and leaves her alone at the table. She manages a few green beans and a spoonful of potatoes without gravy. The rice pudding tastes good, washed down with clear tea. Fighting the dull ache in her back, Mhairi clears the table and puts the food away, dips water from the reservoir at the end of the stove into a dishpan, and starts the dishes. She sets the table for Orville's breakfast in the morning. Tired, sore, and uncomfortable, she goes into the bedroom and, although it is only seven-thirty, pulls on her oversized flannel nightgown, lowers herself carefully onto the bed, and pulls the quilts to her chin.

She is not sure how long she has slept. In the dim glow of the kerosene lamp on the dressing table she can make out Orville's shape leaning over her, rolling her from her side onto her back. "Remove that thing." He tugs at the nightgown.

"Orville, no, please. It's too close to my time."

"You're my wife," he says in a guttural tone. He heaves the voluminous nightgown up and over her stomach, where pearly purple stretch marks gleam in the oily yellow light.

The pains begin the next morning, shortly after Orville has left for the lumberyard. Although she is not supposed to call him at work she cranks up the telephone operator, given the circumstances. Orville's voice is flat and distant.

"I'll be home at the usual time. Call Mrs. Lundy."

Mhairi gets the operator to connect her to Mrs. Lundy, who answers immediately. Within fifteen minutes the midwife is letting herself in at the front door, satchel of birthing equipment in hand. She finds Mhairi already in bed and sets about to make her as comfortable as possible before gathering everything she will need for the birth. Mhairi is silent and passive, communicating only a soft thank you.

Mrs. Lundy's short frame carries a well-rounded, strong body. Her salt-and-pepper hair, mostly pepper, sweeps off her shiny face and ends in a tightly bundled braid at the back of her neck. Well-placed wrinkles at the corners of her eyes are testaments to laughter. When she opens her mouth to speak, a heavy Irish brogue rolls off her tongue and hangs in the air like the mist of her homeland. She exudes kindness and good humour.

Mrs. Lundy has delivered most of the babies in Radford. With her diagnostic eye she measures Mhairi's narrow hips and pelvis against the swollen abdomen. In spite of the belly, Mhairi is thin. Mrs. Lundy believes it will be a difficult labour but she is careful not to articulate this. She brings a basin of warm water to the bedside table and begins to sponge her patient. She sucks in a sharp gasp when she sees the purpling bruises on the insides of Mhairi's thighs and in her groin. Mrs. Lundy is horrified. She has never seen anything like this in all her years of midwifery. Mhairi turns her face to the wall and is silent, shamed.

Mrs. Lundy first met Mhairi and Orville when they moved to this house right after their marriage a year ago. They were a quiet couple, Orville coming and going to and from his lumberyard like clockwork, Mhairi hanging out the washing on the clothesline even in the coldest of weather, or working in her little garden in the summer. Mrs. Lundy thinks Mhairi looks like a child-waif with her slight frame and blonde hair pulled back in a knot. She always seems to be waiting for approval or permission.

Mrs. Lundy studies Mhairi. She is far too thin and pale. A bruise, yellow and fading, is visible just below the sleeve of her white flannel nightgown. The skin on her hands is cracked and sore looking and her eyes are ringed with dark circles. She is clearly exhausted and there is a long travail ahead of her.

Orville changes his mind and decides to pay a visit at lunchtime. Mhairi is by now labouring heavily, sucking in deep breaths and panting them out much too quickly. Mrs. Lundy holds her hand and wipes her face with a damp cloth.

"How much longer is this going to take?" Orville asks in a constipated voice, still wearing his jacket and snowy boots. He frowns and fidgets, clearly repelled by the scene.

You filthy pig, thinks Mrs. Lundy. For years she has regarded him as the sternly polite man at the lumber store. She motions him to the kitchen and his relief is palpable.

Orville is a tall man with a lanky, almost skeletal frame. High cheekbones and hollow temples outline his bony face. Behind the round spectacles clinging tenaciously to his nose, a pair of deep set eyes peers dark and hard. A nervous tic dances beside his mouth. He adjusts the spectacles with a long skinny finger and Mrs. Lundy steels herself.

"It's going to be long and hard for her, I'm afraid. I don't think it will be until later tonight, but it's hard to know for sure."

She stares hard at Orville, her eyes intense and censorious. He stares back. He turns on his heel and slams the storm door on his way out.

There is no dinner waiting when Orville returns at ten to six. He is apparently quite agitated by this and Mrs. Lundy can hear him opening cupboards and rattling dishes and silverware, muttering to himself. She can't help but wonder if he expects her to have supper ready. Finally it is quiet.

Another powerful contraction grips Mhairi. When the pain subsides Mrs. Lundy waits a few minutes before edging into the kitchen.

"Hmph," says Orville. "Is she still grunting?"

Mrs. Lundy's tolerance is well honed by experience, but it is all she can do to keep from slapping him in the face. "It's almost time," she says in a measured voice. "But she's exhausted and she still has some hard work to do."

Orville pushes his chair from the table and disappears into his office, pulling the door shut behind him with a slam. Mrs. Lundy returns to Mhairi as another violent spasm takes control of the frail body. To this point Mhairi has not cried out. Mrs. Lundy can see the slimy dark hair of a little head coming into view and, before she has time to instruct Mhairi, there is a single unearthly drawn-out scream and the baby emerges so quickly she barely has time to catch it. She hoists the child by its feet and slaps the tiny bottom. A squeaky cry scratches through the cool air of the bedroom like the complaint of a small wounded animal. A girl. Mrs. Lundy wraps the infant and turns to place her on Mhairi's chest when she sees the copious bloom of blood spreading on the sheets and towels. She hurriedly puts the baby in the small bassinet by the bed and runs to the kitchen.

"Mr. Christie!" He pokes his head around the door of his office. There is no mistaking the urgency of Mrs. Lundy's voice. "Get a pail of snow, Mr. Christie."

Orville has heard Mhairi's scream and the baby's first cry. He stands immobilized in the doorway.

"What?"

"For God's sake, hurry," Mrs. Lundy shrieks. "We're going to lose her if you don't hurry!"

The commanding exigency in the tone of Mrs. Lundy's voice snaps Orville's mind back into place and he grabs a tin pail and runs outside, returning in seconds with the snow. Mrs. Lundy seizes the pail and disappears into the bedroom. She spreads a thin layer of the snow on Mhairi's belly and through the coldness she frantically feels for the uterus. She massages it almost violently. More snow, more kneading, more snow, more kneading. Mhairi lies in ominous silence, her skin as white as the snow piled on her abdomen. Mrs. Lundy's arms and hands ache from the cold but she continues her rhythmic manipulation. At last she feels the uterus begin to contract weakly. She pushes the snow aside and massages more gently. Mhairi is unconscious when the afterbirth delivers. Mrs. Lundy fetches the woolen blankets she draped on chairs in front of the kitchen stove and wraps their warmth around Mhairi.

Orville sits at the kitchen table. Mrs. Lundy steels herself and dutifully delivers the child to him. When she places the infant in his arms he stiffens in panic. He can feel the warmth of the little body and is astonished to see the rosebud mouth turn hungrily toward the flannel blanket where it brushes the little cheek. For months Orville has denied the reality of a child. Pregnancy disgusted him. Whenever he looked at Mhairi, especially in the last three months, he could imagine nothing more than a huge purple tumour filling her belly. He hated the swollen ugly feet and the puffy look of her face with its blotchy dark patches, the jagged marks stretching her skin. The very idea of birth itself was abhorrent to his mind.

But now, now, he cannot take his eyes from his daughter.

Chapter 8

Millfield Manitoba *January 5th, 1918*

Dearest Mhairi (or should I say Mama Mhairi?) and Orville

At last your treasure has arrived! One more day and she would have been a New Year's Baby! Adelaide Mhairi is a beautiful name. Where did Adelaide come from, was it a name chosen by Orville? In any event, I like your decision to call the wee girl "Laidie." And I am sure she will indeed be a little "lady." I trust also that you are well as I know from Colin that it took Saharah a while to get back to her former self. I have to tell you something quite funny. Three weeks ago I got a beautiful little five-month-old border collie, and I named her Lady! You will be pleased to know I immediately changed the name to Queenie when I got your letter. My neighbours are right about Manitoba winters, I have found out. By the time I get my woodbox filled in the little shed attached to the house, I am white with frost and my boots are so stiff they won't bend. Last week we had a blizzard that piled snow to the height of my door and I was forced to tunnel myself out. I was pleased to meet an old army comrade of mine, Les Linford, who is right from Millfield. He was sent home just before Christmas with a bad leg wound but appears to be recovering well. His family lives right in town so that will be one more place for me to drop in. In the two and a half years since I came here I have come to know a surprising number of people. Last fall on a threshing gang I met a funny Ukrainian fellow by the name of Steve Kalinsky who is just a few years older than I. He came to Canada in 1913 when he was only nineteen to make a place for himself and Anya, his wife-to-be, who was supposed to join him the next year, but in his absence she took up with a (so-called) friend of his and refused to make the journey. Steve is a good person but not at all interested in the ladies any more. His farm is about two miles south of mine so we get together quite often. We also have a new neighbour between our places and Millfield. His name is Tom King and we hear he has come into a good deal of money from somewhere so decided to invest in farming property. He put up a big fancy house last summer and always seems to be bringing something new into his yard. He doesn't seem at all friendly; the McCorries agree with me on this. I have bought five more cows and a sow, which will farrow in the spring. Next year I shall have my own source of bacon! Also in the spring I plan to acquire more equipment, namely a hay rake and stook binder. The McCorries have always been kind enough to let me use theirs but I feel it is time for me to have my own—perhaps I will pass on their favour by helping Steve. I believe I have finished breaking all the land I can at this time and this spring I will have forty acres to plant. There is still available Crown land here, and if my crops are good I may try to purchase another holding or two. We have had some good snows this winter and I hope the dry conditions of last year will not be repeated. My new root cellar is working fine with its stone lined walls and weighted cover. Did I tell you about my first effort? Apparently rodents and raccoons have no problem getting in under lids and through dirt walls and about a third of my vegetables were bitten into and unusable. But I ramble on about farming details that probably do not interest you much. My most loving congratulations again. I only wish I could see my dear little niece.

With much love to all of you

Your Brother Mac.

Chapter 9

Wolf River, 1918

The war years are a good time for farming. Rains fall auspiciously and crops flourish. Harvest weeks are warm and dry, and stay that way until garden produce is in rows of shiny jars in the cellar and sweet hay piled in stacks behind the barn. Ford and Colin McCorrie acquire a 40-acre parcel immediately across the trail that passes their house. They break the land, leaving long strips of sod turned over along its length, ready to be summer-fallowed the next year in readiness for cropping. They buy a new "Waterloo Boy" John Deere tractor, fuelled by kerosene. The tractor's chuffing putt is still an alien sound on the prairie and will eventually eliminate the need for work horses, but both Ford and Colin believe their horses will continue to play a part in their operations for a long time. They purchase a team of sleek black mares, Dusty and Shadow, for Saharah.

The harvest gods conspire to confer good fortune in 1918. Fields sowed in April flourish with timely rains. By mid-July the kernels of wheat swell, soft and tan and fat in their coats of chaff. August heat transforms the green fields to expanses of waving gold as the grain ripens and hardens. Colin and Ford take to the fields with the binder, cutting the grain and tying it into sheaves in one operation. Steve Kalinsky helps the McCorries pile the sheaves in stooks, to be moved to the threshing machine when Charlie Wilton, the travelling harvestman, arrives.

Saharah and Annie prepare for their turn at providing meals for the threshing gang, which will arrive at the McCorrie farm in two days. There will be anywhere from twelve to sixteen men, Ford has warned them. Two field meals a day are expected, unless weather interferes. Annie throws herself into this gargantuan task with gusto, dragging Saharah along for the ride. They fill the pantry shelves with bread and pies and cakes and cookies, along with huge roasts selected from the special beef ring supply. They dig carrots and new potatoes and beets, pick fat ears of corn, and borrow dishes and cups from their neighbours--a favour they will return to the next farms on the threshing circuit.

When the day arrives Annie is up before daybreak, stoking the woodstove out in the summer kitchen. Saharah stays in the kitchen to organize the baskets and tubs, which will carry the meals to the field, and Joey is underfoot with a question for every movement. Annie's mother Ethel and Saharah's mother Ivy arrive to help just after nine o'clock, along with Helen Thompson and her sons, Walter and Duncan. The men mill about the threshing machine, waiting for the first load of sheaves. Mr. Wilton, the thresherman, has brought his own crew to look after his huge steam engine and they baby the machine constantly, oiling its bearings and checking its drive belts, adjusting the engine speed, keeping the boiler pressure constant, and hauling water to keep up the steam pressure.

With the exception of the duties of Mr. Wilton's crew, the work is backbreaking and repetitive. The men take turns pitching the sheaves from the rack into the maw of the greedy machine. There is no group of people more appreciative of a good meal than a threshing gang, and bachelor farmer Steve Kalinsky is probably more appreciative than most. He is usually first in line, piling his food to overflowing on his plate and coming back for second helpings. There is rarely anything left over. The men roll fat cigarettes from their pouches of dry tobacco and clouds of blue smoke waft over the eating area, as this is the only time when they are permitted to smoke. The steam engine's ponderous heartbeat ramps up its tempo. The men scatter to their various functions.

The water boys, Walter and Duncan Thompson, ready their pails and dippers to deliver water to the gang throughout the afternoon. The women gather up the detritus of the dinner hour and head for the house. Preparations begin immediately for the evening meal, five hours hence.

Harvest is over. The week before Thanksgiving Saharah prepares for a trip to Millfield. Her first special dinner planned for the McCorries and Fletchers requires some special trimmings. Colin hitches Dusty and Shadow to her buggy. The horses are well trained, the buggy in good repair, and Saharah is capable. She has made the trip many times. Still, Colin feels a vague apprehension. Only the two of them know she is again pregnant.

"Are you sure you'll be all right?"

"Don't be such a fusspot," she scolds. She adjusts the cushions at her back for comfort. "I've done this before, haven't I?"

Colin leans over the wheel of the buggy and kisses his wife. "I love you, Saharah McCorrie. Take care."

She smiles, gives the reins a light flick, and the horses trot ahead on their own.

Annie has been allowed to go home for Thanksgiving so Grandpa Ford is watching Joey. The twenty-one-month-old is weaned from Saharah's breast and trained to use his little po-po, which he propels across the kitchen floor with his feet. Although Ford pretends crustily that this might be an inconvenience, he is delighted to finally be alone with the child.

Colin waves when Saharah looks back. He tries to shake off the inexplicable disquiet he feels. He returns to the barn to harness Old Jim and Custer to the mouldboard plough. The tractor waits in the yard in front of the barn, but sometimes, especially this time of year when the work is nearly finished and the frantic rush to harvest is past, Colin still likes to use the horses. He wants to turn the sod on a small field of pasture that will be summer-fallow next year and cropped the year after that. He will be finished long before Saharah returns from town.

The ten-acre pasture is bounded on all sides by thick stands of tall poplar and a few ancient oak trees. It's like a room with tall swaying walls and a ceiling of heaven, Colin imagines. He loves its solitude and shelter. The day is sunny and warm for early October. Although brisk southwest air currents lift fine dust into quavering grey sheets along the trail, there is no breeze in the sheltered meadow.

Colin holds the eager horses back slightly. It's strenuous labour and he stops after the first round at the southwest corner of the meadow for some cold tea. Heralding late fall is a faint smell of tall prairie sweetgrass smoke in the air. He wonders if Saharah is enjoying the same far-off fragrance. He squints through the naked-branched poplars scratching at the sky and can make out a tumbled line of grey clouds just above the southern horizon. Colin finishes the last of his tea and guides the team back onto the field. There is perhaps a half hour of ploughing left.

When he comes around to the southwest corner again, he sees the clouds in the south now closer, churning upwards. Greyish yellow wisps extend from the cloud like tentacles and in that instant Colin understands he is looking at a prairie fire. In minutes, the gentle sweetgrass aroma becomes strong and acrid, stinging his eyes and nose and throat like strong lye soap. The horses, eyes wide and nostrils flaring, snort and pull at their traces.

Colin unhitches the plough and climbs onto Custer's bare back. With a dig of his heels he urges both horses out of the meadow and onto the trail. To the south, a violent updraft sucks flames into a spiralling vortex, visible for miles. It swells upwards in huge rolling swirls of all shades of grey with silvery glints like jagged lightning. The greys become more intense lower down, and merge to pitch black near the ground where bursts of the fire beneath stab through the darkness. In the direction of Millfield a dark billowing wall rises to the sky, sucking the sun into its upper reaches. Colin forces the horses on and they veer sideways and whinny and rear. It is all he can do to stay on Custer's back.

Prairie farmers know about prairie fires in the same way that fishermen in their small boats know about rogue storms at sea. They both understand the deadly peril and they know they must pit their every strength against nature to survive. So Colin well knows that a prairie fire fuelled by dry grass and bush and goaded by wind can be capable of overtaking a horse at full gallop. He knows the dense hot smoke can blind and choke and suffocate within minutes, and he knows absolute and total destruction will lie in its wake.

He reaches the McCorrie yard and sees Ford across the trail in the new field with the tractor and a plough, frantically going over the broken sod to reinforce it as a firebreak. *It's a good thing I didn't take the tractor.* On the porch, Joey screams hysterically in the playpen Ford has made for him. Gypsy, frenzied and hoarse, barks and strains at the rope tying her to the fence. Colin frees Old Jim from the traces and digs his heels into terror-stricken Custer's flanks. Custer snorts and neighs like a creature possessed. Colin whips the reins across the horse's sides and back, sending streams of sweaty foam into the air. They hurtle toward the towering wall of flame and smoke and into the sickening miasma where wildly panicked rabbits, several deer, and two coyotes pass in front of them, headed in the direction of the river. Through stinging eyes, Colin helplessly watches them vanish like dreams in an awful morning. Snakes and mice slither and scurry across the trail in a futile attempt at escape. The roar is deafening and ashes and cinders and charred bits fall to the ground. *How close is the fire?* He can still make out the indistinct outlines of trees and bush streaking past. Colin's face is stinging from the intense heat and he can feel the skin of his cheeks and forehead blistering and breaking. A flock of disoriented prairie chickens flies directly into the roaring inferno. Custer no longer registers the desperate jab of the boots or the sting of the reins as they whip his flanks. He makes an otherworldly noise that can only be described as a scream. He rears wildly, throws Colin to the ground, and gallops north, following the panicked wildlife.

The smoke isn't as thick down here, Colin's mind observes detachedly, as unconsciousness rolls over him like a dark warm blanket. It's a blanket that quickly turns to ice.

The acrid smell of wet ashes fills Colin's nostrils when he awakens, chilled and trembling. Hammers pound at the inside of his skull and his eyes are raw with pain. Annie leans over him in a mist of recognition, her gentle hands pressing cold wet rags against the rising blisters on his face and arms. Night folds itself close around him again and he sleeps in fitful dreams of suffering where he cannot draw a breath, charred mice tear at his eyes, and an eyeless stranger scrapes hot sand over his forearms.

When he finally awakens, he is alone in his bedroom.

"Saharah," he calls. His voice is little more than a low rasping from deep in his chest. "Are you there?"

The door, slightly ajar, opens wide enough for Annie's head. The head abruptly backs out and he can hear muffled voices in the kitchen. He calls Saharah again, but it is Ford who pads into the room in his sock feet. He pulls up a chair and sits close to the head of the bed. Colin's eyes focus painfully but well enough to see the anguish on his father's face. "Where's Saharah?" he croaks.

Ford swallows back what feels like a small boulder deep in his throat and struggles to keep his voice even. "Son, she didn't make it. Saharah didn't get through the fire. She…"

Colin tries to understand what his father is saying, but it's like listening to a distant foreign language. Ford's voice falls silent and he holds his head in his hands. Colin's mind strains to piece together the meaning, trying to find some clue to tell him what is happening. He lifts one hand to his stinging face to feel the wet cloth there and sees the swath of bandage on his forearm. The hurting fragments of his dreams float in his mind like sour cream on the surface of bad milk, and there they mingle with foul apparitions: mice burned black and hairless, a stinking dark curtain, a newborn screaming in the flames, horses gone insane, heat burning his eyes, and the smell of the singing hair on his arms. He remembers.

It is two days after the fire. Undertaker Dunham arrives at the church, perched high on the buckboard seat of his polished hearse. Tasselled with shining dark blue cords, the black curtains shield the oak coffin bearing the remains of Saharah McCorrie. Dunham's team of glossy black geldings are trained to a slow walk and the mourners trail behind on foot with Ford and Colin leading. The wind tangles itself in their hair and they pull their coats together against the cold October gusts. Colin's steps are slow and pained and set the pace for the procession. Fred Fletcher supports his distraught wife Ivy, who has never been close to Saharah and now mourns her death not only for the loss of a daughter but for things said and done; things not said and not done. The O'Reillys, their own grief over Rusty's death still painfully close to the surface, follow next and move in their usual close family cluster. They follow the rest of the mourners, which includes most of the population of the Millfield area.

Colin does not hear the funeral service. The rubric of farewell floats far above him like a grey cloud of unrecognized language. He sits, only feet away from the coffin, his bandaged arms and hands held stiffly in front of him. Although he tries, his mind will not dismiss his vision of Saharah's black remains wrapped in her pink silk wedding dress.

In the churchyard Colin kneels by the coffin and rests his head on the rich oak.

"I love you, Saharah McCorrie," he whispers.

News of the fire spreads quickly through the area by way of first-hand accounts. It began as a lightning strike south of Willis Marsh, where the normally sodden bog was nothing but a bowl of white salt-dust. The cattails, reeds, and sedge grasses provided propitious brown tinder. An advancing weather front spawned strong winds which acted as a giant bellows, pressing the fire into a life of its own. There are no holdings on Willis Marsh, so the greatest loss there was hundreds of water birds gathering for the southern migration. Just north of the marsh, Steve Kalinsky turned his horses, cattle, and pigs loose in hopes they might escape, and lowered himself into his ten foot deep well. Above, he said, he could see a continuous sheet of flame which seemed to be sucking air from the well, making it difficult to breathe. Heavy yellow smoke remained above after the fire passed, and when Kalinsky climbed out of the well there was nothing left but smoking blackened land. Henry Davis was caught with his team and a wagonload of goods on a trail south of Millfield. His terrified horses tried to turn and flee but somehow in their disorientation and fright got the harness and traces caught around the doubletree. Davis could not untangle them or straighten the doubletree and was forced to leave the team and run for his life. He managed to get to the Wilford farm in time to join the family in their outdoor root cellar, but he was badly burned and died shortly after he arrived there. Neighbours discovered his horses' roasted remains beside the wreckage of his wagon where dozens of coyotes congregated for a feast. The McCorrie farm was spared, in no small part due to the wide strip of newly broken land across the trail. The wind changed from south to southeast in time to veer away from Millfield, although by then the lightning storm that started the fire was already rumbling close behind the flames. The rain began to fall just as Steve Kalinsky emerged from his well. He told how its first scattered drops hissed to vapour and then turned into a downpour that sizzled and steamed on the hot black earth. On the north side of the trail the only farm buildings destroyed belonged to a young bachelor, Mac Ward, who survived by lying flat in a low spot in a ploughed field near his yard.

The rain came too late for Saharah McCorrie. Searchers located her on the trail the next morning, about a mile from where they found Colin. Her horses' bodies, swollen and grotesque and twisted in the agony of death, lay a short distance away near the charred skeleton of her buggy.

Chapter 10

It is curious—two letters arriving from Mac on the same day. Mhairi slides her silver letter opener beneath the flap of the earliest, postmarked October tenth.

Millfield Manitoba 30 September, 1918

Dearest sister Mhairi,

I am thinking you are probably getting accustomed to my one letter a year. I do think of you much more often than that but it takes me quite a while to settle down long enough to write everything I want to tell you and I'm afraid I do put it off. Are you feeling well? I must admit to surprise upon learning you will be welcoming another wee one in December. But I am feeling badly that things are not going smoothly with Orville, especially since you have no other family around Radford. I understand that he can be difficult, but do keep your chin up. At any rate, I am pleased to hear that he is fine with Laidie. It is still very hot in Manitoba for this time of year and the wind seems to blow all the time on the prairies. The crops this year were not nearly as good as last as we did not get enough rain. Fall work is done early but the cattle are still out on what little grass remains in the fenced pasture. I wish I could turn them out on some of the unfenced prairie but they would be long gone. Steve Kalinsky is having a hard time of it. His land is poor to begin with; about the only crop he can grow well are stones. He jokes that his stones are piled so high he will soon be able to build a house out of them. Our new neighbour Tom King is proving to be as unlikeable as we first thought. I don't know if he thinks he is better than everyone else, but he certainly thinks he is better than Steve just because Steve is Ukrainian. Postmaster Land told me King was down at the post office in Millfield cornering anyone who would listen to him to complain about stupid Ukrainian people spoiling the country. He does not know Steve, who is worth ten Tom Kings. My two-year-old steer "Bifteck" is ready to join the beef ring this fall. I will miss the rascal, but I am learning it is not a good idea to make pets of livestock. We are using up the last of O'Reillys beef right now and the crew will be here next week. Anyway, there are seven new calves this year and on a farm that is how it is; there is a new crop of everything each year, or so we hope. The McCorries are all well. Little Joey is a year and 9 months and manages to entertain everyone with his escapades. Last week he was lost for a few hours and there was great panic and all the neighbours were rounded up to search for him. He was finally found sleeping with his raggy doll under Annie's bed. Actually it was Gypsy the dog who found him. Annie went into her room for a jacket and there was Gypsy with her nose under the bed, wagging her tail. Colin often brings Joey to my place and I have learned to put everything in a high place, especially my tobacco, which he has tried to eat. Telling you all this makes me think of little Laidie. I was so grateful to get the little photograph of her and I can well imagine the beautiful dark red hair you describe. I wish I was able to see her; she will soon be a year old. Please give her a kiss and big hug from Uncle Mac. And a kiss and hug for you too.

Love, Your Brother Mac

PS My apologies, I confess, I set this letter aside and forgot about it. I will be taking it to the post office tonight. I look forward to hearing from you soon.

The second letter was postmarked October 15, only five days after the first

Millfield Manitoba 15th October, 1918

Dearest Mhairi,

You will have barely received my last letter and no doubt surprised at the arrival of another so soon. I must tell you bad news, probably the worst that has ever happened around here: the community has lost two young mothers. There was a horrible prairie fire right before Thanksgiving and I have never experienced anything so terrifying in my life. The worst possible thing was the loss of Colin's wife Saharah. I can hardly bring myself to write it down. She got trapped by the fire on her way to Millfield with her buggy and her two horses. Everyone is devastated by this loss. Thank God little Joey was at home with Ford. Colin tried to ride into the fire to save her but the smoke overcame him and he is still recovering from some burns which will heal long before he does. Saharah's parents have taken Joey for the time being and Annie has agreed to stay on with Ford and Colin.

This tragedy is closest to me because of my friendship with Colin and Saharah, but there was another most dreadful accident just a week before the fire. A young chap in town, Jake Martens, (I only know him to see him) lost his wife when she got badly tangled in a piece of farm machinery. She never regained consciousness. Just like Saharah, she leaves a child, a baby girl.

I lost my cabin and barn in the fire but compared to the loss of Saharah that is nothing; buildings can be replaced. I was fortunate to have a ploughed field next to the yard, and after I turned the livestock loose I ran as far into the field as I could and laid flat with my face down in a little hollow I made to get away from the smoke. We found the cattle and horses the next day down by the river, but the pigs and chickens have disappeared. My friend Steve lost everything too but he survived by lowering himself into his well. Even the soil on his farm was burned away. He and myself are staying at the O'Reilly's; it is just a corner in the loft of their barn but will shelter us for a couple of weeks. I am going to throw together a small log shack with a sod roof to get us through the winter. I have offered for Steve to stay with me until something can be done at his place. Hopefully we will be able to manage without too much argument. He is already talking about that pile of stones of his for a house but I think it may be a while before he can move back there, if ever.

Dear Mhairi, it is with a lot of sadness I send this news to you. I will write when things have settled down and I again have a roof over my head. Much love to you and Laidie.

Don't worry about me, everything will work out.

Your brother, Mac

Chapter 11

Millfield, 1918

On November 11, 1918, at eleven in the morning, the long-awaited Armistice comes into effect. The world celebrates. Even in little Millfield, the citizens parade through the streets of town, waving their Union Jacks in the face of a strong north wind, which slices sleet into their faces. A small band of musicians, their fingers numb with cold, manages to pound out a few rousing marches. The crowd gathers in front of the Town Hall to listen to speeches delivered by anyone who wishes to be heard. They cheer and clap and laugh and smack one another across the shoulders. The taste of victory is like sweet red wine.

But there is little in the way of celebration in the McCorrie household. It is only four weeks since Saharah's funeral. The burns to Colin's arms and hands slowly repair themselves, leaving waxy red scars. He manages to eat a little. Ford and Annie struggle to cope with their own personal sorrow while at the same time showing as much strength as they can muster to support Colin. Little Joey is still ensconced at Grammy Ivy Fletcher's. Several times Ford suggests bringing the child home, but Colin won't talk about it. He just shakes his head decisively each time it is mentioned.

Colin walks sometimes, but on these middle days of November he feels the nascent cold of winter intensely. The ground is frozen and bare and to him, desolate as the wind that harasses with its threats from the northwest. He clutches his arms to his chest to keep warm, perhaps too, to hold Sahara close. He is afraid, but of what, he is not sure. His grief sits heavily within, a great undigested meal of horror and pain and loss.

The first snow falls on November thirtieth. Ford takes his time at the barn and Annie sits in the corner by the stove with her eternal mending, bits of thread, yarn, and fabric scattered at her feet. Colin, unshaven as he has been most of the past month, leans on his elbows on the kitchen table by the window, mesmerized by the fall of the flakes and the way they swirl and pile into loose drifts by the fence. A chickadee lands on the windowsill and stays long enough to examine its reflection in the wavy glass, right under Colin's nose. It explores its likeness with curiosity, pecks at the pane, flies off to a seedy weed top for a moment, and returns. This time it sees Colin beyond the glass and disappears into the snowy air in panicked flight. What is it about a seemingly unimportant small moment of nature that is able to trip a switch in the mind? Colin stands stiffly.

"I want to get Joey today," he says to Annie. "Will you go out and tell Dad?"

Annie tries to hide her surprise and stumbles over her own feet on her way to the closet for her coat and felt boots. She returns from the barn in minutes, a flurry of snowflakes tumbling through the door ahead of her.

"He's going to hitch up the team right away," she says, breathless. "Do you need me to help you get ready?"

A hint of a smile creeps into the corners of Colin's lips for the first time since the accident. "I'll be fine," he says. "Just get me some blankets and extra quilts for Joey." He readies a basin of warm water for a quick shave.

Ivy Fletcher is not prepared for the appearance of Colin and Ford on her front porch.

"I've come for Joey," Colin says. "Sorry I didn't let you know beforehand."

"You can't take him. He belongs here." Ivy's eyes narrow and she thrusts her chin up towards Colin. "Saharah would have wanted him to be with us."

Fred Fletcher stands slightly behind her, eyes cast downward, his hands in his pockets.

Ford is about to say something when Colin steps toward Ivy and Fred. "I think I know how you feel," he ventures, "but Joey is my son. Saharah would never let anyone take him from me."

"How can you say such a thing?" Ivy snaps back, her hands planted firmly on her ample hips."Here it is over a month and you haven't even come to see him. None of you. He needs someone to be a mother and your hired girl certainly isn't up to the job."

Fred stares past Ford to the door and still says nothing. Ford speaks up, his voice deliberate and measured. "Fred would you please tell Ivy to get Joey for us? And his things. If everything can't be ready today, I'll come back for it next week."

Ivy is hyperventilating and flushed, her voice strident. "He doesn't even remember you," she says to Colin. Fred sidles past her and she turns her fury in his direction."Don't you dare disturb Joey. Bill, do you hear me?"

The commotion is too much. Joey pads around the corner, barefoot, dragging a little frayed red quilt and rubbing his eyes. The stillness is thick and charged like the air just before a lightning strike. Time has a way of stretching its momentous markers, so while the silence runs long it is probably only a second or two before Joey's face lights up with unmitigated joy. He runs to Colin with his arms up, launching into a hug.

"Poppa! Poppa!" His arms go around his father's neck and he burrows his face into the wide shoulder. Colin squeezes his eyes shut and inhales the familiar scent of his son. It reminds him of Saharah.

Fred stares at Ivy. Tears of anger and defeat fill her eyes. "Well?" he says quietly."Get his things."

Christmas. Ford drags in a little poplar sapling to put in the living room, and as fast as Annie and Colin can hang paper stars on the branches, Joey grabs them and runs away, flashing his nearly black eyes and laughing wildly during Colin's pursuit and capture, which always ends with a tickling. Joey exhausts himself at last and falls asleep beside Ford's chair on a braided rag mat, clutching the rag boy-doll Annie has made for him. The dog Gypsy comes to lie close by. Now in relatively undisrupted calm, Annie salvages some stars that are still in one piece and fastens them to the tree along with half a dozen silver spoons tied with coloured bits of fabric and many huge pinecones strung on red yarn. She finishes with a chain of popcorn and rosehips.

There has been no communication with the Fletchers since the day Ford and Colin came for Joey, except for the day Fred came by to drop off a bag of freshly washed clothing and some toys that had been left behind. Fred was civil and apologetic but did not stay to visit. Now, on Christmas afternoon, Colin hitches up Custer and Old Jim and prepares the sleigh for the fifteen-minute ride to the Fletcher place. Joey snuggles beneath Ford's old buffalo robe, his mittened hands clutching two little gifts: Annie has made a lace doily for Joey to give to his Gramma and there is a set of two dotted red handkerchiefs for Grandpa Fred.

The Fletchers are surprised to see them. Fred takes Joey from Colin at the door and Ivy immediately begins to cry, snuffling and wiping at her nose and eyes.

Colin points to the little packages. "Can you give those to Grammy and Grampa, Joey?" Joey hands them to Fred.

Ivy retreats to the parlor and returns with a package wrapped in red paper for Joey. He rips it open, casting a flurry of paper and ribbon aside until he comes to a knitted blue dog with a bright yellow collar. For the rest of the visit he will not part with the dog, even to show it to Colin, and this makes Ivy beam.

Ivy pours coffee for the men and brings out a plate of fruitcake, shortbread, and jam-filled cookies. Joey darts back and forth between the adults, filling his hands with cookies and disappearing to eat them under the table with the blue dog. They manage to keep the conversation centered on mundane small talk until the grandfather clock strikes four and Colin rises.

"It's time to go home for chores, Joey," he says. Ivy brings their coats without argument. "Got a hug and kiss for Grammy and Grampa?"

"Big ones," says Joey. He plants soggy kisses on their cheeks and Ivy is crying again as they close the door on the way out.

The sleigh runners squeak across the crisp snow on the way home and Custer and Old Jim snort clouds of icy breath, pink from the sunset that streaks the sky with cold reds and yellows. Joey is again buried under the buffalo robe, this time with the blue dog pressed to his face.

Colin looks in on Joey before he goes to bed. The quilts are rumpled up around his square little chin, his long blond curls tousled on the pillow. Annie's rag doll is in one fist, Ivy's blue dog in the other. Colin can hear a faint little snore like the purring of a kitten.

Chapter 12

Radford, Ontario, 1918

Orville can't abide the sight of Mhairi. In his opinion it is worse than last time—the huge stretch-marked belly and knotted veiny legs, the swollen face, and even, to him, the smell of pregnancy—a nauseating revulsion. But it is his doing. It will never happen again, he vows. From now on, he will find another way.

Mhairi's second labour begins before breakfast the first Sunday of January. She says nothing to Orville. He waits at the table while she, between contractions, prepares two soft poached eggs and two slices of toast with a small dish of strawberry jelly on the side. He eats quickly without acknowledging her and quickly disappears with his coffee. She prepares lunch: cold pork sandwiches dressed with home-made apple chutney and a pot of split pea soup.

By eleven o'clock, he must be told. Mhairi knocks cautiously on the closed office door. "It's time, Orville," she whispers. "I'm going to call Mrs. Lundy."

He clears his throat. "That'd be a good idea."

"Can you take care of Laidie?"

No response. Mhairi leans on the doorframe, waits. At last he comes to the door. "Where is she?"

"She's napping. She'll likely be awake soon."

"Is anything ready for lunch?"

Mhairi nods. She cradles her abdomen, and lifts the telephone receiver to crank her call to Mrs. Lundy.

Within a half-hour the midwife, her bag of gynaecological necessities slung over her shoulder, lets herself in without knocking, bringing with her a flurry of snowflakes. She throws off her woolly black coat and kicks her felt boots into the corner by the woodstove, ready for action. At the top of her mind is her last delivery here. It still weighs heavily.

Mhairi is in the kitchen setting the table for lunch. Millie Lundy takes her hand and leads her to the bedroom.

"That's enough kitchen work, dearie. You've got more important things to do now." She settles Mhairi with a pillow at her back. She untangles the stethoscope from her bag and warms the chestpiece in her pudgy hand. Mrs. Lundy has a faraway look of concentration while she listens to the baby's heartbeat, which is deemed slightly slow but healthy enough. The initial examination continues. It is a relief to find no thigh or groinal bruising this time. She buzzes about on her mission, gathering what she needs from the towel shelves and the kitchen. This will be much easier than the last time, she opines in a whisper.

Mrs. Lundy appears to be right. Between the strengthening contractions she massages Mhairi's back. She checks the baby's progress, noting only persistent little hiccups. There is little change in the heartbeat and she relaxes. She can hear one-year-old Laidie's high-pitched voice trying to make conversation with Orville, who returns an occasional response. Mhairi is quiet. Mrs. Lundy holds her hand and leans back in her chair.

She dozes for a brief moment and jolts awake to the feeling of her hand being squeezed in the vice of Mhairi's birth grip.

"Are you all right, dearie?"

"It's time, it's time," Mhairi cries out. "The baby, the baby's coming!"

Mrs. Lundy conducts a quick assessment. "Just wait a little, love. It'll be very soon, but not for a bit." She grabs her stethoscope to take a final reading on the little heartbeat.

There is nothing. Then, a tiny faint thump followed by another, then again nothing.

"You're right, love. It's now! You have to push if you can. Now!"

Mhairi is hyperventilating. Mrs. Lundy is frantic. Laidie is crying in the kitchen while Orville slams cupboard doors looking for salt and pepper.

"Again love! As hard as you can!"

Mhairi bears down with all the strength she can summon. With an ugly guttural moan she pushes out the child, a perfect little boy. She cannot see, as can Mrs. Lundy, the pale greyish cord wrapped around the child's neck or the bluish porcelain hue of his skin. She waits for the cry of life. The silence is profound.

January 30, 1919

Dearest Mhairi,

Just a little note to tell you I am so terribly sorry to hear about the loss of your wee boy. For you to have named him Mackenzie Ward Christie is a great honour to me. It's so sad that Laidie will not have a little brother. Now you must work at getting yourself well again. I wish I could be there to help you. I will write more soon.

Love as ever,

Mac

Chapter 13

Millfield, Manitoba June 12, 1919

Dear Mhairi,

Well, the winter has been quite an adventure. The O'Reillys most kindly put up with Steve and myself for nearly a month after the fire until we had time to build a small shack for the two of us. It was really pioneer style with poplar log walls chinked with sod and a dirt floor. Ford McCorrie let us cut sod for a roof, that is hardly ever done anymore, but that is how most of the early settlers started out around here I am told. In one thing we were fortunate, being that the weather has been mild, otherwise we would not have been able to use sod at all. We moved in just before the first snowstorm and the little drifts along the inside walls quickly showed us where the chinking needed attention. We could not get any more sod by then so the next day we got some old rags from Annie and forced them into the cracks. It was actually quite cosy all winter. I might say too cosy, as Steve and I shared the one room and by the time the spring melt started to drip through the sod roof we were getting quite testy with one another. We hired ourselves out for the winter to Ford McCorrie, doing chores and such like. It worked well for Ford as Colin is only now beginning to be able to carry his share of the work after the fire. We will go on this way a few more weeks and then I plan to start a new house and barn. Steve is going to stay with me for another year and hopefully it will be more peaceful as he will have a room of his own. In spite of our many differences we are still friends. It will be until next year before my own land will be ready for crops again, although I did have a few acres that were not touched by the fire. McCorries and O'Reillys fields look good already. Tom King has two hired men from down east that do most of his work for him. His fields look good too so far. He has bought a herd of Angus cattle and pastures them next to my land. He put up barbed wire fences all around and I believe some of them encroach on my property in places. I am not looking forward to bringing that up with him as he can be miserable. I'll let you know what happens. I hope you have managed to avoid that terrible influenza that is spreading across the country. There have been four deaths in the Wolf River area but no one I knew personally. The strangest thing is that it seems to hit healthy people the hardest. All of the deaths here have been young; two men, a 15-year-old girl, and a year-old baby. Around here they are warning people to stay away from crowds and gatherings. So please take care of yourself and Laidie.

Love,

Your brother Mac

Chapter 14

Millfield Manitoba 30th July, 1920

Dear Mhairi,

Again, time has flown with much happening. The best news is that Steve finally has his own house. Now my extra bedroom is available for you and Laidie to come and visit. I guess I should not have been surprised that Steve used his pile of stones. Apparently his family had a stone house in the Ukraine and he knew just what to do. His walls are about two feet thick and plastered and whitewashed inside. It is very cool in there in the summer heat. He was also lucky with his well and only had to make a new cover for it. I was surprised when he made three bedrooms, but it has been seven years since his experience with Anya (I think that was her name) and perhaps he is looking around again. This is something he keeps to himself. Growth is starting to return to his land but the topsoil is thin at best and he is talking about fencing the whole thing for cattle to run and I think that just might work. Well, the pasture fence problem with Tom King is finally resolved. The whole experience was unpleasant. He tried to tell me I hadn't any idea where my property line was so I went and got my Survey Certificate and showed him and he grabbed it out of my hand and tore it in half. Ford McCorrie took me to meet Denver Atchison who is his lawyer, and it didn't take long for Mr. Atchison to set Tom King straight. Mr. Atchison told him if he didn't have the fence moved within two weeks, we would sue him. If there was ever any chance of things being civil between King, myself, and the McCorries, I am afraid that will never happen now. Did I ever mention to you that I ran into an old war buddy of mine, Les Linford, who lives here? Les is a sad example of what war can do to some men. He looks fine but is what they call 'shell shocked'. He came out to the farm one day earlier this summer to help me with some fencing and a storm came up with thunder and lightning and he started yelling and dived headfirst under the stoneboat with its load of posts and he just laid there crying and shaking. I finally talked him into coming out about an hour after the storm blew over. And he did not even seem to remember any of it. I had heard some things about Les being shell-shocked but that is the first time I saw him like that. Some of the fellows I was overseas with were shell shocked and it is a terrible thing, but I never saw anyone as bad as Les. He does a lot of drinking now and cannot seem to keep a job. I hoped I might be able to help him but I don't think it is possible. I don't know where he gets his liquor, but Colin says there is an old fellow north of here in the valley that makes some pretty powerful home brew. Colin and Ford are doing fine and Joey is 3 and a half and quite the little man. Annie is still their hired girl and she seems quite happy there. She has become quite the cook. I now have ten cows with calves but I only milk one whose calf was born dead. My sow had fourteen(!) piglets in May and I will be able to sell them come fall. At last I am beginning to make some headway with farming. Next year I may even be able to buy my own tractor. Thank you for the picture of Laidie for my birthday. It is amazing that I can love her so much just from pictures and things you tell me. Give her a kiss for me.

Your brother, Mac

Chapter 15

Millfield Manitoba August 12th 1922

Dear sister Mhairi,

No, I am certainly not angry with you! It would seem that my last letter to you went astray, and that was quite some time ago. I cannot even remember what I wrote you about. At any rate, I was about to write anyway. I have had a bit of bad luck with my wheat. We had wonderful growing weather this year and it was looking like my best crop ever. July 29 was a hot day and I was on my way to my little hayfield when this huge blue and green cloud formed up fast and it got very windy and cold. I turned to head home and was just about there when I could hear this sound like a galloping herd of a hundred horses and that was when I realized it was a hailstorm. I had never seen one before but heard about them from Colin. I just made it to the barn and hurried in the horses for shelter when it hit; white balls of ice as big as crabapples. It was all over in minutes. I jumped on one of the horses and rode out to the field and I have never seen anything so completely demolished. My wheat was beaten into the mud, nothing left of it, and my oats did not do much better. This means I will have to be a miser and a beggar again for a while. It is a real setback for me. The hail fell in a wide path right through my land but seems to have missed everyone else. They tell me that's how hail can be. I hear Tom King was in town having a good laugh at my bad luck. Other than that things are all right I guess. My cattle are in good shape and I have put up a good supply of hay. Colin and Ford are both fine. Neither of them seems to have any inclination to find another wife and Annie takes care of the household very well. Once in a while she will even walk over with some baking. The last time she brought two saskatoon pies and asked me to take one to Steve as it is too far for her to walk to his place. Ford and Colin made a watering dugout in their pasture this summer. They hauled dirt out with the horses pulling scrapers. They piled the dirt around the sides so whenever it rains the water is collected in the hole. The cattle just love it; they wade in up to their stomachs. It helps them keep flies and mosquitoes off too. And wouldn't you know it, two days after they finished digging it, Tom King brought in a gang from over by Bainesville and had them make one for him. It is big enough to put three of McCorries dugouts inside it. Ford says the soil over by Kings' is a lot sandier than here and he says it probably won't hold water very well. But no one can tell Tom King anything. Joey is getting big and I think he is going to be tall. He is a mischief though and sometimes scares people. Last week he found a little squirter oil can and Colin found him under the most skittish horse they own, OILING its legs! Apparently a new family has moved to the old Helgason place in the Riverview District east of here, I believe Colin said their name is Popham. I might have mentioned the Helgasons to you. The parents both died in the big flu epidemic three years ago and their three boys were sent somewhere to live with their grand-parents. Anyway, according to Colin, the Pophams have a son and a nineteen-year-old daughter and he is trying to convince me to go over there on some excuse so I can see what she looks like. I'm not sure if he is curious for himself or if he is trying to be a matchmaker. I must sign off Mhairi, it is getting late and I am nodding off. I will send this letter to town in the morning with Ford. He is going in to pick up a piece for his tractor. I hope this letter reaches you and does not disappear like the last.

Love to all, your brother Mac

PS: Do you have any more pictures of Laidie?

Chapter 16

Millfield Manitoba 15th June, 1923

Dear Mhairi and Laidie,

The first thing I must do is thank you for the family picture of the three of you. I couldn't have asked for a better Christmas present. You have not changed at all! Laidie is getting so grown up with her long hair and I am having a hard time imagining her going off to school in two months. Everything is going well here. Thanks to all my wonderful neighbours I made it through the winter without starving! My crops are all safely in the ground, including the 40 acres I bought in '21, which was summer-fallowed last year. My herd of cattle is still growing. The calves are in very good shape with the rich milk they get. I just milk off what I need and they get the rest. Most of the farmers here separate the milk from the cream and sell the cream, then giving the skimmed milk back to the calves to drink out of a pail. Those calves take a lot longer to fatten as you can see why. I now have a little chicken shed. I am getting enough eggs to sell in Millfield and that gives me a little extra cash. My friend Steve has been lucky too. He fenced most of his land *to let cattle run and I think it was a good decision as his farm is so marginal. He built a small windmill by his well and it keeps a water trough full for the cattle. Steve always surprises me with all the things he knows how to do. You always ask about the McCorries and they are all fine. They are truly like a family to me. Joey turned seven in January and can hardly wait to go to school in fall. He is a smart little tick. I thought he should have gone to school last year but Colin wants to keep him as long as he can, I guess. Ford and Colin have always been hard workers and I believe they manage their place well. Annie is still their housekeeper and I must say how much she has changed since she first started working for them. I used to think she was rather plain and quite simple but she has really come out of her shell and is very pleasant to be around. She still brings treats of baking to myself and Steve and even offered to help us with spring cleaning on her own time. I declined, as I would have been ashamed for her to see some of the corners in my house, but Steve told her he would think about it. I get the feeling Annie likes Steve more than she lets on. The church in Millfield held a box social last Saturday to raise money for new hymnbooks and Steve and Colin and I went to it. Each girl brought a fancy wrapped lunch for two and an auctioneer sold the boxes to the highest bidders. The man who bought the box got to eat the lunch with the girl who provided it and also won the privilege of being able to dance with her. I was surprised when Steve bid from 25 cents up to 2 dollars for Annie's lunch and she was smiling from ear to ear. I really have to admire Steve for being so kind to her. Tom King was there, of course, and he bid up to the sky for Mabel Harrison`s lunch. Mabel is the telephone operator in Millfield. She makes a point of knowing everybody`s news and doesn`t think twice about passing it on. I'm thinking Tom enjoys getting all the gossip first hand. When Miss Edina Popham's lunch box was held up there was a lot of bidding, she being a new girl. I must have been feeling rich, as I bid 4 dollars and 50 cents for her lunch, being determined to eat with her. Edina Popham is a very pretty girl, with long dark hair held back in curls (something like you have done with Laidie in the picture). Her lunch was excellent and she is a good dancer too. And Colin, bless his heart, won the bidding for Miss Effie Dunham's lunch. She* *is the elderly spinster sister of the undertaker. When it was time to go home I offered to take Edina in the buggy but she would not hear tell of it and went off in a big huff to her father who was waiting outside for her. I couldn't find Steve and someone told me he had taken Annie home early because she was tired. All in all it was a good time, especially the square dancing, which is very popular here. I forgot to mention that Les Linford showed up in time for the dancing but was so drunk not one girl would dance with him. He tried to pick a couple of fights and some of the men forced him to leave. My next job will be haying, and if the weather cooperates I shall be well finished before threshing. Oh, and my garden is doing well too. Love to you all, and a special hug and kisses for Laidie.*

Your loving brother, Mac.

Chapter 17

Millfield Manitoba 30th June 1924

Hello, dear sister,

You will be amazed at my news! Steve Kalinsky got married to Annie Elliott last week! For the second time in my life I had the honour of being a best man. Steve and Annie managed to keep everything a big secret for most of the past year so it was quite a surprise to everyone. Annie looked beautiful at the wedding. You would not know she was the same person who first came to work for Ford after Ruby died. When I think back on things I know I should have realized sooner what was going on. Ford knew, as Annie had to tell him she was leaving. In the first few years Annie was there, there was a lot of sadness and grief and the last thing Ford and Colin could deal with was cooking and cleaning, but it is different now. Ford and Colin will manage, but I suspect she will be showing up with pies and bread and likely even sneaking their mending home to do. The only person not happy with the situation is little Joey. When you think of it, Annie is the closest thing to a mother that he has known. At the wedding he reached up and slapped Steve in the face and ran away to hide. Colin was angry with him and spanked him but I think everyone knew why he did it. Annie felt terrible but Joey wouldn't even talk to her. Poor little fellow. Speaking of weddings, Tom King married the telephone operator, Mabel Harrison. They are an obnoxious pair, quite suited to one another. She has left her job to enjoy King's money, and never lets anyone forget how superior they are. You are probably wondering about Miss Edina Popham? I was quite fascinated by her at first, but she turned out to be not as nice as she looked. I believe she has been badly spoiled, as she insists on getting her way and gets quite nasty about it. She has been hired on for this fall as the teacher at Wolf River School, which is a little down the river from here and fairly close to the Popham place. That will be a good place for her as she will be able to be the boss of everyone. That's fine for me to say, isn't it, as I am finished with school. I wonder what Joey will think of her? Do you remember me telling you about Les Linford, the fellow who was shell shocked? Well, his father found him three weeks ago in a bluff of poplar trees, hanging dead. I guess he just couldn't take that fear that was always with him. Even though he has made a fool of himself rather often, I always felt sorry for him as I remembered him in the trenches as a brave man. It is terrible what war can do, even years after it is over. As is usual this time of year I have a little break after seeding. I am going to Millfield tomorrow and hope to buy myself a tractor. My farm is getting busy enough that it is too much work for the horses. Colin is coming by shortly and we are going to repair some fences so I will close for now. My usual love to Laidie.

Your brother, Mac

Chapter 18

Millfield Manitoba 27th August, 1925

Dearest Mhairi,

I think it is longer than usual since my last letter! That is a sign of how busy I have been. Farming is going extremely well here in Manitoba. I have another 40 acres to my name so it is a good thing I got my tractor last fall. When you plough with horses, you can do about two and a half or three acres a day but with a tractor I can do 20 times that. The banker saw fit to let me buy a truck too. It is a 1925 Model T pickup, which is coming in handy for trips to town and hauling just about anything that will fit into it. It is a handsome vehicle with a dark green wooden box and matching dark green spokes on the wheels! I am still working with the McCorries and we will be cutting and binding next week if there is no rain. McCorries got another 80 acres south of the trail. They also bought a manure spreader, which saves a lot of hard work. They pull it with the tractor and it throws the manure out onto the field. I get to use it in exchange for labour in the fall. The big news around here is the twins. Steve and Annie have twin girls that were born in July. They named them Catherine and Nadia. Steve is popping the buttons off his shirt and it looks like Annie is going to be a very good mother. Did I ever tell you that Steve took Annie to the eye doctor over in Bainesville? She got eyeglasses and she is a different person with them. I'm starting to think she was never slow, she just couldn't see. I can picture Laidie with the twins; she would be a real little eight-year-old mama wouldn't she? I look at Joey and Catherine and Nadia, and pictures of Laidie, and I can't help but feel I am missing something. Most of the men my age around here are married, most of them to teachers. It seems every time a new teacher comes to Wolf River School she is grabbed up within the year. That all changed with Edina Popham. I think it will be a long time before there will be another new teacher as no one is in a hurry to grab Edina. I built a piece on the back of my barn to make room for ten more cows for the coming winter and also built two large granaries to store my wheat until I sell it. My wheat crop this year is going to be early and looks like there will be a heavy yield. There is a low spot behind the barn and I have made a ditch large enough to drain the water out and the land will become part of the pasture. Colin and Ford are doing well too. I wish you could meet them. Young Joey will be starting Grade 2 in a few days and he still likes school in spite of Miss Popham.

Have things improved any with Orville? You know, you and Laidie will always be welcome to come to Manitoba and make your home with me if you want to. Don't forget that extra room I have.

Your loving brother,

Mac

Chapter 19

Radford, Ontario 1926

Mhairi struggles to open the swollen slit of her left eye. The yellow and white pattern of the linoleum presses cold against her right cheek. From somewhere she can hear Laidie wailing uncontrollably, huge hiccups punctuating her sobs. Mhairi gasps at the sharp pain in her ribs. She pulls herself up into an awkward position, half sitting, half leaning against the table leg. She remembers.

She remembers how she tried to broach the request pleasantly, carefully, right after lunch. "Orville, I've been thinking it might be nice for Laidie to meet her Uncle Mac. He's asked us to come for a little vacation in July."

How Orville's jaws clenched visibly. "You're not going anywhere."

How she should have realized this was a final answer.

"It would only be for a couple of weeks. Mac has offered to pay for the train trip."

"He's nothing more than a trouble-making failure putting ideas into your stupid head. I *said*… you're not going anywhere."

She remembers the snapping back of her neck when his hand struck her squarely in the face. How she raised her hands to protect herself. How Orville's fist plowed into her stomach and knocked her to the floor. The awful struggle to draw air back into her lungs. The pain of his fingers digging into the soft flesh of her arms like vises, dragging her to her feet. Another backhanded slap to the face, and finally the boots, Orville's immaculately polished boots, striking her over and over in the ribs and stomach. And, as if in a nightmare, Laidie's high-pitched screams fading away into black mist.

How long has it been? The hysterical crying continues. Mhairi struggles to her feet, steadies herself first on the table and then on the cupboards, and makes her way to Laidie's room. She locates the child under the bed, wrapped in a blue quilt and shaking convulsively. She has vomited on the floor.

"Please come out, Laidie. He's gone."

The gulping sobs continue.

"It's all right Laidie. Please come out."

The room tilts from side to side and Mhairi eases herself onto the bed. After a moment she feels a cold little hand on her leg. Between paroxysms of terror, a small voice asks, "Is that you, Mama? You aren't dead?"

"Yes, it's me, Laidie. I'm right here. I'll be all right. He's gone now. You can come out."

Laidie crawls out dragging the blue quilt, soggy with tears. Mhairi wraps it around both of them and they huddle on the bed. Laidie brings her hand to the swollen and purpling face, her touch as light as the settling of a butterfly. "Mama, I'll take care of you."

Oh, she should have known. How could she have imagined for a moment that she and Laidie would have been allowed to travel to Manitoba to see Mac? After all, she is not allowed to go for groceries alone, or even to leave the house during the day when Orville is at work. He comes with her to buy clothing, even her brassieres and stockings. Everything must meet his specifications and approval. He has not agreed to have a telephone put in, even though many in Radford already enjoy that convenience. She must hide her letters from Mac and read them secretly or risk having them torn from her hands and savaged by derogatory criticism. The letters do not come as often now. Although Mac has never been a prolific letter-writer, it seems he has almost abandoned her. She wonders.

There is one thing for which Mhairi is thankful. Since the stillbirth of the wee boy seven years ago, Orville is no longer interested in exacting his marital rights, a welcome turn of events to her. His lust and cruel appetites, once so overpowering, have ceased to exist. Or have they? Again, she wonders.

Laidie has fallen asleep in Mhairi's arms, still shuddering with the occasional hiccup. Mhairi peels away the damp quilt and eases the little girl to her pillow before pulling up the comforter. She forces herself up from the bed. The bruises are settling in, darkening and swelling, and every movement knifes pain through her body.

She goes to the stove and fetches a dipper of warm water from the reservoir. She wipes the sink basin with a rag and pours the water into it slowly. A green face rag hangs on the hook by the basin. She soaks it in the water and brings it slowly to her face. She knows the water should be cold to suppress the swelling, but she needs it to be warm. Comfort must be warm, not cold. The rag soothes the throbbing flesh around her eye. She takes three aspirin tablets from the drawer beneath the sink and swallows them with a sip of water from the pail on the cupboard. She cannot bear to touch any part of her stomach and rib cage, where great purplish blooms are already opening their ugly petals on her skin.

The clock in the living room chimes five. Mhairi has one hour in which to prepare supper.

Millfield, Manitoba, September 2, 1926

Dearest Mhairi,

I'm sorry it didn't work out for you and Laidie to visit this summer. We will just have to plan for another time, won't we? It is raining again, the fourth day in a row. Just about everyone around Wolf River is finished threshing so the moisture is welcome. The threshing gangs seem to get bigger every year and the meals get better. All the ladies are intent on outdoing each other with their cooking. Ford and Colin and myself really look forward to the harvest as we get better food then than any other time of the year. Well maybe Christmas. As we do not have any women to take their turn at meals, we make up for the shortfall by helping to supply beef and eggs and potatoes and whatever else they can use. The crop yields are again beyond expectations. It leaves one wondering if it is all too good to be true. They say wheat prices are going to hold over the next year. People are optimistic about just about everything. Steve and Annie Kalinsky have a new baby, a little boy (Peter), the end of July. The twins are just turned one, Annie is a busy lady. You would like Annie. She is a down to earth person, honest and kind. I often talk to her about you and she hopes she will meet you some day. The Kalinskys had a sad time last month: one of Steve's good cattle dogs died after dragging himself home with a bullet in his side. He had been gone three days. There is no way to know for sure but Steve has his suspicions that Tom King might know something about it. I ordered myself one of those new battery operated radios from the hardware store. Looking forward to listening to news and hockey games this winter. Millfield has finally finished putting in electricity and waterworks. It seems strange to be able to see the lights of town from here. Actually, Millfield is progressing quickly. Doctor Millan now has a partner, a Doctor Smythe from Nova Scotia. The community built a small hospital, all with volunteers. It has 6 rooms and they plan to add another 6 in two years. Mrs. Collins (where I stayed when I first came to Millfield) will be boarding any nurses who come here to work. By the way, thank you for the latest picture of Laidie. I wish I did not have to imagine the colour, but as you say dark auburn, I'm guessing her hair must be like mine, including the curls. I'm happy to hear how well she does in school. Do you think she could write me a letter and put it in with your next one? Along with some of her drawings that you have been telling me about? I have become quite close to Colin McCorrie's boy Joey. He is nine now and smart as a whip. He rides a horse as well as his father and thinks he knows everything about farming. Having grown up with mostly adults, he is old for his age. I can only dare to imagine the shenanigans he and Laidie would cause if they were to meet. It looks like the rain is letting up. I will take advantage and go to town to post this letter. Write soon Mhairi.

Love from your brother, Mac.

Chapter 20

Radford, Ontario, 1927

The air in Orville's office is thick with the smell of stale cigarette ashes, humid newspapers, and ripe banana peels. He raises the sash window and props it up with a ruler before turning his attention to the letters on his desk. A letter from Millfield, addressed to Mrs. Orville Christie, tops the pile. Orville deals with the rest of the mail, saving the Millfield letter for last. He opens the envelope methodically, tearing first across the end by the stamp, inserting his skinny middle finger in the opening, and tearing down the top fold. He spreads the paper open.

Millfield, Manitoba, June 10, 1927

Dear sister and niece,

I'm hoping this finds both of you well. Things have been busy here since I last wrote you. I spent much of the winter improving my house. I made cabinets for the kitchen (I had some help from Steve) and finished the extra bedrooms. Walter Crampton came and showed me how to plaster the walls and that was quite an experience. Now that everything is painted, it looks better than I ever thought it would.

> *Every time I go into those rooms, I picture you and Laidie there. Will this be the summer you come to visit?*

Orville smiles, a scornful mean little slit. He lights a Player's Navy Cut and sucks the smoke deep, blows it out slowly through his teeth. He leans back in his chair.

> *Millfield is growing by leaps and bounds. We have more and more of what we need right here at home and people are happy they don't have to go to Bainesville all the time. A group of farmers around here started up a co-operative creamery last fall. As I don't have enough cream or milk to sell I'm not sure how the business part of it works but I can now go there to buy fresh butter. They make cheese too and it is as good as any I've had anywhere. They deliver milk right to the door in town but of course we farmers have our own supply at home.*

Orville scratches his genitals. He scrutinizes Mac's tidy script. He flicks the ash from the end of his cigarette and deliberately allows it to fall to the floor.

> *The Royal Canadian Legion opened a branch in Millfield last month and of course as a veteran I can go any time I want. Up until now veterans have not really had any place to go to that they could call their own. It's strange, but most people do not realize how important this is to us. Only those of us who have gone through the terrible experiences of war understand how important it is to be able to talk to others who have been there. Even so, a lot of the veterans don't want to talk about what they saw and did. Once those things become part of your brain you can never get rid of them. I speak from experience. The Commerce Club has nearly finished construction (mostly volunteer) on an entertainment building for the community. They wanted to call it The Millfield Opera House but that got shot down because some people thought it sounded a bit highfalutin. They settled for the Millfield Town Hall and it will be used for dances and concerts and the like. Bob McTavish and his brother plan to bring in movies starting this summer and are hard at work setting up a projector system in the hall. The Legion is talking about building a skating rink behind the*

hall and a group of sportsmen are talking about a curling rink. So, as you can tell, Millfield is progressing nicely.

A fleck of ash falls on the top corner of the letter and Orville watches a brown circle of scorch form beneath it. He bats the ash away just short of ignition. He hears Mhairi in the kitchen opening and closing cupboard doors, setting the table for lunch.

I have no news to report as regards the McCorries, except to say they continue to do well. Joey McCorrie has taken a growth spurt this past winter; he is 4 ½ feet tall. Since he started listening to the hockey games on the radio he has taken the notion he wants to be a hockey player. Colin tells him there is a flaw in his plans as he is not interested in learning to skate. Tom King is showing off his latest purchase, a 1927 Nash Coupe with white tires. Normally he doesn't have anything to do with me unless he wants to lord it over me for something, so of course he and Mabel made a point of bringing the car over to show me last week. My stomach is growling and I see it is time for supper so I will close and get this ready to take to the mail tomorrow. My invitation to you and Laidie still stands, just let me know when you would be able to come.

Love, Your brother, Mac.

PS Thank you for the drawings, Laidie. I love the way you put a spot of color in each of them. You are a wonderful little artist.

Orville folds the letter and puts it back in the envelope. He pulls a small key from his watch pocket, unlocks the bottom drawer of his desk, and tosses the letter on top of the others. He looks at his watch. Noon. Time for lunch.

Chapter 21

Radford, Ontario, 1928

Orville Christie is immune to the intoxication of spring. From the sweetness of warm April sunshine he storms into the kitchen. He throws the day's mail on the kitchen table where it sprawls across the yellow and blue flowered oilcloth like a spilled deck of odd-sized cards. He hurries into his office. Something is obviously wrong, more wrong than usual. Mhairi can hear him shuffling through papers, opening and slamming shut the drawers of his desk, muttering angry unintelligible words. After a few minutes he reappears, slams the office door, and goes back out into the sunshine, slamming the kitchen door as his final punctuation. Slamming is Orville's forte.

Orville never leaves the mail unattended. First he sorts it, leaving behind anything he deems unimportant enough for Mhairi to contend with. The rest goes into his office where he methodically deals with each piece before filing it in his wooden cabinet. Then he bundles the envelopes for the burning barrel in the back yard. But in his mysterious preoccupation this morning he overlooks the mail, forgetting his routine. Mhairi pushes the yellow gingham curtains of the kitchen window aside slightly, just enough to see him half way down the block. He walks with long purposeful strides through the dirty slush and holds his head down against the spring breeze. Once she is satisfied he is really gone she gathers the few pieces of mail together and places each letter carefully to one side as she looks at it. Two bills, one from the butcher shop, one from the iceman. A little advertising paper from Newton's Food and Drugs. And a letter from Mac.

She cannot remember the last time she received a letter from Mac. Her last several to him have gone unanswered and she has all but given up hope of hearing from him again. She goes to the window again, just to make sure there is no sign of Orville, and it is safe. Once in her bedroom she tears open the envelope. She is fearful of bad news.

Millfield, Manitoba, March 30, 1928

Dear Mhairi,

It is such a long time since you've written and I'm afraid I must have offended you somehow. If that is the case, please write and tell me what is the matter, because surely you know I would never intentionally hurt your feelings or make you unhappy. It concerns me deeply when you do not answer my letters. Whatever the reason, please let me know what is wrong.

I miss hearing about Laidie. I know she is past ten now and I imagine she must be getting to be quite a little lady. I would love a newer picture of her. We are enjoying an early spring this year and the snow is mostly gone although the ground is still frozen. The Farmer's Almanac tells us it is going to be a good year for planting, with dry fall weather. Ford McCorrie swears by that Almanac. I'm not so sure, but I will say that they have been right a few times. Cattle prices are still good and I have had six new calves arrive already. This is one of my favorite things about farming: the young animals in the spring. There is now a chicken hatchery in Bainesville and I plan to take the truck over there the end of April and pick up forty or so chicks. There is already a family of kittens in the loft of the barn and I am going to take one of the litter over to Kalinskys for the girls. As I write this it occurs to me that I had better take two, as the twins do not share kindly with each other. Spring is the time for cleaning the barn out and I will be spreading manure on the fields I can get to. It's heavy work, as I have to fork everything onto the stoneboat, then the horses walk on their own across the field as I fork everything off and then it is in for another load. You are probably wondering what in the world is a stoneboat? Not what it sounds like, that is for sure. It is just a little flat rack with no sides that rides on sled runners. In the summer I put wheels on it and we use it for hauling the stones that we pick off the fields. There are a lot of stones here, although I am gradually getting them cleared away. I'm sure I have told you about my neighbor Steve who had so many stones on his land he built a house out of them. Everyone around here is doing very well. Wheat has been good for a few years in a row and all the hard work is paying off. It is time for chores, Mhairi, and I have a sow that is getting restless. I might have a litter of piglets by morning! Rather, the sow might. So I must say goodbye for now, hoping I will receive word from you soon.

Love to both you and Laidie,

Mac

When you do not answer my letters?

Mhairi rereads the puzzling phrase. There have been no letters to answer. Or have there? A worm of suspicion squirms in her mind. It's all too clear. How could she not have realized? What a stroke of luck to have a chance to see the mail today! Suddenly the memory of the little pile on the kitchen table strikes her with panic. She folds Mac's letter and stuffs it into her apron pocket before hurrying back to the kitchen where she spreads the letters in haphazard disorder, hoping they look the same as Orville left them. He is already back. She can hear him stomping the wet snow off his boots at the back door. Did he look through the mail when he picked it up earlier? He enters, dragging a draft of spring air behind him, and Mhairi turns to the kitchen sink in an effort to hide the beating of her heart, which she fears must be punching outwardly at her chest like a wild animal trapped in a bag. Orville helps himself to a dipper of water, scoops up the mail, and retires to his office without a word. Mhairi starts dinner.

Laidie's joyful song can be heard long before she can be seen.

"The farmer in the dell, the farmer in the dell, Hi-ho, the derry-o, the farmer in the dell." Her exuberance is unmistakeable. She is celebrating spring.

"The farmer takes a wife, the farmer takes a wife, Hi-ho, the derry-o," she pauses mid-song while she gets the door open, "The farmer takes a wife. Hello, Mama!"

Mhairi smiles at the child. Laidie can be counted upon to lift spirits wherever she goes. "Did you remember to bring your lunchbox home tonight?"

"The wife takes a child, The wife takes a child, yes I did, derry-o Mama, deary-o Mama, yes I did," she sings. She kicks off her boots and holds out her arms for a hug.

"Put your things away, sweetheart, and come and help Mama get dinner ready. Wash up first, please."

There is no argument or complaint. Laidie hangs her coat and book bag on her hook by the door. She is a willing child, has always been. She soaps her hands in the basin of water in the sink and dries off on her own pink towel. Mhairi sets out dishes and silverware and Laidie arranges everything perfectly. She, like her mother, knows exactly how things must be. It's extremely important to keep Father happy, to avoid upsetting the delicate balance that can tip from calm to rage at the slightest provocation. Still humming "Farmer in the Dell" she sets out the three twins, as they call them: salt and pepper, cream and sugar, bread and butter. She goes to the sideboard to get napkins. Mhairi opens jars of yellow beans and beets to go with the potatoes, already boiling, and checks the little chicken in the oven. The rice pudding is cooling and everything will be ready by the appointed hour.

Orville emerges from his office on the dot of six. He hasn't been seen since his earlier retreat with the mail and he is still restless. The meal proceeds without incident. Laidie finishes first.

"May I please be excused, Father?"

"You may. But come here first."

She slips out of her chair to stand at his side. He offers a hint of a smile. "And how is my Princess Laidie? Did you have a good day at school?" He pats her dark red hair, fingers the braids, and rubs her back up and down.

"I'm fine, Father. I had a good day."

"Do you have some schoolwork for tonight, Princess?"

"Yes. A little."

"Good girl. I'll come and help you with it later."

Laidie's freckles darken. Mhairi bows her head and concentrates on what is left of her rice pudding. A sharp pain begins in her left eye and she knows a headache is imminent. "Excuse me please, Orville."

He takes his time. "Yes." He pushes back from the table too.

Mhairi quickly clears the leftover food to the icebox. "Laidie. The table. I'll come back and finish the dishes in a little while. You finish your schoolwork and have a bath, sweetheart. I'm going to lie down."

There is nothing to be done for one of Mhairi's headaches. She goes to the bedroom, leaving her door ajar. Orville has not shared this room with her since the death of the baby boy eight years ago, when he moved to the small bedroom upstairs. He has not touched Mhairi since. She knows he goes elsewhere.

She can hear Laidie's voice. "The wife takes a child, the wife takes a child, Hi ho, hi ho, hi ho, and hi ho…the wife takes a child." Laidie clatters the dishes into the sink and in her skull Mhairi can feel the reverberation of each piece of china. After a moment of quiet she can hear the sound of Laidie dragging the book bag from its hook, spilling its contents on the kitchen table. A pencil falls to the floor and the sound feels like the snap of a finger behind Mhairi's eyes.

Laidie spreads her arithmetic before her. Orville is in his office but the door is open and he has been waiting. He comes to sit beside her, pulling his chair close, watching as she does each problem. He clasps and unclasps his long fingers and runs them through his slick hair. Laidie can smell his shaving soap and the starch on his shirt. He rubs her back in a large and slow circular motion.

"All right, Princess Laidie. Time for your bath. You can finish this in the morning."

Through the partly opened bedroom window, early evening air flows across Mhairi's bed and spreads its fragrance through the room. She hears the sloshing in the big tub and she pictures it with its claw feet spread wide and gripping the floor. The water sounds like stormy waves, wind-driven rain, overflowing sinks. A child's song runs through Mhairi's head, weaving its way through the ache. "The rat takes the cheese, the rat takes the cheese…hi ho the derry-o… the cheese stands alone…hi ho, hi ho the derry-o…"

Chapter 22

Millfield Manitoba, April 24, 1928

Dearest Mhairi,

I am shocked but not really surprised to learn that Orville has been taking my letters. I wish we could know how much mail he actually has stolen over the years. Thank you for the address of Mrs. Millie Lundy. From now on I will send all letters directly to her. Dear sister, we must begin to plan a way to get you away from Orville. There is not a day goes by that I do not worry about the way he treats you. Do you think it would be possible to come out this summer? I understand how careful you have to be, so take your time and think everything through. I would need a couple of weeks at this end. The ever-productive Kalinskys have another boy! The little fellow was born a week ago, his name is Simon. Annie's mother, Ethel Elliott, is over there helping out. Steve says Annie won't admit she needs help but I think he is happy to have Ethel there for a while, even though he and Ethel don't speak to each other half the time. I broke my left thumb three weeks ago, got it jammed in a belt on the tractor. I went to see Dr. Smythe at the hospital and he said I was lucky that was all that broke. He looked at it and left me with a nurse who splinted and bandaged it. She is Alice Rose Fuller, new in Millfield, and came from Brandon to work in the hospital. She boards at Mrs. Collins place (that is where I lived for a couple of months when I first came out here). She is a mighty fine young lady and wants me to come back and have the splint checked every two weeks. Ford and Colin are just about ready to start planting their wheat and I will start shortly after. There was a good bit of snow this past winter and the fields should be in good shape. Last fall I cleared another 20 acres and as soon as I am finished seeding I am going to burn up all the brush and pick the stones off it, so it should be ready to plant by spring 1929. Tom King had his men dig out a drain on his north field last fall. When the snow melted all the water came on to my land and sat, so that field will have to dry out before I can get onto it. For this year I think I will put oats there. In the fall I will have to figure out some way to drain it, maybe into some of Steve's land that is swampy anyway. Unlike Tom King, I will talk it over first with Steve. Please thank Laidie for her latest batch of drawings. I am having trouble figuring some of them out, but don't tell her that. Her pictures don't seem as happy as they used to. I don't know… dark colours, eyes with blue tears. Is she all right? You can tell her I made a poplar frame for her picture of you and it sits on my bureau. I'm glad to hear she is doing so well in school. Young Joey McCorrie is a corker of a boy. I hear tell he has Miss Edina Popham pulling her hair out. The two of them are the same in some ways, like being stubborn and smart at the same time. The difference is, Joey has a sense of humour and she doesn't. All the same, everyone says she is a good teacher. She drives herself to school every day in her little democrat buggy. Ford said he heard her mother was doing poorly. No one will talk about what is wrong with her but Alice Rose thought she probably didn't have long to live. It's chore time, Mhairi. I will take this to the post office tomorrow when I go to have my thumb checked. Write soon. And God bless Mrs. Lundy.

Love, Your brother, Mac

Millfield, Manitoba, December 3, 1928

Dear Mhairi and family,

Just a little note to put in with your Christmas package. I hope it will arrive early. You will notice I have included a package of handkerchiefs for Orville, just to keep things smoothed over and unsuspicious. In addition to your package I am sending a little more cash (look inside the gloves) to add to your escape fund. I hope Laidie likes the book I picked for her. I saw Edina Popham in Millfield at the general store and asked her opinion of what a twelve year old girl might enjoy. She assured me that Magic for Marigold by L.M. Montgomery is a new book this year that is very popular. The art book is intended for her birthday. I often wonder if Laidie minds having a birthday so close to Christmas. Do you remember me telling you about Alice-Rose Fuller, one of the nurses at the hospital? I have been seeing her on a slightly more than friendly basis ever since my broken finger healed. She says she is looking forward to meeting you. You will like her; she is very down to earth and kind. And very pretty too, tall and blonde. I am trying to decide what I might get for her for Christmas. I wish you were here to help. I am thinking perhaps I might get a book for her, too. I don't have much imagination, do I? She will be going home to Brandon for the Christmas holiday so I must find something before she leaves. Annie sent Steve over yesterday with some shortbread and fruit cake for Christmas. I don't know how she has time to bake with four little ones, the oldest just past three. Steve is a lucky man. Now, if we could just find someone for Colin! But I don't think he will ever get over losing Saharah. All is well here. Wheat is sold, hay put up, woodpile stacked high for winter. Try to have a good Christmas, sister. Time will fly by and before long you will be safe here.

Love from your brother, Mac

Chapter 23

Millfield, 1929

The wheat yields of 1928 are spectacular across the prairies and the fields around Millfield contribute to the overabundance. The McCorries' crop brings record prices and Ford and Colin bask in the face of such security.

The next year, 1929, begins with auspicious promise. The weather is favourable and a crop nearly as remarkable as the previous year's is harvested. Prices soar to over $1.60 a bushel and a golden flood of wheat flows to prairie elevators. In Millfield, long trains of grain cars stretch along the railway track, waiting to transport the bounty to Winnipeg. But markets are glutted. The stage is set for a huge agricultural disaster. News of a huge economic crash on the stock markets makes its way into prairie communities in late October.

"I'm not too worried about anything that happens down east," Ford says to Colin. "Besides, all our investments are right here on the farm. I don't think it'll affect us at all."

Colin wants to agree. "I hope you're right." But a deep gut reaction nags at him.

Ford leans back in his chair and puts the finishing touches on the cigarette he is rolling. "If we keep getting grain prices like these, we'll see it through, no matter what happens with the stock markets."

He looks out the kitchen window to his farmyard and its sturdy buildings. Fat chickens scratch the ground for feed. Two milk cows absent-mindedly chew their cuds over by the fence. Pigs squabble loudly in their pen behind the barn. Further out, cattle and horses graze the remains of the little summer pasture.

"Yep. We're in pretty good shape. We'll be fine."

Colin hangs on those words. The future of the farm stretches into the haze of his imagination. He visualizes Joey, now just on the cusp of his teenage years. He sees an enterprise built on the groundwork laid by Ford and himself. He knows how significant the next few years will be.

But what he and Ford cannot see are the elevators, ports, and ships the world over filling to capacity with western grain. He cannot know that the Wheat Pool does not hedge against the falling prices of glutted markets. Already encumbered by a huge unsold surplus of grain bought at untenably high prices, it is impossible for them to resell the wheat on world markets for even a minuscule profit. The possibility of the Pool's impending default on bank loans and its ultimate bankruptcy is unthinkable.

So 1929, a year that begins with such prosperous promise, closes out the calendar with predictions of financial gloom after another, albeit lesser, market crash further punishes the stock markets in mid-November. Even Ford, looking back on the boom times of the twenties with their busy factories and flourishing agriculture, begins to wonder how long this pessimistic outlook can last.

He and Colin cannot know of the dark scenario biding its time in the transforming atmosphere above. The ominous predictions of 1929 will fade to insignificance in the face of what is to come.

Chapter 24

Millfield Manitoba, March 31, 1929

Dear Mhairi,

Spring is coming to Manitoba early this year. Most of the snow is gone and crows have been back for over a month already. Colin saw a meadowlark last week. Ford is itching to get out on the land, as he always is, but he is usually ahead of himself by two or three weeks. Wolf River is up over its banks in places but no one seems to be too worried about major flooding unless we get a lot of rain in a short time. I have ordered some lilacs and caragana to plant around the yard. The tree nursery man at Bainesville told me they would be a good choice as they are hardy and long-lived. They will be ready to be picked up at the end of April and I think I will get a crab-apple tree when I go to pick them up. Do you remember the crab-apple tree we used to have growing up? The McCorries have a big one and Ford says it takes about six years before I will have any apples to speak of. I think I forgot to tell you that Ike Evans from the Riverview District talked me into buying six sheep from him last fall. They are all ewes and they are all due to deliver babies within the next two months. Ike assured me they are easy to care for and profitable too. He will come and shear them for me when the time comes. Queenie, of course, is delighted. Herding comes naturally to her as a Border Collie and she can hardly wait to get to work. I will have all my machinery ready to go in a few weeks and hopefully the weather will co-operate and allow planting without any problems. I am looking forward to another year of big crops. I have decided to sell off some of my cattle as my herd is really far larger than I need. Steve and Annie will take the milk cows and I will just keep two for myself. Steve and Annie are fine, by the way. They are expecting another blessed event! I will be spending Easter with them; Annie is cooking a big ham dinner for the McCorries and myself. Alice-Rose has gone home to Brandon for Easter weekend. I miss her, but of course she wants to see her family.

Take care of yourself and Laidie. My plans to have the two of you join me have not changed, even with Alice-Rose in the picture.

Love, Mac

Millfield, Manitoba, July 18, 1929

Dear Sister,

Well, since my last letter I have decided I will never be a sheep farmer. Sheep are the strangest animals. All winter the ewes were as friendly as could be, but when the lambs started coming they became totally different animals. They used to let Queenie sleep right beside their pen but one of the biggest ewes, when she gave birth to her lamb, butted Queenie halfway across the barn. They aren't too friendly with me either if I try to get close to the lambs. I put them out on the pasture a few weeks ago and they are eating the roots right out from under the grass. I always pictured sheep as white and soft, but these are dirty and matted. Ike Evans came two weeks ago to shear them and their wool was so matted with burdocks and blue bur that he said it wasn't hardly worth anything. As I do not care for lamb or mutton even slightly, I sold the lot of them to the Pophams over in the Riverview District. Apparently they have had sheep before and know what they are getting into. Speaking of the Riverview District, they challenged the Wolf River District to a baseball game next week. We don't know much about actually playing the game, but Colin and I have agreed to take turns pitching and catching so we don't have to do so much running with our gimpy legs. I am already wondering if that is going to be a good idea. I got everything planted from the Bainesville plant nursery. Young Joey McCorrie helped me. The lilacs and caragana should give nice shelter from the west and north. The crab apple tree I have put at the end of the garden furthest from the house. The Millfield Fair is just over. It is getting bigger every year. Ford McCorrie showed his team of heavy horses but something happened to his harness setup and he was disqualified. He is suspicious that Tom King was lurking around the barns the night before. Annie Kalinsky, who bakes the best pies and biscuits for miles around, did not even place in the competitions because one of the judges noticed what looked like mouse droppings on the edge of a plate. Annie is one of the cleanest women I know and if there were mouse droppings anywhere near her baking, someone else put them there. Ethel Elliot (Annie's mother) says it is very strange that Mabel King walked off with the red ribbon prizes. Everyone knows that Mabel pays Mrs. Fletcher to do all her baking. There is a lot of talk about the Kings as you can imagine. I guess we should not be so suspicious, but sometimes things seem like more than just co-incidence. I have been helping McCorries clean their barn and loft for barn dancing. This is something a lot of farmers do out here. It is a break before harvest and haying starts. Charlie Maxwell and his brother Vernon on their fiddles and Mrs. Maxwell chording on the piano provide the music. And a foot-stomping affair it is; the dust just bouncing out of the cracks in the loft floor. The McCorries charge 25 cents a person for the dance. People bring their children and babies (the babies somehow manage to go to sleep behind the piano and the older boys and girls spend their time seeing how far they can slide on the dance area of the floor) and everyone has a great time. The ladies provide sandwiches and cake and coffee, and there is always some stronger refreshment being served outside at the bottom of the back stairs to the loft.

The first dance is next Saturday night and I am hoping to take Alice Rose. I have not had a chance to ask her yet as she has been very busy at the hospital, I have not seen her for three weeks. I have to go into Millfield tomorrow so I will go around by the hospital and talk to her. I am looking forward to your next letter.

Love, Mac

Millfield, Manitoba, September, 1929

Dearest sister,

There is not much news around here. Harvest went well; we only had two short delays because of rain. Bumper crops of wheat all around; everyone's granaries are full to overflowing. They are paying $1.60 for wheat, not as good as several years ago but still good enough to make a nice profit. There was a bit of a scare last week with the Kalinsky twins. They wandered away when Annie was busy with the other two little ones and she thought they were with Steve. No one realized they were missing until Steve came in to eat supper. The word spread like wildfire and huge groups of searchers went out in all directions. Nobody had any idea even which direction they might have gone. Most of the searchers from town went home when it got dark as they probably would have got lost too if they had stayed. All the Wolf River people kept looking all night. Ethel took the two little boys so Annie could go out and help hunt for the twins. It got cold that night and Annie was frantic because she couldn't remember whether they had coats on or not. The town people *all came back as soon as the sun was up and you could hear the girls' names being called in all directions. In the end, the one who found them was Joey, bless his heart. He was not allowed to go out into the flats and sloughs in Willis Marsh but as it turned out he didn't need to. Catherine and Nadia had wandered over the trail to my place and found what they called a cave in one of my haystacks and that is where they spent the night. The two of them were just sitting there with their arms around each other, hearing all the calling but afraid to answer back in case they were in trouble. It made me think of all the times I swore at those sheep for the damage they could to a stack, and in the end it was one of those chewed-out holes that sheltered the girls. That is exactly the kind of place Joey would have explored. Other than that, nothing is happening except that I have not been feeling well this last while. I have a dull pain in my back that just won't go away and I don't feel like eating. Even Annie's occasional gifts of baking go unfinished. By the way, Alice-Rose has gone back to Brandon. She is getting married on Thanksgiving weekend.*

I am looking forward to the next letters from you and Laidie. Plans continue. I always feel better when I hear from you.

Love, Mac

Chapter 25

Millfield Manitoba, January 30, 1930

Dear Mhairi and Laidie,

Thank you so much for the Christmas gift of hand-knitted socks and the latest picture of Laidie. She is a beautiful thirteen-year-old. She reminds me a lot of our mother, don't you think? Speaking of thirteen-year-olds, my dear dog Queenie died in late November. Thankfully the ground was not frozen solid and I was able to dig a grave for her beside the lilacs, her favorite spot. I hurt my back doing so and it is still bothering me. Colin McCorrie insists I should get another dog right away but I think I will wait. There will be some purebred Border Collies available next spring in Bainesville. After Queenie, I wouldn't have any other kind. I am glad I bought lumber last fall for the final stage of my house. Money is going to be tight come spring. Ford McCorrie bought a new car, a dark blue Chevrolet. Ford is optimistic to a fault; I think he may regret the car if the economic situation gets any worse. I don't intend to make any purchases until next summer at the earliest and only then if things are better across the country. Tom and Mabel King are still flying high. Mabel has a hired girl now, even though she herself has nothing to do. They are both getting fat! There is not much snow this winter so far and after a dry fall some people are saying it could be the start of a drought. Somehow I don't believe that will happen. Rains on the prairies always seem to come when they are needed. What is it they say? Rain follows the plow? The huge harvests of wheat from the past few years have started to pile up on us out here in the west. Granaries are overflowing and I have grain piled on the ground. There is nowhere to sell it, and even if I could, the price per bushel is now lower than the cost of seed. The McCorries and the Kalinskys send their regards; they are all looking forward to meeting you and Laidie next summer. I understand it is best for Laidie to finish her school year in Radford, but that doesn't stop me from wishing you could come right away. Still, we have to be careful and make sure we do everything right so that Orville doesn't find out and put a stop to everything. I will sign off for now, Mhairi. I seem to be more tired than usual lately and I have to force myself just to get up in the mornings. My cattle and chickens await and with this sore back it takes me longer to get my chores done than it used to.

Much love, Your brother Mac.

Millfield, Manitoba, May 1, 1930

Dearest Mhairi,

Winter has dragged on and on. I am not feeling any better than I was a month ago. My back is still very sore and the pain seems to be in my stomach as well. I have lost some weight, although that is probably due to my lack of desire and energy to cook for myself. Annie sometimes sends a pie or some stew over with Steve when he comes, so that helps a lot when I have an appetite, which is not often. The Docs, Millan and Smythe, can't seem to figure out what is wrong.

I myself think it is just a long drawn out case of influenza and I am sure things will improve once you and Laidie are here. The land is very dry this spring because there was not a lot of snow cover this past winter. I don't know how I would manage without the McCorries and Steve. They help whenever they are able and they both refuse to take any pay for their work. Steve says they will take it out of my hide once I am better. I have decided not to get a car. It is becoming very obvious that money is going to be scarcer than I thought. There is still no market for wheat and it makes me wonder if the expense of sowing crops is worthwhile. It will depend on the weather, I guess, and whether the Wheat Pool can start to move some of this huge surplus of wheat we are sitting on. I have sold some of my livestock, prices were poor though. I have kept two milk cows and three steers (for the beef ring). Colin is still trying to convince me to get another dog to replace Queenie. He knows someone who has Border Collie pups ready to give away. I am tempted, but will wait until you and Laidie arrive and you can help me pick one out. Annie and Steve, by the way, have yet another addition to their family: a little girl, Irina Ethel, named for her two grandmothers. Nadia and Catherine are just five, the boys Peter and Simon are four and three, I think. The twins are just like two little mothers, a lot like Annie, and smart as a pair of foxes. Steve says enough is enough and Irina will be the last. We shall see, I guess. I am expecting you will send a letter by return post to give me the dates for your travel. As soon as I hear from you I will mail the train tickets to Mrs. Lundy, along with some extra money for you. Please be extra careful now, Mhairi. We can't afford for Orville to find out and ruin what might be your only chance to get away from him. Please let Millie Lundy know how grateful I am for her help and friendship to you. It would make me very happy to be able to meet her someday. I have some business in Millfield tomorrow morning with my lawyer, Denver Atchison. I will tell you about it when you arrive.

Your loving brother, Mac

PS: Once you and Laidie are here safe and sound, I know I will start to feel better.

Chapter 26

Radford, Ontario, 1930

June 15th, 1930. TELEGRAM

MACKENZIE WARD PASSED AWAY SUNDAY JUNE 14 STOP FUNERAL JUNE 17 STOP REGARDS AND SYMPATHY STOP G MCCORRIE

Orville stands behind Mhairi, reading the telegram over her shoulder. He loosens his collar and peers through his thick spectacles. He turns away with a hint of a smile stretched over his thin lips. Without a word he turns and leaves, letting the screen door slam behind him on his way out.

It is Monday and hot already at 8:30. Mhairi is unable to absorb the news of the morning, not just yet. After some time she pushes away from the table. She piles the breakfast dishes into the sink, fills it with steaming water, sprinkles a handful of white soap flakes on the surface, and watches as they settle like snow. She hauls the gas-motor washing machine from its corner in the kitchen and fills it with hot water from the boiler on the stove. She then sets up the rinse tub on its stand and sorts and loads the first pile of laundry into the washer. Setting the lever, she watches as the washer launches into its rhythmic agitation. She returns to the sink, finishes the dishes, sweeps the floor, and closes the windows against the mounting heat. Back to the washer. She pulls the lever to stop the agitation and swings the wringer to a position between the washer and the tub. She usually uses a large wooden stick to dig out the wet pieces and feed them into the wringer. This morning, she thrusts her bare hands into the water, oblivious to the heat. Her fingers redden and swell as she lifts each piece of laundry up to the sucking slit. She always approaches this part of the process with great caution. Everyone knows about Mrs. Danforth over on the other side of Radford. She tempted her fingers too close to the rollers when feeding in a towel and had her arm pulled in to the elbow along with the fabric. Her husband heard her screams and was able to turn the wringer off, but not soon enough to prevent the machine from stripping skin and flesh from her arm. Mrs. Danforth is horribly scarred and never regained the use of her arm and hand. But this morning Mhairi is not thinking about Mrs. Danforth and her mutilated arm. She pushes the wet clothes into the greedy maw. The laundry passes through the rollers and drops on the other side into the rinse tub with its blued water. She dunks each piece up and down to remove the soap and swings the wringer to a new position over the clothesbasket. With the last bedsheet she glances away just long enough for the hungry rollers to nibble at her fingers. The hot pain shoots up her arm. By the time she hits the release bar on the top of the wringer assembly her left hand is fully engaged in the machine. She somehow manages to spring the rollers and extricate herself.

The pain is a tangible thing. It forces Mhairi's mind into focus. *Can it possibly be true? Can Mac really be dead?*

She leaves the laundry unfinished, forgetting to worry about Orville's probable reaction. She dry-swallows four aspirin for the hot throbbing in her hand and wraps her entire arm in a cold wet towel. The wet laundry sits in its pile in the basket, going nowhere. Mhairi returns to the kitchen table where the telegram lies atop the remains of breakfast. She smooths the yellow paper and reads it again, in disbelief. She rests her head on her forearms between the dirty dishes and a strawberry jam spot on the tablecloth. Tears meld with the crumbs on the table and dilute the spot of jam into a sticky red puddle.

Mhairi takes the telegram to her bedroom. She lifts a small metal lockbox from the bottom drawer of her bureau along with a small red velvet bag, which she empties onto the bed. The fingers of her good hand rummage in the pile of old jewellery for a key. It opens a green brocade-covered box where important family documents are kept: their marriage certificate, records of Laidie's birth and baptism, the deed to their home, and a grainy photo of Mhairi's parents. A bundle of letters from Mac spanning twelve years, tied with string, is carefully organized from first to last.

She takes the bundle out to the back porch and sits on the cane rocker and slides the worn envelopes out of the string. The letters have been read and reread over the years, but Mhairi especially wants to study the last few. *How could I have missed knowing how sick he must have been? Why didn't he tell me?*

It is eleven thirty. In half an hour Orville will be home for lunch.

Chapter 27

June 15, 1930

Millfield Manitoba,

Dear Mr. and Mrs. Christie,

I am very sorry for the loss of your brother Mac Ward. I sent you a telegram but I want to be a little more personal.

I know you must have a lot of questions. I was a good friend of Mac's and I know he would want me to try to explain what happened. He was fine until late this past winter when he hurt his back. He was not sure how it happened but it did not get better and he was in a lot of pain, which spread to his stomach area. He came down with stomach flu and he had a hard time keeping his meals down and started to lose weight, but he told me he didn't feel much like eating anyway. The last while he was very thin and not looking good at all and the pain seemed to be getting worse all the time. The doctor in Millfield could not figure it out and finally took Mac into the hospital so he could help more with the pain. Mac was only in the hospital for three days when he died and the doctor says he now believes it had something to do with the pancreas. The doctor says his back injury probably didn't cause it.

Mac's friend Steve Kalinsky and me are arranging the funeral. I don't expect you will be able to make the trip but everyone will be thinking of you. Everybody around here liked Mac and he was a good friend and we will all miss him.

Mac's lawyer Denver Atchison asked me to tell you he will be getting in touch with you through your lawyer if you could telephone him to let him know who your lawyer is and how he can be reached. Atchison's telephone number is Millfield 306-4 or you can write him at Box 19 Millfield, Man. I am thinking you will want to reach him as soon as possible so the telephone would likely be best.

I send sympathy to you from our family of Ford (my father), myself, and son Joey, and from Steve and Annie Kalinsky, who were also close friends of Mac.

I will mail this tomorrow (Monday) and hope it will not take too long to reach you.

Colin McCorrie, Box 19, Millifield, Man.

Denver Atchison, the Millfield lawyer, sends a letter to Orville's lawyer in Radford. He outlines the terms of Mac Ward's last will and testament, written and signed only three weeks before he died. Everything Mac owned is left to Mhairi.

Orville takes charge immediately. This turn of events is what he has been waiting for. Mhairi would like to have taken time to consider her options, now that her plans to escape to Manitoba are obliterated, but she doesn't dare articulate this to Orville, who is already at work on the logistics of moving to the prairies.

His lumberyard business is on a rapid decline following the market crash of the previous year. Cash is in short supply everywhere. Plans that may have been in place for construction are either on hold or cancelled and no shipments of new lumber are arriving. Anything already in stock is reduced in price and gathering dust and Orville knows it is only a matter of time before the bank will be knocking at his door. Of course, Mhairi knows nothing of this.

It will be about a month, Orville says, before affairs are settled and they will be ready to leave. Let the bank have the house and the lumberyard, he sneers.

"What are you two looking so miserable about?" he demands of Mhairi and Laidie. "I'd think you'd be happy to get a free farm. The farmers on the prairies have been doing better than anybody. We'll be well-off."

Mhairi and Laidie are silent.

"You'd better start packing things," he barks. "It'll take you longer than you think." He slams the door on his way out.

Now that's ironic, Mhairi thinks bitterly. She has so many boxes already packed and hidden in various places, waiting for the trip to Millfield. If Orville only knew…

Laidie goes to her room and Mhairi sits at the kitchen table, head in hands. She was anticipating such relief at leaving Orville and at being in Manitoba with Mac. Now there is to be no such liberation.

What was to have been an escape is now a sentence.

The Christies step from the train onto the hot plank platform in Millfield. It is just after two and the mid-August temperature is close to 90 degrees. Hot wind presses itself against them, flattening their clothing against their skin and filling their nostrils and eyes with black dust. They are sweaty from the long trip and the dust sticks to their skin and clothing, which is already grungy from four days of travel. Mhairi and Laidie are in light cotton dresses but Orville is pompously outfitted in a black suit with vest and tie. The collar of his white shirt is yellow and oily, already collecting dust. He loosens his tie slightly and squints through his spectacles at what he can see of Millfield, which is very little, as the train station sits on the north edge of town.

A team of horses pulling a wide wagon makes its way down the street and pulls up to the platform. A tall man with blond hair poking out from all sides of his straw hat swings his legs over the wagon seat and lands on his feet in the dust. "You must be the Christies."

Orville smiles thinly and extends his long-fingered hand. "That we are." He is repulsed by the badly scarred face of the man before them. He gestures to the two standing behind him. "This is my wife Mhairi and my daughter Laidie."

"Pleased to meet all of you! I'm Colin McCorrie, as I'm sure you've figured out. Did you have a good trip?"

Mhairi takes a breath as if she is about to say something but Orville cuts in. "Yes, it was all right, but too long. And the train wasn't up to what we're used to."

Colin regards Laidic. "Mac talked to me a lot about you," he smiles. "I wish it was him picking you up today instead of me."

"Well then," Orville interjects with an overweening smile, "we wouldn't be here if Mac was still living, now would we?"

Colin doesn't answer. He has decided in less than a minute that he does not care for Orville Christie.

Colin would have preferred to bring the Model T to the station but decided upon the wagon so he wouldn't have to make another trip for the Christies' belongings. He and Orville load three heavy trunks and over a dozen boxes into the wagon and Colin helps Mhairi and Laidie to climb aboard before he and Orville take their place on the seat up front. The horses strain to establish some momentum and the wagon finally rolls down the street to the south end of Millfield where they turn east towards Mac Ward's farm.

The temperature has risen since they left Millfield and out on the open prairie the hot wind is free to sweep the land. The vast circular horizon is blurred with dust, like a far-off rim of smoke. Strange mirages bend the air into watery pools and heat ripples wash the fields.

Mac's farmyard comes into sight. It is as Mhairi imagined it would be: clean and well-kept, the buildings organized into a little square of civilization out here on the vast prairie. Lilacs and caraganas circle the yard. A flock of brown chickens flutters away in a panic at the approach of the wagon and a large pig roots in the dry soil by the barn.

"I think Mac left everything in good order. We've been looking after everything for you." Colin draws the horses to a halt in front of the house. "I'll help you unload right here, and I'll come back with some supper for you in an hour or so. Our hired girl is a great cook."

"Mr. McCorrie, thank you so much for bringing us from the station. Mac put us in good hands with you." Mhairi smiles. This is definitely a friendly face, despite its scars.

"Please call me Colin," he smiles.

Orville starts pulling trunks and boxes from the wagon. They land on the ground in puffs of fine dust and Colin helps drag them to the porch. Mhairi and Laidie carry the suitcases and smaller boxes into the stiflingly hot house.

Orville knows nothing about farming. To his credit, however, he is not afraid of hard work. Things would be easier for him if he would admit to needing help, but that is not his nature. Everything is tackled and solved by trial and error, a process not suited to a man of such volatility. Fortunately for Orville, the neighbors have harvested Mac's meagre crop and scavenged together some winter feed for his livestock. The community welcomes the Christies with no reservations. They are, after all, Mac's family.

Chapter 28

Wolf River, 1930

The dust is a hot grey powder under Joey McCorrie's bare feet. The thermometer insists it is summer, but the calendar pronounces otherwise. Joey drags his steps, his toes lifting the dust into lingering puffs, drawing out this last morsel of freedom like hard candy dwindled to a flat sliver on the tongue. He arrives at the last possible moment. The brass hand bell, harbinger of cold weather and short dark days and dusty blackboard walls, clangs at the end of Miss Popham's arm. From a fifteen-year-old perspective, the bell is the embodiment of involuntary detention and relentless boredom. He would rather be doing almost anything else, but here he is, about to enter his last year at Wolf River School. The children are lined up like little soldiers in front of the door with the smallest and youngest at the front. Joey takes a deep breath and huffs it out and, in a display of show-off adolescence, runs to the end of the line and slides his bare feet to a grinding stop in a hot swirl of dust. The line files into the school, each child muttering 'excuse me' as they pass in front of Miss Popham.

There are desks to be assigned, rules to be explained, and paperwork to be completed. Joey tries to listen to Miss Popham's voice but it drones over his head like a persistent mosquito. He is otherwise preoccupied trying to steal sideways glances at the new girl. She is leaning forward, her arms crossed on the table, a cascade of auburn hair hiding most of her face. His eyes go from the long hair to the inkwell on the corner of his desk. The girl is just out of his reach, he decides. But thirteen-year-old Gracie Marie Martens on the bench directly in front of him has long braids, shining and dark and much easier to dip. She turns and flashes her violet eyes and smiles before he can make his move. He grins back at her and settles down to hear what Miss Popham has to say.

There are five new students. Miss Popham formally introduces each of them, beginners first: little Jamie O'Reilly and the identical and precocious Kalinsky twins, Nadia and Catherine, who create quite a stir with their presence; Emma Walker new in second grade; Danny Delorme who has come from Massinon is in Grade Five and can speak French. And Adelaide Christie, whose family has just moved to Mac Ward's farm from Ontario, is in grade eight. Miss Popham has every student, new and old, stand and state his or her name. Laidie rises when the teacher nods that it is her turn.

"My name is Adelaide Christie. But everyone calls me Laidie," she announces pleasantly.

Miss Popham frowns, her forehead creased into two sharp lines between her dark eyebrows.

"In *my* classroom, everyone is called by his or her proper name. You will be referred to as Adelaide as long as you are here."

Joey puts his head down and covers a grin. It has always been a great source of annoyance to Miss Popham that his given name is Joey.

Laidie Christie is a year younger than Joey although they are in the same grade. She is tall for her age with striking coppery hair and dark eyes. One might think a town girl from Ontario could be a little snobbish in the company of unsophisticated farmers' children, but Laidie is gracious and kind. Even Miss Popham, who doesn't usually exhibit much friendliness, openly allows herself to like Laidie.

For the first time in Gracie Marie Marten's extremely sheltered life she has a friend near her own age. Confidences and secrets flutter between the two. They eat lunch together and whisper and giggle. Laidie helps Gracie Marie with mathematics and shows her how to sketch. They play checkers at recess time and Laidie always loses. Gracie Marie braids Laidie's hair like her own. Gracie Marie has a gift of perception. She registers the flicker of chemistry between Laidie and Joey; a kind of spark new to her limited social exposure. It is the one thing she cannot bring herself to mention to Laidie.

At the end of the day they leave the school headed in opposite directions. The friendship cannot exist after four o'clock. Gracie Marie has no mother. She and her father live with her grandmother Helena

Martens, a strict old-school Mennonite woman who knows no grey areas. There is only one way to do things, and that is Helena's way.

By the time the school year closes, Joey and Laidie are inseparable. They spend any available time with the horses along the river trails. He teaches her to ride bareback, shows her how to put on a bridle, and how to get the gentle beasts to nibble oats from the palm of her hand. He loves to explain how farm machinery works and if she isn't interested or doesn't understand, she doesn't let on. He takes her up into the tree house built by his father Colin and his friends, now shaky and dangerous but still clinging tenaciously to the trunk and branches of a great oak.

When summer arrives on the backs of hot dry winds from the southwest, Laidie and Joey meet whenever they can, which usually means they must wait until Joey has respite from farm work and Laidie has a chance to escape from home when her father is not there. Laidie's signal is her red shirt on the clothesline. Joey can see it from the McCorrie back yard and answers with a sugar-sack dish towel thrown over the high part of the fence. When these requisites are fulfilled, they meet along the pasture trail that connects their farms. They swim in Wolf River or walk along its banks in the tall grasses. Some days Laidie brings paper and charcoal and she sketches: flowers, the river, horses, whatever she fancies. Joey fiddles endlessly with birch bark, turning the pale strips into boats and canoes and boxes and birdhouses. He makes her a birch bark bracelet.

They lean on the trunk of a huge basswood in the shade and they talk. They talk as if each must find out as much as possible about the other, as if they must account for all the spaces of their lives. Like sentient old lovers they finish one another's sentences and thoughts, hearing not only what is said, but also what is not said.

The horses wander to a low spot in the river to drink. Joey picks at his teeth with a tiny twig. Laidie has been sketching but is not satisfied with her efforts. She puts the paper and charcoal back into her bag.

"We went to Toronto in the summer when I was ten," she begins out of the blue. "Mother took me on the streetcar downtown and I was really excited but the swaying and the squeaking on the tracks gave me a headache. She didn't believe me and by the time we got to where we were going I was sick to my stomach. That's the only time I ever remember that the two of us got to go somewhere without Father, because he had some important business to do by himself."

"So where did you go on the streetcar?"

"It was a really huge store and there was everything a person could ever think of buying, all in that one place."

"What did you get?"

"Nothing. Mother said she only had enough money to buy the things on Father's list. She didn't even get anything for herself."

"Why didn't your father go himself?"

"I'm not sure. He wouldn't talk about it. All I know is we just had one hour to get back and meet him at a giant lumber store."

"Doesn't sound like a very good trip."

"Well, that part wasn't as good as I thought it was going to be. But that wasn't all. Father took us to the Riverdale Zoo. That's the only time I ever remember him taking us to anything special."

"I've never been to a real zoo. What was there?"

"Well, there were bears and lions and tigers, even an old elephant that was tied up by the gate where we went in. There were quite a few cages of monkeys and a hippopotamus and a lot of birds. I can't even remember the kinds."

"What was best?"

"I'm not sure." She draws her forehead into a frown. "But I know what was worst. The black bears. The polar bears had a big place and even a pool to swim in, but the black bears were down in a dirty round cement pit. It was hot and the only thing they had in there was an old dead tree to climb on. They were begging for peanuts but a lot of the people were taunting them, throwing all kinds of things at them and laughing and they had nowhere to hide. I felt sorry for them. I think Mother felt the same way I did but Father thought it was funny that they couldn't get away. Sometimes I still have dreams about those bears."

"What do you dream?"

"I dream that I fall into the pit and I can't get out and everyone walks away and the only person left is Father, and he's laughing at me. Then the bears start coming toward me and I have no place to go and then I wake up. I really don't want to talk about it anymore."

A short silence. A change of subject.

"Did I ever tell you about the river?"

"What part?"

"Well, um, how about how it got its name?"

"That sounds interesting."

"My dad told me that when the first settlers came around here, there were big packs of gray wolves running around. One of the settlers was out hunting deer one day and he tracked a big buck down here to the river, but before he could shoot him, three wolves attacked from behind and killed him. So they called it Wolf River. But that was a long time ago. I've never even seen a wolf, myself."

"I saw a wolf in the Riverview Zoo. The poor thing lived in a cage that was so small he could hardly turn around. He just stared at people with his yellow eyes as if he hated everything about the world. I guess he probably did. I'll always remember those eyes." She is thoughtful for a minute. "Do you think there are any of them left around here?"

"What? Eyes?"

She pokes him in the ribs with a fist. "Don't tease like that. No, wolves, silly."

"Well, once in a while somebody says they saw one, but I think maybe they're just coyotes. The district used to pay the settlers for wolves' ears and my dad says they're pretty much wiped out now."

"Do you mean they killed them just for their ears?"

"No, they killed them mostly because they were attacking the cattle, but they were afraid of them too."

"So what's that got to do with the ears?"

"The farmers had to prove that they killed them. The district office kept the ears so people couldn't get paid for the same wolf twice."

"That's really sad."

"Well, I guess that's what they thought they had to do to keep everyone safe."

"Do you think the wolves were that dangerous, or did that settler that got killed do something he shouldn't have?"

"Don't know. Maybe they were after the same deer?"

"Maybe."

"Gramp says they mate for life. He says if one of them loses a mate they might take another one, but some of them never mate again."

"After all this talk I'll probably think there's a wolf behind every tree when I come down here," she giggles.

"Don't worry. I'll save you. And then I'll throw you into the river."

Laidie makes a gesture of mock fear. She nods toward the river.

"Does it ever flood?"

"I never saw one, but my dad says it does. He says there was water all the way to the trail and it even washed away haystacks and woodpiles. What was it like in Radford? Did they have a river there?"

"We had a little creek in Radford behind the school but I don't think it could be called it a river. We used to sneak down there at noon hour sometimes, until Bobby Armiston got caught smoking in the bush."

"You never told me about your school."

"Not really much to tell. It was all right, I guess. The stuff we learned is the same stuff as we have here. My teacher was Miss Kennedy and she was really nice. Not like you-know-who."

They both laugh and knit their brows in a copy of Miss Popham's famous glower.

"I guess the biggest difference is that there were whole classrooms that only had one grade. And the schoolyard was a real playground with swings and teeters and grass, not just a patch of field like Wolf River."

"Do you miss it?"

"No."

Joey chews on a blade of grass. "Do you know how to whistle with grass?" he asks.

"Can you show me?"

He chooses a wide green blade and stretches it over the top of his thumb, then presses the other thumb tight against it. He brings it to his lips and blows, hard, and a loud screech cuts the air.

"That wasn't a whistle, that was a scream," Laidie laughs.

They spend the next half hour whistling grass until their fingers are green and their lips sore from the sharp blades. The birds have stopped singing, choosing instead to vacate the area. It is quiet.

"Don't you have any aunts or uncles or grandparents?" Joey asks.

"Why do you ask?"

"I don't know. You never talk about any relatives."

"I guess that's because I don't really have any. But you must have known my Uncle Mac?"

"Yep, I knew him pretty well, everybody around here did. He and my dad were really good friends. He had red hair, just like yours."

"So, what about your family?"

"There's just my dad and I, and, Gramp. My Grandma Ruby died a long time before I was even born. She had a bad appendix and they took her to Winnipeg on the train for an operation but it was too late. She died on Dominion Day and Gramp never went to a Dominion Day celebration again."

"That's terribly sad."

"And my mother…I think I was about twelve before anyone told me what happened to her. She burned to death in a prairie fire when I was two. I don't remember her at all."

Tears well up in Laidie's eyes. "I'm really sorry, Joey. I think she must have been a wonderful person to have a son like you. You have a great dad. Not like mine."

"What do you mean?"

"You know how strict he is. It's just mean. And he…" Her voice fades away. "And Mother just goes into the bedroom and cries."

"I'm sorry, Laidie. Sometimes I wish you could come and live at our place." He drapes his arm around her shoulder and hugs. "I guess it's time to round up the horses and head for home before your father gets back."

Chapter 29

Wolf River, 1931

It's a July afternoon, Sunday, thick with heat. Joey and Laidie race the horses along the river trail and out toward the little hay meadow and draw up in the shade of the cottonwood grove. The horses, slippery with sweat, snort their approval. They dismount, drape the reins loosely over the horses' necks, freeing the animals to graze on the sparse dry grass.

"When do you have to go home?"

"They won't be back from Bainesville until late. So, I guess, six or seven. How about you?"

"Whenever I want." Joey pulls out his battered pocket watch. "It's only two. We'll have time to stop at the river for a quick swim on the way back."

They stretch out in the shade beneath the cottonwoods. Jagged bits of sizzling blue sky stab through the green leaf-lace overhead, inventing dapples of light in the tall grass.

"Can you believe it's almost two years since we moved to Wolf River?"

"Hmm. Feels like you've lived here forever."

"I know." Laidie loosens the bundle of dark red hair at the back of her neck and lets it fall over her shoulders. "But forever goes both ways."

"What do you mean?"

"I hope I *will* be here forever."

"Hmm. Are you going to play ball next Sunday?"

"I wouldn't miss that game against Riverview for anything. After last time…"

They both shake their heads at the memory of Riverview District's last inning rally to win the game. Joey shakes his fist. "We'll show them who the ball players are."

Laidie rolls over onto her stomach. "Have you seen Gracie Marie all summer?"

"Nope. Oh, yeah, once. She was helping Jake fix fences along the trail. But I wasn't close enough to talk to her."

"I really feel sorry for Gracie. She isn't allowed to do anything but work. I'll bet she'd love to go swimming in the river, just once. We should ride over to their place and ask her."

"Her grandmother would never let that happen. Besides, I'm pretty sure she'd be too shy to take off her long dress and her bonnet."

"Maybe. Still…"

"That low spot in the river would be good for her. You know, the place where you can see all the gravel and stones at the bottom?"

"We've never gone swimming there. How come?"

"Because, dopey. It's not deep enough to swim, let alone dive."

"Dopey? You're the one that's dopey." She sits upright and straddles him, tickling his ribs until he grabs her arms and pins them to her sides.

The giggling trickles away, fades into a long silence. She rolls off him and they lie facing one another.

For one suspended moment their eyes meet and hold in surprise, and in that moment their connection to each other is immutably altered. They are startled and unprepared, as if caught in one of those sudden summer thunderstorms that rears up without warning, swirling away everything in its path. Joey's breath catches in his throat and he touches Laidie's face and traces his fingers around her chin and is so close he can smell her, sweaty and musky and hinting of soap. She clasps her hands around the back of his neck and pulls him closer until their bodies touch and he kisses her. He is hesitant at first, until she pulls back and takes in a deep breath, and he kisses her open mouth and she holds him so tightly he can barely breathe. He leans away just enough to tug her blue blouse up and over, and she helps him pull off his shirt. The touch of skin on skin fires their adolescent passion to the ultimate arousal. They are unrestrained, almost feral in their coupling.

Laidie's long auburn hair spreads in a wide tangle on the grass beneath her and she watches Joey as his eyes rest on the nubs of nipples on her breasts. The sun dips under the lowest branches and its angled light makes a golden haze in the hot dusty air and swallows the dapples on the ground. Evening subdues the breeze and the rustle of the great heart-shaped leaves of the cottonwoods dies to a whisper.

It is a summer of secrets. The birdsongs in the deep river-bottom forest ring clear and melodic, and time stretches endlessly. Joey and Laidie go often now to the shallows, far from the regular swimming hole, where the shadowed river flows clear over its bed of polished rocks and pebbles. The slow-moving water washes cool on their skin and Laidie's burnished hair floats on the surface around their shoulders. They lie on the mossy bank, drying in the hot breeze. Joey raises himself on his elbows, and in the coruscations of the water he spies a flawless round white stone. Some miracle of erosion has carved an exact circular opening in its centre. He wades in and scoops it out for her. It gleams wetly in her hand. "Keep it forever," he tells her. And she laughs, like music.

"No, wait, I changed my mind. Let me have it, just for a couple of days," he pleads. "Then I'll give it back to you. I promise."

Laidie pretends to pout and returns the stone to him reluctantly and he goes and puts it into the pocket of his shirt which lies nearby on the rocks. He comes back to her and they make love again before splashing back into the water.

It is last week of August. The hot dry spring and summer has left the land choking with drought. The poor and thin fields wait to be harvested, though Ford and Colin can see there won't be any yield to speak of. The threshing gang is scheduled to arrive on the McCorrie farm the first week of September, so it is urgent to get the sparse grain cut and bound into sheaves.

The crew arrives on time and in less than a day they harvest the poor and shriveled kernels of wheat. Quality does not make much difference. There is no market for grain anyway. Once the pathetic crop is stored in the McCorrie granaries, Colin gets the fall fieldwork underway. The land is nothing but dry black lumps and the plough chews it into dust to feed the wind.

Joey needs to see Laidie again before school starts, but there is still much to be done in spite of the wretched harvest. He works hard and fast to help finish the tasks of autumn. He cultivates the cracked-earth garden with the horses and a small plough so it will be ready for spring. He cuts a late crop of sparse hay and a week later he and old Custer head to the field with the hay rake. Custer drags the rake over the thin windrows until the long rattling curve of its greedy teeth is full and Joey trips the lever with his foot to disgorge the hay into piles. He finishes the raking just as the sun slides into the thick red dust along the horizon. His gaze wanders to Laidie's cottonwood grove at the far end of the hayfield. He heads Custer for home. The white stone in his breast pocket has waited for three weeks. It will have to wait a few days longer.

Joey delivers a yearling calf to John Maxwell's farm and adjusts his route home to come by Wolf River School when classes let out for the day. He hasn't seen Laidie for five weeks, since just before school started up again at the end of August. He arrives at the school just at four and waits at the crooked wire gate for the children to pile out of the door. Laidie is not among them.

Gracie Marie Martens edges over to him. "I guess you're looking for Laidie?'

Joey nods. "Where is she?"

"I don't know. She wasn't here yesterday either. Charlie said he thought she had the flu. Do you want me to tell her you were here?"

"Can you just give her this?" he says, pulling from his shirt pocket something wrapped in a brown handkerchief and tied with string. "And this?"

The second item is a square parcel wrapped in brown paper and also tied with string.

Gracie Marie takes the first tiny bundle and turns it over in her hands, feeling its weightiness. Joey hands her the other package. "Sure, I guess so. I'll give them to her as soon as she comes back."

"You can tell her I have to start cutting firewood for winter tomorrow. Dad and I have a lot of fences to fix too, but I'll be back to see her as soon as I can."

Gracie Marie nods. Joey turns his horse and rides away, fast, and she clutches the smallest parcel close, feeling the warmth of him still in the folds of the handkerchief. She slides the box-shaped package into her schoolbag and hesitates while she shifts the weight of the small handkerchief-wrapped bundle from hand to hand. She considers for a short moment the possibility of stealing a quick peek at the contents but buries it instead in her deepest pocket. She resolves to give it and the box to Laidie at the first opportunity

Chapter 30

Millfield, 1931

Laidie's pink checked blouse chafes against the welts on her back. The slightest movement awakens stinging pain and will not allow her to put her punishment out of her mind or, rather, the beginning of her punishment.

She stands on the Millfield Station platform alone in the same spot as she did two years ago. She is alone, not because there are not others with her, but because she is not allowed to stand with them or speak to them. Orville and Mhairi are at the other end of the platform with their trunks and crates, he board-straight and stiff-jawed and staring down the train track, Mhairi a few feet behind him with her head down and her back to Laidie.

It is cold. Ragged grey clouds scud overhead, driven by the northwest wind, which rips off the few leaves that remain on the oak trees beside the station and throws them into corners where they swirl in endless little gyres. Laidie faces into the wind so it cannot slap her jacket against her throbbing back. The pungent smell of stubble smoke and damp field ash fills her nostrils. Hundreds, perhaps thousands of Canada geese, the wind behind them, trail their dark skeins southward across the sky. Their plaintive honking drifts in and out of the wind. In a sad harmonic discord the whistle of the approaching train melds with the call of the geese.

It was only a week ago. Laidie plays the scene over in her mind: Orville questioning her debilitating fatigue; Mhairi noticing her daughter's firm breasts pressing too fully against her blouse; Orville finding her retching away her breakfast in the back yard beside the chicken house; Mhairi's inquisition into the most personal of Laidie's bodily functions; the fearful admission.

"You're nothing but a slut. A whore and a slut!" With full force, his hand strikes Laidie on the side of her face. Little jagged bits of silvery light dance in her peripheral vision. He slaps her again on the other side.

Mhairi takes a step forward. "Orville, please…"

"You back up, stupid woman. If you knew how to be a decent mother this wouldn't have happened."

Mhairi stands her ground. Orville's fist grinds into her stomach and she gasps for air.

"Now, back the hell up or you'll get worse than that."

He turns back to Laidie and grabs the front of her blouse. Buttons fly as he rips it from her body. The blooming breasts are clearly outlined beneath the white undershirt. He yanks the undershirt over her head in the same motion as he slides his belt from his pants. Mhairi tries to protest and the belt catches her in the neck and she falls to her knees. He turns his full fury on Laidie. The belt slashes across her already tender breasts and her hands and arms. She falls to the floor near Mhairi and the beating continues. Orville stops just short of blood. He is still dangerously furious. No one moves.

"Now, get up and start packing, both of you. We'll be on the train out of here tomorrow. I'm not going to stay around here to have myself shamed by you." He returns the belt to its loops.

Moving from Wolf River has been previously discussed, but only in the context of economics. What is left of the field crops after drought and grasshoppers is negligible, not even worth threshing. For nineteen cents a bushel, what's the point, Orville says. It's not worth the work. There is nothing in the garden and the well is running low. Farming has not lived up to Orville's expectations, even with free land and buildings. *It's worth nothing, never will be.* This latest development cements the decision to leave, to just walk away.

Orville agrees to allow Laidie to go to Wolf River School one more time to get her belongings, as long as she goes at the end of the day. She walks into the schoolyard just as school dismisses. Gracie Marie rushes over.

"Laidie! I'm glad you're over the flu!"

"Hello, Gracie Marie." Her face is swollen and tear-stained.

"Laidie, what's wrong?"

She throws her arms around Gracie and buries her face in her shoulder.

"I have to tell you some really terrible bad news," she manages between convulsive sniffs. "We're moving to Winnipeg. Tomorrow."

Gracie Marie's mouth falls open. "But you can't," she wails. "This is going to be such a good year!"

"I want to stay, too. But I have no choice. We're going on the train tomorrow. And I don't have much time. I've got to get back right away,

I promised." She pulls two envelopes from her pocket. "Gracie, you're my best friend and I'm really going to miss you. This is for you."

Gracie Marie opens the envelope to find Laidie's little silver heart-shaped locket.

"Are you sure, Laidie? This is such a special thing."

"It's not too special for you, Gracie. I won't ever forget you." She knows Gracie will not be allowed to wear the locket. Helena Martens says it is a sin to adorn the body.

There is something else in the envelope; a charcoal-sketched portrait of Gracie Marie. Almost photographic in its perfect blending of greys, it is a remarkable likeness. Laidie has colored the eyes a brilliant violet blue.

Tears well up in Gracie Marie's eyes. She wraps her arms around Laidie in a tight hug. Laidie fights to hold back a cry from the pain of the pressure on her wounded back and breasts.

"And Gracie, will you give this to Joey?" She holds out a stiff, flat package. "And you have to promise me, cross your heart and hope to die, that you won't tell him where I've gone. You can't. Not ever. You are the absolute only one who knows."

Gracie Marie hesitates. Deception is an alien concept to her. "What will I say if he asks me?"

"Please, Gracie." She is begging now. "Please don't let me down."

Gracie Marie nods.

"I have to hurry now, Gracie. I have to help Mama."

Laidie begins her last walk home from Wolf River School. The October sky is crisp and blue with only a few high wispy clouds. There is little wind and the sun comforts the throbbing welts on her back. Then she hears her name. Gracie Marie is in pursuit.

"Laidie, wait! Wait for me!"

Laidie turns and stops. "What's the matter, Gracie? Are you all right?"

"Yes, I am. But I almost forgot something. It was in my desk." She holds out a small bundle tied in a dark brown handkerchief and a square package wrapped in brown paper. "Joey asked me to give you these."

Orville knows someone in Winnipeg who helps find the family a house, a small bungalow on Hampton Street. The rent is twenty-five dollars a month. There are two bedrooms and a tiny office, so Orville is content. He finds work right away at a small lumberyard and Mhairi sets about unpacking. But there is still the matter of Laidie to be dealt with. She spends the days in her room, blinds pulled down and curtains drawn.

Mhairi has to talk to her.

"Laidie, your father and I have decided you'll have to go back to Ontario to have the baby. You'll have to give it up to be adopted."

"I won't do it." These are the first words Laidie has spoken for days. "I'll kill myself before I'll give away my baby."

"And your father is likely to kill you if you don't. Laidie, there is really no choice. You have to do this, darling."

"Please Mama. Please do something." She is sobbing, and the sound reminds Mhairi of the time Laidie hid under the bed after one of Orville's violent rampages. "I don't want you to get hurt on account of me, Mama, but there must be something you can do. I just can't give away this baby."

"Laidie, who is the father? Is it the McCorrie boy?" Laidie turns her back.

The girl's utter devastation is tangible. Mhairi has no doubt of Laidie's intentions. She has one card to play. Denver Atchison, Mac Ward's lawyer, holds a letter that will implicate Orville in any harm that might come to Mhairi or Laidie. She convinces Orville that Laidie is suicidal. He capitulates.

They formulate a plan. Laidie goes to live with Mrs. Lundy in Radford. Mhairi feigns a pregnancy, easily passed off in Winnipeg, as they know so few people in the city. Still, next-door neighbors are curious. *Yes, we do already have one daughter, yes, that was her you saw here last week. Oh, she was just visiting us, to help out when we moved, you know. She got so homesick we agreed to let her go back to school in Ontario for the rest of the year. To be with her friends, you know. But she'll be coming back to help once the baby is born.*

All ties with Millfield have been severed except to the lawyer Denver Atchison. Laidie will be allowed to keep her baby. The Christies will legally adopt the child and she will be raised as Laidie's sister. But there are irrevocable conditions, to which Laidie must agree. She will never contact the baby's father or have any connections whatsoever with anyone in Millfield, even Gracie Marie. Absolute and infinite secrecy is the ultimate cost to Laidie. It will be a high price to pay.

Orville and Mhairi meet Laidie at the downtown train station in mid-April. She steps from the train holding her tiny wrapped bundle. She is only a child herself, with her dark red hair loose and falling over her shoulder onto the pink and white blanket. A tiny hand tangles delicate white fingers in the long strands. Laidie savors this moment. It is the last time she will officially hold this child as a mother. Mhairi steps forward to take the infant, who is named Blythe Corrie Christie. Orville says nothing, not even hello. Laidie can see the clenching of the muscles in his jaw and the nervous tic twitching beside his mouth. He leads the way to the exit.

Chapter 31

Wolf River, 1931

Lying is wrong. There are no grey areas; it is a matter of black and white. No matter what the circumstances, it is a sin. Gracie Marie struggles with the dogma. What is a lie, really? Is there a difference between a deliberate, malicious lie and a lie to help or spare pain? Is a lie better than the truth if the truth causes heartache? She can hear the voice of Oma Helena Martens reciting the verses. *Lie not to one another, Colossians. God hates a lying tongue, Proverbs. Thou shalt not bear false witness against thy neighbour, Exodus.* But Oma also emphasized the sacredness of giving your word. *Let your yea be yea and your nay, nay, Matthew.* So what about breaking promises? Is that not the same as a lie? Isn't it even worse, if someone is depending on you? If you are entrusted with a secret and someone asks you to reveal it, what do you do? Do you protect a promise with a lie?

"Come for supper, Gracie."

Helena waits until Gracie Marie and Jake are seated and brings thick sliced sausage, kielke with onions and cream, and buttered green beans to the table. She launches into her ritual lengthy prayer of thankfulness and forgiveness before nodding her head as a signal to begin passing the food. They eat in silence. When the meal is finished, Helena again bows her head and the three repeat the Lord's Prayer.

Jake runs the farm homesteaded by his late father, but his mother Helena is the undisputed and unyielding boss. Her religious beliefs inspire every decision. Whether wheat or oats will be planted in a certain field, whether to buy or sell livestock, when to begin harvest—every decision is influenced by her faith. She is a powerful presence. For Jake, this is good. He is no longer able to make decisions. Truth be known, Jake does not care, and has not cared for years.

There was one time when Jake Martens veered from his mother's edicts, and that was when he met Élodie Beauchemin. In 1916, Élodie came from St. Boniface to the Wolf River area as a schoolteacher and quickly established herself as a free-spirited and irrepressible young woman. Nineteen-year-old Élodie drew attention wherever she went. Her musical laughter preceded her arrival on any scene. A wild charismatic magnetism imparted to her a beauty far beyond mere physical appearance. Long dark hair hung around her face in loose waves and, depending upon the light, her large eyes were either violet or blue. Every eligible bachelor in the area relentlessly sought Élodie's hand but she was inevitably drawn to Jake Martens. Jake was everything Élodie was not: shy, conventional, religious, plain looking, and quiet. He often watched her from afar, but the first time they actually met was accidental. She was galloping her horse along the headland trail from town when a darting movement of some creature in the bushes spooked the animal and a runaway ensued. From where he rode in his field, checking the germination of his early-sown wheat, Jake could see Élodie's long dark hair streaming behind her as she bent low over her horse, clinging tenaciously to the flying mane. He made pursuit on his own horse and finally stopped the panicked animal by riding hard alongside until he could grab the flyaway reins. The first thing Élodie did was laugh. Jake dismounted and stroked her snorting horse to calm it. In one motion Élodie slid from the animal and flung her arms around Jake's neck in an uninhibited thank you. They walked the two horses back as far as the edge of Jake's field, and by the time they arrived there, Jake knew he must have Élodie.

Helena Martens was furious. Élodie was Catholic, and furthermore she was "wild and sinful," an oxymoronic juxtaposition of attributes. But for the first time in his life, with Élodie by his side, Jake stood up to his mother. He announced they had decided to get married. He promised to continue looking after the farm, but Helena vowed he would no longer be welcome to live on the homestead.

That was fine with Jake. At the end of June he and Élodie went to nearby Bainesville so they could marry in the Catholic church there.

They rented a tiny house in Millfield from Mr. Dunham, the undertaker. If the house had ever been a sombre place, it was no longer. In Élodie's presence the walls rang with sounds of laughter and music and visitors. Jake was intoxicated with their passionate lovemaking. He put Helena's rules behind him and sailed into life with Élodie.

He continued to work the farm and care for the livestock, and in spite of Helena's anger with his choice she could not refuse his help, as there was no one else for her to turn to. Élodie wanted to work alongside Jake on the farm and when he mentioned this to Helena the thought of it rendered her apoplectic. Jake stood tall and declared there would be conditions to his ongoing assistance. So Élodie came and went as she pleased, except into Helena's house. There was nothing Élodie would not tackle.

When Élodie announced she was going to have a baby, Jake's joy was complete. Helena's only reaction was a sour and disinterested shrug.

Gracie Marie was born in April of 1918. By summer, Élodie was once again at Jake's side on the farm. Depending upon what they were doing, she would either bring little Gracie Marie along in her basket or leave her with Saharah McCorrie to watch over. Either option infuriated Helena.

Élodie was helping Jake with the haying during one of those times when Gracie Marie was at Sahara's. The hay crop was cut and lying in windrows, waiting to be raked into piles. Jake showed Élodie how to operate the hay rake by pressing hard on the lever with her foot when the rounded teeth of the rake were full of hay. The teeth lifted to release the hay into a long pile and Jake followed the rake on foot, gathering the piles into small stacks to be picked up later by the team and rack. The hay crop was heavy and he lagged far behind Élodie and the rake.

Saharah McCorrie was uneasy when Jake and Élodie didn't show up to get Gracie Marie before suppertime. She sent Colin over to the Martens' farm after supper to see if there had been some trouble. He could see the hay rake and the team of horses at a standstill on the far side of the hayfield. There was no sign of Jake or Élodie. Two hawks glided far overhead in wide silent circles, their sharp eyes on the lookout for mice routed out by the rake. Evening breezes were already dissipating the heat of the day. Long fingers of shadow clawed out over the west side of the field. Colin gave Custer a sharp dig in the ribs with his boots and made straight for the hay rake and team of horses.

At first he could see nothing. He dismounted and walked around the rake. There he found Jake, blood-soaked and silent, cradling Élodie's mutilated body.

Silence. Jake was rocking tenderly back and forth, back and forth, as if trying to soothe a hurt child. Colin took off his jacket and laid it over Élodie, then threw himself on Custer's back and rode the horse hard and sweating the two miles to Millfield to get Doctor Millan. He arrived back at the hay rake just before Millan, who pulled up trailing a churning cloud of grey dust behind his Model-T. The two men pried Élodie gently from Jake's arms. They wrapped him in a blanket from Millan's car and lifted him into the vehicle where he sat, continuing to rock gently back and forth, in his mind still holding his wife's body.

They turned to Élodie. What little was left of her clothing was soaked with blood. When Millan gently lifted her up and forward he could see that her long hair had been ripped from her head. There was nothing to be done. Tears welled in the doctor's eyes and overflowed. The two men sat, leaning against the Model-T, trying to make sense of the accident. Something, perhaps a hidden rock, caused Élodie to lose her balance and fall forward, they decided, landing behind the horses. The curved rattling prongs of the rake would have been upon her in seconds. She likely didn't have a chance to scream out. Her hair must have become tangled in the turning wheel in order for her scalp to be torn away so completely. Millan could see the back of her head had been crushed and was sure she must have been unconscious almost immediately, perhaps kicked by one of the horse's hooves as she fell. Jake probably didn't even realize anything had happened until he saw the team and rake approaching without a driver, dragging something unspeakable in its curved teeth.

The doctor took Jake back to the farmhouse and Colin stayed with Élodie. He heard Helena Martens' jagged screams cut high through the deepening twilight like a dull rasp and then he saw the red back-lights of Dr. Millan's car fading down the road on the way to fetch Undertaker Dunham.

Colin and Saharah brought Gracie Marie to Helena Martens the next morning and Jake, shivering and caked with dried blood, was still sitting catatonically on the porch where Millan left him the night before. Helena could not get him to move so had draped a couple of quilts around his shoulders and sat next to him all night. Colin carried Jake inside and helped Helena remove the gruesomely stained clothing, then waited while she sponged the encrusted blood from his face and hands and body. At last Colin was able to lift him to his bed. It was over a month before Jake uttered a word. A great dark lacuna came to occupy the part of his brain where Élodie had lived and he never spoke her name again.

Gracie Marie knows nothing of any of this. She has been told her mother died when she was only a baby. As no one will speak of it, she assumes it must have been some sordid disease. She once asked her father about Élodie and he turned his back on her question and walked out of the house and far across the pasture. No one knows she has two pictures she found in a box of things that Jake brought years ago from the little house in town. One is a portrait of a laughing Élodie, her dark hair falling on bare shoulders. Her eyes flash and sparkle with the love of life. The other is a small photograph of Élodie holding a baby, and Gracie Marie knows it is herself. Élodie's eyes are cast down toward the baby and she glows with an aura of love.

Gracie Marie with her melodic laugh is the quintessence of innocence and virtue and honesty, these qualities moulded and vigilantly protected by Helena Martens. Although Gracie Marie has the violet eyes and dark hair of her mother, Helena is determined the similarity will go no further.

The first week of October is sunny and dry, and a west wind blows for the tenth straight day. The trees along the river have cycled through green and yellow and brown, red and orange, and their leaves lie in a loose carpet of profusion and sweet heady decay. Thousands of Canada geese thread their dark v-skeins southward across the sky, honking a distant promise of cold on its way. Still, the sun is warm wherever there is shelter from the wind. Along the trail, determined dandelions and goldenrods bloom in a riot of yellow. Fluttering leaves of saffron and red still cling to the trees along the river.

Joey rides up on old Custer as the doors of Wolf River School swing open and the children tumble out, but Laidie is not among them. He waits, thinking she is probably helping the teacher. After fifteen minutes he enters the school to find Miss Popham alone at her desk, pressing papers onto the firm jelly of the hectograph, smoothing them with the palm of her hand, and peeling them off to reveal purple-lettered script.

She looks up at him. "Yes?" she asks, eyebrows raised in haughty black arches.

"Uh," Joey hesitates. "Is Laidie, uh, Adelaide away today?"

Miss Popham smiles to herself and looks down at the hectograph. "Miss Christie no longer attends school here." She knows Joey needs, must have, more information but remains deliberately and infuriatingly silent. She applies a blank white sheet to the hectograph and lines it up carefully.

"She, uh, do you know where she's gone?"

"Yes, as a matter of fact," she says sanctimoniously, "I do. Well, partly at least." With the heel of her hand she smooths the paper, examining it intently for any small wrinkle.

By now Joey's heart is pounding with apprehension, but he knows Miss Popham well enough to realize he will have to play along with her callous little game.

He musters his most polite tone and forces a casual smile. "Miss Popham, I would be most grateful if you could tell me where she is."

His voice is controlled but Miss Edina Popham can hear the urgency buried in his words. She clears her throat and takes her time. "Well," she says, slowly peeling the finished paper from the dark jelly, "I understand the family has moved away. To where, exactly, I don't know. That is all I can tell you." She turns back to her hectograph and it is evident she has spoken her last word on the subject.

Joey leaves the door open on his way out and goes to get his horse. The sunlight feels darker and the wind has grown cold. Leaves and dust spin in eddies beside the trail. Old Custer plods along, head down. A pair of Canada geese flies overhead, so low Joey can hear the rush of wind sifting through their wings. Out of the corner of his eye he sees a flash of blue on the side of the trail ahead. It is Gracie Marie, waiting for him.

"I saw you at school tonight, Joey. I was cleaning the brushes out back."

"Oh."

"I have something for you. She reaches into her schoolbag and pulls out a small flat package. and passes it up to him. "It's from Laidie."

He takes the package and puts it in his jacket pocket. "Where did she go, Gracie? Did they go back to Ontario? I know she would have told you."

Gracie Marie has thought long and hard about what to do. A lie or a promise? It is an irrevocable decision. She cannot look at him. She stares down at her feet, shoves her hands into her pockets.

"I don't know. She wouldn't tell me."

Chapter 32

Wolf River, 1935

There are some rains, yes. Clouds pass over day after day; mostly just distant pieces of fluff, but occasionally one will burst forth with a downpour. It is never a gentle shower—it seems the clouds have decided it will be everything or nothing. The last deluge dumped three inches of rain two miles south of the McCorrie place, most of it in the area of Willis Marsh, where moisture was not needed. The sloughs around Steve Kalinsky's farm are nearly full and his lowlands flourish with thick hay. There has been rain in Millfield too, turning the streets to trails of sloppy mud. The townspeople are guiltily apologetic whenever they see a dust-dry farmer at the Post Office or in Parker's General Store. *There's no justice,* they say. *But it looks like more rain might be on the way. For sure next time it'll be out your way.*

The *Free Press Prairie Farmer* arrives at the post office weekly, full of depressing news about the situation which, as hard as it is to believe, is far worse in Saskatchewan. The grainy black and white pictures tell the stories; deserted farms sleeping under hot black drifts, tops of fence posts poking out in rows above insidiously creeping dunes of soil, piles of dust climbing the sides of houses and barns; families loading all their worldly possessions on hayracks and wagons to make the slow trek west in search of better times; starved bodies of cattle lying in barren pastures where they fell; families lining up for relief food and supplies from down east.

Ford McCorrie, once the epitome of optimism, now dwells morbidly on the reports from just over the Manitoba-Saskatchewan border. He reads and rereads the *Prairie Farmer*. Colin hides the newspaper when he can get hold of it and tries to engage Ford in positive conversation.

The two men sit at the kitchen table with their breakfast coffee. Colin nods toward the window. "Looks like it might be a better day today. Bit of wind should help cool us off."

"Hmph. All the wind is going to do is blow in more dust. It's bad out west and it's just a matter of time 'til it's the same here. We'll be starving too."

"We're not as bad off as a lot of people, Dad. We aren't going hungry."

"For today."

"We still have livestock and chickens. There's lots of stuff in the root cellar. The well is still flowing."

"It's bad, Colin. You're burying your head in the sand. In the dust."

"Come on, Dad. This isn't like you. Why don't you come to Millfield with Joey and me this morning? We're leaving in fifteen minutes or so."

Ford shakes his head. "Got work to do. Anyway, I'm too tired to go anywhere."

The thermometer nudges the one hundred degree mark for the third day in a row. Like the breath of the devil himself, the wind rises, whipping in from the southwest. From the kitchen window Ford can see a dark dust behemoth rising and stretching across the near horizon. There is no such thing as a far horizon these days, he muses. Within minutes a black cloud sweeps across the prairie, reducing the sun to a pale disk. Fine black topsoil fills the air and sifts into every crack and crevice.

Ford sits shirtless at the kitchen table, staring at the remains of his sandwich and listening to the wind from the furnace of hell. It batters the house and rattles the windows and hurls its dry innards at the walls. He pushes his chair back and it scrapes across the grit on the floor. He dips himself a glass of tepid water from the pail by the sink. His throat is dry and sore from breathing in the parched air and he is tired, so tired. But there is work to do. There is always work to do. He puts on his dirty shirt, wipes the sweat from his face, and pulls his brown handkerchief over his nose before he goes outside.

Lucy, dear old Lucy, is sick and coughing and he wants to check on her. He shuffles across the farmyard to the well and pumps a pail full of water. He slips into the darkness of the barn and sets the pail down in front of the old Jersey cow. She has not touched her hay ration and she hangs her head and turns away from him. There is not much change in her cough but Ford can see the rapid heaving of her sides as she struggles to pull air into her lungs. Short of breath himself, he sits down beside her, lays his arm across her back, and gently rubs her bony ribs and spine. She lifts her head and looks at him dolefully and he can see dust turned into mud in the discharge around her eyes and nose. There is nothing more he can do. Lucy will be gone by suppertime. When Colin and Joey get back from Millfield they will help move her out of the barn.

This is where they find Ford, his arm still draped across the dead cow's back.

Chapter 33

Wolf River, 1936

Fickle spring, they say. Teasing warm breezes, blue skies, bullying cold rain. Scarves, mittens, woollies, washed, folded and stored away, hastily called back into service. Crystal icicles dripping from rooftops; short-lived tantrums of brittle cold. Unpredictable.

But they forget. Winter can be fickle too.

The New Year of 1936 launches with bone-chilling cold and relentless wind. Storm after storm pummels the prairies. Drifts variegated with streaks of blown soil build up in bizarre formations wherever there are trees or buildings. On unprotected land the violent gales keep the fields swept clean of snow. Sometimes the sun comes out for a spell, taunting that somewhere in the world there is warmth.

One morning a broad blue arch of sky lifts the grey clouds in the west. It advances quickly, widening as it pushes the weather system eastward. By evening the temperature rises to twenty-five degrees Fahrenheit under a sharp quarter moon.

The wind blows straight from the south for four cloudless days and nights. The air, heavy with a blue haze of humidity, smells of warmth and thawing manure piles and soil offering itself to the sun. People talk, hopefully. *Wouldn't it be nice if this warm spell stayed around? Yep, there's a little black starting to show in the fields over by the Watson farm. Maybe there's goin' t' be an early spring? Nah, I think it's a tad too early to hope for that. Anyway, it don't matter. We'll enjoy it while we can, eh?*

The fifth day dawns mild and clear. Sunlight struggles to penetrate the dingy window of Colin McCorrie's bedroom. He has been up for some time, awakened by a spell of paroxysmal coughing. His right ankle, broken in his riding accident many years ago, throbs painfully. He gets up and dresses, takes three aspirin, and goes to the kitchen to see if there are any live coals in the wood stove. Soon the smell of barley coffee, strong and nutty, hangs in the air. He makes a pot of thin porridge.

"Joey? You awake yet?"

"Nnnh. What time is it?"

"Past eight."

Colin pours himself a coffee in Ford's favorite cup and spoons out a bowl of porridge. Joey emerges, tired-eyed and stretching.

"G'morning."

"Damned ankle is giving me some grief this morning. I'm thinking we're in for some bad weather," Colin mutters. He sprinkles a dusting of white sugar on the porridge. "Can't remember the last time it was this sore."

Joey is skeptical. "Don't know, Pap. Looks like another pretty nice day."

Colin pushes his chair back and stretches.

"My ankle doesn't lie."

Joey goes out to do the morning chores, Ribbett following joyfully at his heels. *Only a dog could be so fucking happy in the morning.* These days there is barely enough to keep Joey busy for half an hour. He pumps water into the ice-encased cattle trough and fills a pail to take to the barn for the chickens and the sow, who screams in raucous anticipation when she hears the door creak open. The cattle hurry to the trough for their once-a-day drink and Ribbett herds them back to the barn for their ration of miserable hay. On his way in to the house Joey fetches a pail of fresh water from the pump. He sets it inside the door and goes to the woodshed for an armful of split poplar to fill the woodbox by the stove, just in case his father is right about the weather.

Colin fights through another bout of coughing and gets up to pile three more pieces of split poplar into the stove. He returns to the threadbare cushions of the wine-colored chesterfield and settles himself in with Zane Grey's *Riders of the Purple Sage*. He has taken up reading this winter, working his way through Ford's small eclectic library. The book cupboard holds, among other titles, *The Voyage of Dr. Doolittle,* Hemingway's *A Farewell to Arms* and *The Sun Also Rises*, *This Side of*

Paradise and *The Great Gatsby* by Fitzgerald, some Zane Grey westerns, and several books of Saharah's—like *Kilmeny of the Orchard* by L. M. Montgomery, and *Pollyanna.* The books comfort Colin. Every page has felt the touch of his father or his wife.

The day wears on with mounting humidity. By mid-afternoon a bank of cloud gathers on the western horizon like a rolling range of dark hills. The wind eases to the southwest and then to the west and its temperature plummets as if it was skimming a glacier. When the cold front punches into the moist air a haze of ice crystals swirls and sparkles like suspended sugar.

Steve Kalinsky stands outside on his back door step, stretching his suspenders over the shoulders of his woollen underwear. In the warmth of the kitchen behind him he can hear Catherine and Nadia arguing over which book belongs to whom and the boys, Peter and Simon, engaging in some kind of noisy contest punctuated by hysterical laughter. Little Irina is complaining in her high voice about an imagined injustice perpetrated by her brothers. Annie's voice rises over the din and all goes quiet. Steve smiles, scans the clear sky, and inhales a deep breath. He can detect the scent of snow in the air. He is tuned into the weather as few people are: alert to the subtleties of the wind and clouds, the differences in the way sound carries, and the behavior of animals.

He puts on his shirt and coat and heads to the barn to feed his stock. Local rains last year returned some moisture to his marshland and sloughs, giving him a better crop of hay than most farmers. He turns the cattle and horses out and they hurry to the trough for their daily drink. The dog herds them back to the barn where Steve forks a careful ration of hay into each manger. Compared to the beef cattle that stay outside all winter with only wooden fences for shelter, the horses and milk cows have the luxury of the barn. If you can call it luxury; the wind forces its way into the fine cracks of the walls and when it snows and drifts collect in dirty piles by the door. Steve feeds the chickens and pigs before checking the critical rope leading from the barn to the house. Every farmyard on the prairie has such a rope: it can spell the difference between life and death.

He can make out the rising grey mass in the west. Pushed by the mounting wind, it collides with the moist air over the prairies. A cloud of ice dust forms instantly. The sun, so bright only minutes earlier, appears to suck its light back in to itself.

Gracie Marie Martens and Oma Helena form dark heavy dough into loaves and set them, covered with a sugar sack, on the table close to the stove. Helena Martens keeps part of the sourdough mixture from each baking to provide leavening for the next batch. But the dough never rises as it should, partly because of other grains milled in with the wheat flour. Still, it is hearty food. Along with the many jars of vegetables, wild fruit, and preserved venison and chicken stored in the cellar, there will be enough to get through the winter.

Jake Martens puts aside his whittling: a mallard duck sleeping with its head tucked under its wing. Along with his deer, horses, dogs, geese, and pigs, the duck will join his little pine menagerie. Jake's head aches, as it always does when there is a rapid change in air pressure, although he has no way of knowing this is the reason. He goes to the row of hooks by the door for his coat.

"Where are you going, Jake?" There is a worried tone in Helena's voice.

Jake doesn't answer. He pulls his overshoes on over his grey felt boots, struggles into his coat, and pulls on a knitted hat. Today is one of his silent days.

Helena follows him to the door and watches as he makes his way across the rough snow and ice in the yard to the barn. There are few chores to do. A horse, a gaunt milk cow and her pitiful weaned calf, two pigs, and several Plymouth Rock hens are the only creatures remaining from the Martens' once-thriving stable of livestock. Everything else has either died or been sold for next to nothing.

"Is he all right, Oma?"

"He'll be fine, Gracie Marie." She looks out the window above the sink. The sunlight of the morning has given away to clouds and whipping wind. She can barely follow Jake's progress. A maelstrom of white sucks in the wide outline of the barn. Helena hopes the guide rope is still secure; it has not been used for a long time.

"You can wash up these mixing bowls, Gracie. I'm going to get some wood from the shed. We'll bring up a jar of venison for supper."

The wind is by now a howling gale and blowing snow drives the cattle to the shelter of the board fence. Steve Kalinsky returns to the warm haven of his stone house. This storm reminds him of one in the Ukraine when he was a teenager. He and two of his friends struck out to a neighbor's, for no other reason than to challenge the elements. Steve still relishes the thrill when the three of them arrived safely at the neighbor's farmhouse, the laughter and celebration with vodka and hot black bread and cheese. They stayed the night, unconcerned about their distraught families at home.

He wolfs down the sausages and potatoes that Annie has ready.

"I'm going to go over to Colin's and see how he's doing."

Annie looks at him as if he is crazy. "Are you daft? Steve, you can't go out in a storm like this."

"Why not? This is nothing. Nothing like the storms back home."

"You can't even see to the hay shed."

"It won't be dark for hours yet. And most of the way is sheltered."

Annie plants her hands on her hips. "I don't want you to go."

"Why don't you bundle up some of that good bread for Colin and Joey? I'll be back in time for supper."

"Can you just tell me why?"

Why? Why does one have the urge to face a storm head-on, if not to prove an ability to conquer the elements? What is it about extreme weather that elicits foolhardy boy from grown man? Is it some deep-seated atavistic vestige of survival, or a sinister subconscious yearning? Is it the delicious love of risk and danger? Steve cannot explain, even to himself.

The afternoon passes quickly with *Riders of the Purple Sage*. Colin dog-ears the page he is reading and gets up to make supper. He peels a scabby potato and slices some salt pork into a frypan. Annie Kalinsky sent Steve over last fall with several jars of rhubarb preserves. There are seven jars left in the pantry and he opens one for dessert. He goes to the window and looks out into the strange diffused grey of late winter twilight. A brisk breeze drives a mixture of sleety snow across the yard. *My ankle doesn't lie.*

After supper Joey goes out to milk the cow and check on the pig and chickens. He dumps a small scoop of oat chop in the trough for the pig and places a little pile on the floor for the six hens that scramble around his feet to claim their share. In the short time it takes him to finish the few chores, the rising wind has transformed the night to a roaring whiteout. Joey feels for the rope from barn to house. With one hand grasping the handle of the milk pail, the other pulling its way along the rope, he stumbles through the deepening drifts to the house. A blast of wind and snow follows him into the kitchen.

Helena Martens peers out the kitchen window anxiously. She can see nothing.

The six loaves of dark bread bake in the oven, filling the kitchen with a comforting aroma. Gracie Marie opens the jar of preserved venison and warms it in a pot on the stove. She brings up a small jar of rose-hip jelly from the cellar and sets it on the table.

"Oma, I'm going to have to go the barn to get Papa. Something must be wrong. He needs me to bring him in."

"I'll go, Gracie. You get supper on the table."

No, Oma." Her voice is firm, determined. "It'll be too hard for you to walk in the snowdrifts with your sore hips. I'm going."

Helena does not argue. Gracie Marie pulls on her felt boots and overshoes and coat and takes the coal oil lantern from the shelf by the door. She lights a splinter of wood in the woodstove, touches it to the oily wick.

Helena watches from the window. She registers the light from the lantern for only a moment before it disappears into the swirling white curtain. She can't tell if Gracie Marie has found the old rope half buried in the snow by the house.

Gracie Marie pulls at the rope until it lifts from the drift. It appears to be firmly attached at the other end and she follows it, pulling herself along. The wind is vicious. It cuts into her face and stings her eyes and sifts through the fibres of her hand knit mittens. *This is taking far too long. It can't be this far.*

Helena Martens is frantic. She struggles with her boots and coat and scarf and follows Jake and Gracie Marie into the blizzard. She is heartened to find the rope and begins her journey along its length. She is knocked into the deep snow by something, something that falls on top of her. It is Gracie Marie, on her way back.

"Oma! Is that you?"

Helena cannot speak. Her mouth and eyes and nose are filled with snow. Gracie Marie reaches into the snow and helps Helena to her feet.

"He isn't in the barn, Oma. He's gone." Helena falls limp and Gracie Marie struggles to get her up again.

Steve Kalinsky is well dressed for a blizzard. Thick woollen socks, knit by Annie, add to the warmth of his felt boots and buckled rubber overshoes. His long woollen underwear itches next to his skin under a heavy flannel shirt and woollen pants. Finally, a hooded deer hide coat, bought from one of the Metis that come into Millfield from time to time, covers him from head to knee. His hand knit mittens line a pair of leather ones, and a striped scarf holds the hood in place around his face. Annie studies the insanity. She knows he cannot be stopped and so she has done all she can.

Four loaves of bread nestle in a canvas sack thrown over his shoulder. He hugs Catherine and Nadia and Annie. Peter and Simon roll and dodge around his legs. Irina is engrossed with a rag doll at the kitchen table.

"Don't worry, my loves. I'll be back before you know it."

Steve, in addition to his awareness of weather, has a finely honed sense of time and direction. He can feel, somehow, when he is facing north or south, even without any visual advantage. When he reaches the end of the short lane from his house to the road going north, he turns right to the east. He can see a few feet ahead, enough to make out the edges of the road. It should take twenty minutes at a brisk walk to get to McCorries.

The wind grows in intensity. Visibility decreases to nothing. Occasionally the ghostly shadow of a tree or fence or clump of grass emerges for a second, only to be gulped back into the white. The snow is deeper on the road than Steve expects and walking is becoming hard work. He stumbles, just enough to cause the sack of bread to slip from his grasp. The loaves spill around him and he scrambles for them in the deepening snow, finding three of the four. His mittens are full of loose snow, which quickly melts in the warmth of his hands. The momentary distraction is disorienting. He stands, turning from side to side to re-establish north in his bodily compass, then heads again due east.

He perspires heavily from the extra exertion of plodding through the hardening drifts. His hands are wet inside the mittens. The chill of the wind continues to deepen and a cold dampness envelops him. A huge gust tears his scarf loose and it flies away into the blizzard. *Just a short rest. Just enough to catch my breath.* He shivers; a tooth-chattering tremor. A fleeting moment of clarity. Steve fights the urge to stay at rest. He forces himself back to his feet on limbs that feel like lead. He believes he is still on the road.

In the late afternoon darkness, the battering of the wind is even more threatening. Deadly, powerful, invisible, it rattles the windows, pounds against the walls, and wails a warning dirge. Colin and Joey try to listen to the radio. Foster Hewitt is doing the play-by-play broadcast of the Toronto and Montreal hockey game but the reception is sporadic and static-infested. They turn it off and start a game of cribbage. Ribbit the cattle dog, so named for his love of eating frogs from the shallow dugout, curls on the braided mat in front of the stove, his legs chasing an elusive dream.

"Fifteen two, fifteen four, and two pair is eight." Colin pegs his score. "One more hand and I'll have you skunked."

He rubs his chest, sore and aching from his cough. He deals. They pick up the new hands and studiously decide what to discard to the crib. Joey grins and tosses in what he believes will be two useless cards.

Ribbit jumps to his feet from the depths of his dream. The hair on the back of his neck stands in a quivering ridge and he erupts with a deep growling volley of barks.

"Hey, Ribbit, what is it, boy?" Colin reaches to calm him but the dog rushes to the door, still barking and growling. "There's nothing out there, Ribbit. It's just the wind."

"C'mere, Ribbit." Joey holds out his hand. The dog ignores him and paws frantically at the door.

"Maybe he just has to go out and pee," Colin says. "Why don't you put a tie on him and take him out along the rope for a minute?"

The dog continues his barking and pawing while Joey puts on his coat and boots. The second the door opens, Ribbit bolts into the howling darkness, ripping the cord tie from Joey's hand.

"Shit. What do I do now? I'll never find him out there."

They can still hear the dog, further away but no less frenzied. The barking turns to a long howl, back to a series of barks, and again to a howl.

"Something's wrong." Colin grabs his coat and the coal-oil lantern and he and Joey follow the sounds into the blizzard.

Catherine and Nadia are in bed, joining Peter and Simon and Irina who have already been asleep for hours. Annie paces from the kitchen to the living room, back and forth, back and forth, too many times to count. She vacillates between being furious at Steve for his foolishness and wondering how she will plan for his funeral.

His supper of cabbage rolls and hot bread waits in the warming oven.

Chapter 34

Wolf River, 1936

Gracie Marie forces her scrawny old horse through the drifts to the McCorrie place the morning after the blizzard. Steve Kalinsky is there, nursing frostbitten nose, cheeks, and fingers from his foolhardy trek to the McCorries' in the storm. Steve is fortunate that Ribbett found him collapsed in a snowdrift forty feet from the house. Still, when the men leave to look for Jake, Steve is at the front of the line of searchers, even before he goes home to Annie and his children. The dozen or more men called by Colin and Joey criss-cross the snow-covered fields on horseback or on snowshoes and push as deep into the trees and bushes as the drifts allow. They persevere for two days, during which time the temperature never rises above thirty below zero. The vicious cold forces them to abandon the search, but it does not matter. Everyone knows Jake Martens will not be found alive.

Gracie Marie struggles stubbornly to carry on the farm work. She carries pails of water from the pump to the barn for the pig and chickens; she drives the horse and cow to the water trough. She spreads dusty straw for the animals and forks the manure into piles by the door where it freezes into hard mounds. The hayfork blisters her palms and her fingers are sore and swollen from trying to squeeze milk from the gaunt cow. The pathetic calf is finally dead and she drags it outside behind the barn. Gracie Marie is nothing if not tenacious. But there is little energy left to deal with Helena's growing dementia.

The vast snowdrifts of winter recede leaving ugly patches of snow mould on the dead grass. Narrow trails of packed ice are all that remain of the winter pathways to the barn. Every morning Helena Martens drags on her heavy winter clothing and slips and slides along these treacherous surfaces on her way to the outbuildings. She could walk on the bare ground if she wished, but these are the pathways Jake took; these are the pathways that will lead her to him. Behind the barn and along the barbed-wire fence line she searches and squints, peering into the ragged bushes, shading her eyes to focus on the black fields and the horizon. Without fail she returns just before noon.

"God knows where he is, Gracie Marie. We must have faith. God will show him the way back. We have to have dinner ready."

Gracie Marie nods. It is easier to let Helena believe in her God, easier to carry out this bizarre daily ritual than to try to convince her that Jake is not returning.

Harry Popham and his son Arthur cut their horses across the little hayfield on the corner of the Martens farm on their way to Millfield. The weather is pleasant enough for the first of May, sun shining warmly and wind not yet whipped to frenzy. They skirt the adjoining pasture and walk the horses along the sagging fence line at the west end of the hayfield.

At first Harry thinks the brown thing curled low against the strands of barbed wire is a dead deer. He pulls closer and realizes, shocked, what he has found. Jake Martens is lying on his side, his dead face decomposing and unrecognizable and his blond hair ruffling in the wind like dry grass. His heavy jacket is unbuttoned and the bones of his bare hands claw at the putrid air surrounding him. Arthur Popham vomits.

Harry and Arthur continue on to Millfield, now at a gallop. They return with Dr. Millan and the undertaker Dunham to identify and deal with the body. Arthur vomits again. Millan has tears in his eyes.

"This was the same field, you know."

Harry sends Arthur home and goes with Dr. Millan to break the news. Gracie Marie says nothing. She has known since the night of the blizzard. The words drift over Helena but do not settle. Ignoring the men, she pulls her old winter jacket from its hook by the door and heads out on her daily mission. The ice pathways have long since disappeared and a warm spring wind is whipping up the dust in the yard.

"Be sure to have dinner ready, Gracie. Fresh bread and borscht. And some boiled sausage."

"It's impossible, Joey. She can't keep this up."

"I know. But you won't be able to tell her that."

Colin drains his barley coffee and pushes back from the supper table. "Well somebody has to. Times are bad enough without people standing by and watching her kill herself."

Joey takes his dishes to the sink. "I don't know what anybody can do. I know her well enough to know she won't give up."

"There's a difference between giving up and taking help." Colin chews on the stained stub of his crooked rolled smoke and rasps away at his cough. "Doc Millan was out there the other day. He says the old grandmother's completely lost her mind. He's worried she's going to wander away one of these days."

"There's not much we can do about that."

"The Doc wants Gracie Marie to put her into Mrs. Collins' rest home."

"How could they afford that?"

"She gets old age pension. It's not a lot, but it'd be enough to cover it."

"I still don't see how it has anything do with us."

Colin is becoming frustrated. "Christ, Joey, she's not much more than a kid. Someone's got to step up and lend a hand. I think we should take her in."

Joey is flabbergasted. This is an unforeseen development. He looks at his boots and mulls over the idea in silence. All the time he can feel Colin's eyes drilling into him.

"Well?" Colin coughs again, his chronic dry hacking. He draws another pull of smoke into his lungs.

"I'll think it over."

"Don't think too long."

It's not that Joey dislikes Gracie Marie or that he doesn't want to help. There is simply too much of Laidie Christie in the equation. The two girls were best friends. How much might Laidie have confided? Would she have told Gracie about their love-trysts? Probably not. That information would have been too private, even for a best friend. But Gracie must certainly have realized they were more than friends, if not how much more. Joey still believes she knew where Laidie went when the Christies moved away without forewarning, and he has always been aware of Gracie's veiled feelings for him.

What do you think, Laidie?

Helena Martens is deposited at Mrs. Collins' old folks home in Millfield and Gracie Marie arrives at the McCorries' at the end of May. Colin and Joey load her sickly horse and cow and two pigs into the back of the truck and move them in two trips, along with any usable feed, which isn't much. Four hens ride in a crate in the cab. Gracie, in spite of her indomitable spirit, sees the move as personal defeat. Head down, she carries her things into the big McCorrie house. This is the first time Joey has seen her without her little Mennonite bonnet.

Annie Kalinsky's old room is now Gracie Marie's. When she isn't occupied with "hired girl" duties, this is where spends most of her time. The men wonder what she does in there but they don't ask. They invite her to sit in the living room in the evenings and listen to Edgar Bergen and Charlie McCarthy or the Happy Gang or Foster Hewitt's animated account of a Montreal Canadiens game, but she politely refuses.

It's a long forgotten pleasure to have a woman cooking again. Gracie Marie can invent a meal from the most meagre of supplies. The shelves in the McCorrie cellar are augmented by whatever was left at the Martens farm: several jars of preserved venison and chicken, two coils of spicy pork sausage, homemade dry noodles, a bunch of onions hanging from their stems, beets and carrots packed in sand, and potatoes already growing sprouts. There is rhubarb jam and preserves, a crate of questionable eggs, and a crock of salted cabbage. Gracie Marie has never heard of recipes. Her head holds all the information required.

When the wind is not in full attack, she works on the garden, a sad patch of ground on the east side of the house. It is as dry as any desert except for the water she hauls in pails from the water wagon, which Colin fills from the shrinking river with his little hand pump. She hoes thistles and digs dandelions, both of which thrive in the heat and drought, and she somehow manages to coax modest growth from the earth. She cans what cannot be eaten and saves seeds for next year. Nothing goes to waste.

Oma Martens' lessons are well-learned. Except, that is, for the faith she worked so hard to instil in her granddaughter. Gracie Marie has abandoned belief in a God who does not answer prayers as Oma promised. Another lie. A God who allows the burden of drought to destroy farms and take lives. A God who took her parents in horrible ways. She believes things are simply as they are. She believes in what she can control: hard work and loyalty, kindness and honesty. Although she has almost forgotten what it feels like, she believes in laughter. And she believes in love.

There are no bounds to the optimism of a farmer. He looks at a handful of dusty wheat and sees germinating sprouts and fields rippling like green lakes and rose-golden piles of grain in their bins and money to take to the bank. "Next year" always holds the possibility of better times, better weather, and better prices. As long as there is a seed, a farmer will take the risk. He can resist no more than a gambler can walk away from the temptation of a poker game. *One more hand, I'll win it all back.* So once again, seeds are faithfully committed to the ground. The hot wind blows, desiccating the rich soil and rendering it impotent. The green shoots quickly outgrow the meagre reserves of moisture and by the middle of July, there is nothing left. Hot southwesterlies push the temperature higher and higher, topping 100 degrees for days on end. The air fills with fine particulate dust and the huge prairie skies turn a volcanic grey. Trains stop service until soil drifts can be cleared from the tracks. *The Free Press Prairie Farmer* reports of mounting death tolls from the heat.

Through July and August, Colin and Joey spend most of their time working to keep their cattle and other stock alive. The water level in the well remains low but a deep aquifer replenishes it nightly, so the animals do not suffer from thirst. Colin hears that some families in the area have had to butcher their cattle because they had barely enough water for themselves. The few McCorrie cattle forage the pasture for food but there is little to find except Russian thistle. When the tops are eaten, the animals grub out the long woody taproots, loosening the soil to the ravages of the wind.

In some areas the fences are nearly buried and in other spots the soil has literally blown out from under them, leaving the posts dangling from the barbed wire in the wind. Colin is obsessed with the repair of these fences. Joey does not agree with the urgency, but there is not much else to do. The McCorries are hard workers and it goes against the fibre of their nature to sit and brood and do nothing. So they fix fences, battling the ubiquitous dust that stings their eyes and grates in their teeth and infiltrates their lungs. The wind is unremitting in its vindictiveness, burying and destroying the repairs in a matter of weeks, or sometimes days.

The insidious blackness creeping into Colin's lungs is deadly. By October his chronic smokers' cough turns into wrenching spasms that leave him without breath. He is weak, his head aches continuously, and his eyes and nose burn. He is still adamant in his refusal to have Doc Millan pay a visit, but concedes he needs help. He allows Gracie Marie to care for him.

Gracie draws upon her knowledge of Oma's countless home remedies, most of them honey-based and some of which require courage to ingest. She mixes black pepper with honey and administers it by the spoonful to loosen the cough. She serves thick-sliced onions as if they were apples, or chops them and stirs them into honey. She trudges to the river to forage the dusty banks for coneflower and yarrow, which she brews into hot honeyed tea. She makes a cough syrup of honey and vinegar. She sends Joey to Millfield for more honey. The only thing that does not require it is a mustard plaster. This she constructs from dry mustard powder mixed with flour and water and spread between thin flour sack towels. She spreads it on his chest like a large warm pancake and covers him with a blanket and watches the clock to be sure the plaster does not stay there long enough to burn his skin. Joey hovers nervously.

Nothing helps. Colin wheezes with every breath. No position brings him comfort or relief from the pain in his chest. He coughs and gags, expectorating a muddy greenish sludge. Gracie refuses to leave him, even sleeping in the chair at his bedside.

Ivy and Fred Fletcher come every day now to see if there is anything they can do. Ivy usually brings a hot meal in the evening, but Colin cannot eat. Ivy is alarmed at his high fever. In spite of his refusal to see the doctor, she and Joey agree that Millan must be fetched at once, regardless of Colin's wishes. By the time Joey and Millan arrive back at the farm Colin is incoherent and delirious. The doctor shakes his head. His voice is flat and devoid of hope.

"I've seen a few other cases like this. It's dust pneumonia." He rubs his sleeve across his eyes. "I might have been able to do something if I had seen him earlier."

His failure to save Ruby McCorrie eighteen years ago still weighs heavily on his mind. In a way he believes that event is directly connected to Colin's death, because like his father Ford, Colin has refused to see a doctor in all that time.

The day of Colin McCorrie's funeral, the shrieking north wind strafes cold black clouds of dust across the land, forcing fine powdery silt in around the windows of Millfield Presbyterian Church. The building is full. Joey and Gracie Marie sit slightly apart in the front pew. Joey's grandparents, Ivy and Fred Fletcher, are beside him and the Kalinsky family joins Gracie Marie on the other side. Right behind are Annie's parents, the Elliots, and the ever-proliferating O'Reilly clan. The Popham family is clustered tightly a few rows back. Edina sits right on the aisle and cranes her neck to get a glimpse of Colin's open casket at the front of the church. Doctor Millan, his head bowed, stands off to one side near the back. Even Tom and Mabel King are there, basking in their schadenfreude. The church is cold. Kerosene lamps flicker dimly and there is little comfort in the pastor's words.

The cemetery on the south side of the church is somewhat sheltered from the dirty blast and everyone braves the elements to see Colin laid to his final rest between his wife Saharah and his parents Ford and Ruby. His good friend Mac Ward is alone in a plot ten feet away from the McCorries; a plot intended to accommodate his sister Mhairi and her family one day.

Élodie and Jake Martens rest here too, off in the windy western corner of the churchyard near the evergreens. Before her father's funeral in the spring, Gracie Marie had never seen her mother's grave.

The post-funeral visitors are gone. Joey sits at the kitchen table, head on his arms, surrounded by gifts of baking and ready-to-eat dishes, some still warm. He has no appetite. The reality of his aloneness descends upon him like a heavy blanket of dark wet wool. He rises slowly and goes to his room and pulls the door shut behind him.

Gracie Marie loosens the dark knot of braid coiled at the back of her neck and lets her hair fall down her back. She sits on the edge of her bed for a long time before pulling on her flannelette nightgown. She crawls under the quilts, but her feet are cold and she cannot fall asleep. There is too much to think about, too much to try to understand. She is overcome with empathy for Joey. She gets up and pulls on a pair of Oma's knitted wool socks and pads out into the kitchen. The gas lamp on the table is extinguished but a yellow sliver of light leaks from beneath the door to Joey's room. She hesitates only slightly before giving a gentle tap. There is no response and she opens the door a crack. Joey is sitting on his bed. His shirt and tie are discarded in a pile on the floor. He knows she is there but says nothing.

"Joey? I'm terribly sorry. I know how you're feeling right now."

He looks up at her. "I know you do."

She sits beside him. "When Papa went out into the blizzard, I knew what happened. But I couldn't let myself cry until everyone else knew too. Then it finally was real, but I still couldn't cry. I still can't. And now this is real too. It just happened different, but I knew, just like you did. I knew it was going to happen but I couldn't let it be real. Until today. And now...."

She puts her arm around his shoulder and rubs his back. He turns and buries his face in the soft white flannelette of her nightgown, searching for the mother-comfort he so craves. Instinctively, Gracie Marie enfolds him.

"Joey, Joey…"

He holds her tightly and she feels the warmth of his breath on her breast. Gracie Marie does not have time to be afraid. Trembling, they fall back onto the bed and she cannot remember when and how the clothing between them disappears. She feels his skin, his body pressing against hers. Her body. It has often given her hints and pulsings and cues but now it demands realization.

The space above and around and beneath them is a cold blackness of loss, emptiness and grief, but at their centre is a sanctuary of comfort and pleasure, however temporary. Then they lie in one another's arms and the sorrow floods back, thick and too heavy to bear. At last, they cry. Later when Gracie Marie believes Joey is asleep she tries to leave. He pulls her back.

"Please don't leave me alone tonight, Gracie. I can't stand to be alone."

Blue sky is rare this spring. Gracie Marie takes advantage of the clear morning for an early start in the garden. She marks out planting rows with binder twine and sticks and murders some persistent weeds. Portulaca isn't particular about whether it has favorable growing conditions and presents a constant challenge. Oma used to say you could pull up a piece of portulaca and hang it on a barbed wire fence and it would still grow. Gracie is determined to defeat it.

She looks up from the garden to see a horse and buggy rattling down the lane. It's Fred and Ivy Fletcher. Fred waves (he is always friendly) but Ivy looks in the other direction as they pass by. Fred pulls the buggy around to the side door and they are out of Gracie's sight.

Joey is still inside. He sits at the kitchen table, surrounded by bits of leather and wire and twine, struggling to repair a dilapidated piece of harness. He looks up to see Ivy Fletcher in the doorway of the McCorrie kitchen, her hands on her hips, face flushed deep red.

"People are talking, Joey." *No hello, it's a nice morning, how are you?*

"What about?"

"You know what about."

"No, I don't. Now what's wrong?"

Joey can be extremely frustrating. She knows he does it intentionally: forcing her to go into detail when he knows all along what she is talking about. Ivy folds her arms over her large bosom and takes a deep breath. "You and Gracie Marie. The two of you living together under the same roof."

His silence forces her to go on.

"It was different when your father was here. But now…"

He looks at the flowers on her apron, the worn-out pieces of harness spread on the table, the hangnail on his thumb. "It's no different now."

Ivy has made her point. She is not about to argue. "You'd best talk to her."

Fred is waiting for her in the buggy. The conversation is over.

The possible outcome of this terse discussion is something Joey has already considered. It would certainly be practical. It is already passionate.

He finishes up the harness and takes it out to the barn. The sun climbs towards noon and a breeze out of the west gathers strength. The dust stirs and gathers itself into rolling banks along the horizon.

Chapter 35

Wolf River, 1936

The burgeoning clouds of airborne silt darken the early September sun and turn mid-morning into twilight. Edina Popham lights the kerosene lamps at ten in the morning so the children can read. She has every imaginable crack and crevice stuffed with strips of rag to keep out the pervasive dust. The school is so tightly sealed that the lamps flicker. The stifling heat is unbearable.

At precisely noon Edina pours a little water into the small basin on the shelf at the back of the room and the students line up to wash their hands with strong homemade soap donated by Annie Kalinsky. The smallest children go first, some are barely able to reach the basin. Dirty water runs to their elbows and into their sleeves. Everyone washes in the same water, including Edina. When she is finished she pours the dull grey soup into a pail below the shelf, to be used again when the dirt has settled.

The jam pail lunches sit unopened in front of their owners until Miss Popham says grace. "For this food may we be sincerely thankful. Teach us to share and help us to live with kindness. Amen." She has recited this grace so often that sometimes she does not hear herself say the words. She walks among the desks and inspects the lunches.

Billy Walsh and his sister Evaline always sit together, but today there is only one lunch pail in front of them.

"Did you forget your lunch today, Billy?"

"No, Miss Popham. Mama didn't have enough for two lunches so today just Evaline gets to eat."

"May I see your lunch, Evaline?"

Evaline opens the paper wrapping on a thin white sandwich, the lone item in her pail.

"What kind is it?" Miss Popham questions softly.

The child's ears redden and she looks down at her folded hands. "Salt and pepper, Ma'am."

The children are listless from the stale air and beg to go outside for the rest of the noon hour to play Anti-I-Over but Edina won't hear of it.

"What?" she asks. "The air is too dirty. You can't see from here to the gate. Goodness, you would lose the ball in the dust the first time you threw it."

They know she is right, but they are disappointed. She goes to the cupboard behind her desk and brings out her old stereoscope and allows them to look at bright slides of faraway places like Africa, Switzerland, the Grand Canyon, and Australia. *Faraway places. I wonder what I could have done with my life if I hadn't stayed here.*

Edina is thirty years old and ensnared by circumstance. She never wanted to come to the Wolf River area in the first place, but she was only seventeen at the time, too young to be left behind when her father and brother decided to become farmers. *What if I hadn't taken this teaching job? What if I had left after two years like I planned? What if Mother hadn't died? What if the weather hadn't turned on us?* None of it matters any more. There is nowhere else to go. Besides, her thirty-five dollar monthly pay cheque is essential to the Popham family finances.

Edina is bitter. Over the years she has built a protective shell of unapproachability around herself and works diligently at being unlikeable. At first this was to avoid attachments, to allow her to leave expediently when the time came. There was only one man she would have allowed to draw her from that shell, but Colin McCorrie was never able to get past the loss of his wife; never allowed himself to think of another partner. So Edina kept the wall high and unbreachable. This unsociable behavior is now an ingrained part of her psyche. Still, she is recognized as a good teacher. Her students, while they harbour a modicum of fear of her legendary discipline, are fond of her. She is fair and proper and grows more benevolent with the passage of time as the realization becomes clear that this classroom is the closest she will come to having children of her own.

Beneath the rising gusts of wind she can hear the hissing sound of sand and silt battering the school, eroding the wood siding and pitting the windows. In spite of the rag-packed cracks, tiny black drifts form in the corners of the windowsills. Edina squints through the dusty windowpanes. She can't see anything, even the water pump which is only twenty feet from the school. Last year *The Free Press Prairie Farmer* printed a cautionary story about some mid-western American children who were sent home from a country school in a dust blizzard. Several became lost and perished in the storm. Since then it has been agreed in the community that Miss Popham will keep the students at school in such an emergency. She is trusted implicitly. She gathers her charges around her desk.

"I can't let you go home today because of the storm. We will all have to stay here tonight. Now, I need some of you older ones to help me." She scans the worried faces. "Tom and Andy, Danny, Jamie, and, let's see, Maria and Emma. Can I count on you?"

They all nod seriously. Miss Popham presses her face to the window. She can still see the flagpole, less than ten feet from the corner of the school.

"All right then. Danny, I want you and Tom to go together to take down the flag. And untie the flag rope and bring it in. Cover your faces."

The Union Jack is shredded to tatters by wind and blowing soil. The boys drag the rope into the school porch and Miss Popham stretches it to its full length. Twenty-five feet. It will be long enough to reach to the well.

"Andy, you and Jamie tie one end of this to the boot scraper. Walk straight out to where you think the well is and move back and forth sideways until you find it. Take the extra pail so we can have enough to fill the drinking water crock. No matter what you do, stay together and don't let go of the rope. Emma and Maria, I would like you to take the smaller children to the back and keep them busy. Boys, don't forget to keep your faces covered."

So far all is well. The boys bring enough water for drinking and washing. The three horses in the school barn will have to wait until tomorrow. Miss Popham reads a chapter of *Treasure Island* every day after the noon hour. Today she carries on through several chapters. The children fan lazily with paper fans. It is almost pleasant. She has them stand and stretch, walk around the classroom, touch their toes ten times, and get a drink of water from the Redwing crock with the spigot at the bottom.

She convenes the children once again. "I know you are all hungry but we will be all right. Everyone will have to go outside to use the toilets before night. We'll use the rope again. It won't be long enough, so we'll have to find something to tie on the end of it. Do any of you have anything we could use?"

"I have a long skipping rope," offers Nadia Kalinksy. "So does Catherine."

The other girls chime in. It seems they all have skipping ropes, most of them just lengths of braided binder twine. By the time these are tied together and attached to the flag rope there is more than enough length to reach the toilets.

"We will go in groups. I'll take the lantern and go first with Tom and Danny. I'll tie the rope to the door of the toilet. Then we will come back and take the rest of you. We'll take the first and second graders to start with, so be ready. No one is to move until we get back. Do you understand?"

There is a hushed whisper of 'yes-ma'ams.' Simon and Peter Kalinsky move close to the security of Nadia and Catherine. Miss Popham gathers her little group, all of them clinging to the rope. They cover their faces with their handkerchiefs or shirttails or whatever they can find and disappear into the furnace of savage grey swirl.

Chapter 36

Wolf River, 1936

"I guess we should probably get married," he says to Gracie Marie's back.

She doesn't answer. She is vigorously shaking a cup of cream in a Mason jar, watching for the first pale hint of butter to emerge. She has on an old grey shirt of her father's, tied at her waist, and Joey can see the movements of her small but muscular frame through the worn cotton.

"Gran says people are talking about us. Not that I care, but..."

The Mason jar moves faster, back and forth, swishing the cream in foamy circles. Gracie's dark hair is gathered high and tied with a piece of yellow yarn. Stray wisps of dark curl cling to the back of her neck.

"I guess she thinks we're living in sin, whatever that is. So what do you say, Gracie?"

She shakes the jar furiously. The cream splits into yellow globules of butter floating in buttermilk. *What about love?* She sets the jar on the kitchen table in front of her and turns to face him. The old grey shirt is unbuttoned, and he can see her cleavage, damp with sweat. There are greasy spots on her loose pink skirt where cream has leaked from the butter jar.

"I agree." She examines the soiled skirt. "I think that would be the right thing to do."

They say their vows two weeks later at the Millfield Town Office in front of Mr. Collins, the Justice of the Peace. Two town employees witness the short ceremony. Gracie Marie wears Laidie's silver heart-shaped locket at her throat. Her wavy dark hair falls around her face and today her eyes are violet. She is beautiful. Joey positions his grandmother's wedding ring on her finger. They step outside and Mr. Collins follows with his camera.

"I always take a picture of couples I marry."

He shepherds them into position on the steps in front of the wide town office double doors. "Don't move, now." He considers for a moment before clicking the shutter. "I'll take one more to be sure. When the pictures come back from Winnipeg you can come in to have a look. They're twenty-five cents if you want one."

The newlyweds climb into the old Democrat buggy and Joey slaps the reins lightly against the horse's back.

"Well, that's done with. I guess we should stop in to see Gran and Gramps on the way home and tell them the news. They'll be happy we're not going to hell."

The horse moves at a slow trot, its shodden feet stirring up smoky puffs of dust. Gracie glances sideways at her husband.

"Would it be all right if we went to see Oma for a few minutes too?"

Joey turns the horse towards Mrs. Collin's old folks home.

Gracie smiles and nods and turns her face away. *I'll make you love me. I will.*

The only real change at the McCorrie house is the integration of Gracie's and Joey's belongings into the big bedroom. "You go ahead and sort things out," he tells her. "It doesn't make any difference to me where you put anything."

Their belongings are unremarkable: clothing, a few books, Joey's shaving box, Gracie Marie's small box of memorabilia from her mother's life with Jake, her neatly folded rags for her personal days. She puts the portrait of her mother in its brown leather frame on the corner of the oak dresser which once belonged to Ruby and Ford. There is still a small box of Joey's things left to sort and she lifts it onto the bed. It holds the typical hoardings of a boy—shiny and colorful stones, a tiny jackknife, a broken slingshot, a shiny red pencil, unsharpened, a handful of school papers, and an envelope. Gracie recognizes the envelope immediately. She, after all, carried it close for several days, waiting for a chance to deliver it to Joey. Wondering all the while what it could be; resisting the temptation to peek inside. *Well, now I'm his wife. Go ahead and sort things out, he said.*

She opens the envelope and slides out a beautifully detailed charcoal sketch of a pair of wolves standing on a riverbank. The animals lean slightly towards each other, obviously mates. The charcoal greys run from pale as pearly cloud to near-black shadows beneath the trees. Only the wolves' eyes are colored—a deep golden yellow. She recognizes Laidie Christie's initials tucked into the grass at the bottom of the sketch. Gracie turns the photo over. Written on the back in immaculate little script are the words, "Love you forever."

Gracie returns everything to the box except the picture. She leans it against the mirror on the dresser and stands back to admire it. *She was so good at drawing. So good at everything.*

She feels Joey's presence behind her and turns to find him standing in the doorway.

"Where did you find that, Gracie?" His voice is husky, deeper than usual.

"It was in that old box of things of yours," she answers lamely. *Is he angry with me?*

The silence is weighty, sucks the air from the room. Gracie picks up the sketch and hands it to him.

"Do you want me to put it in a frame for you, Joey?"

"I'd like that." He hands it back to her and turns and rushes out as if he must be somewhere at once and has forgotten the time.

They sit on the side verandah facing the struggling garden, Gracie tip-and-tailing a few yellow beans. Joey, shirtless, cleans his rifle in case a rabbit or prairie chicken waits for him somewhere down by the river tomorrow. The early evening sky is steely with dust and the heat of day cloys stickily to their skin. There will be no twilight. Day drops into night behind the thickness of air-borne grit—grey to charcoal to black. The myriad chirps of crickets play against the wind, a frantic rhythmic song of heat.

Gracie's old blue shirt is unbuttoned low. Her skirt is hiked, albeit modestly, above her slightly separated knees to allow the breeze to cool her pantiless privates. She sets the finished beans on the floor and leans back in the old porch chair.

"Do you ever wonder about our families, Joey?"

"I dunno. What do you mean?" He works the bore brush through the rifle barrel several times.

"They were all so small. My Oma left all her family behind when she came to Canada with my Grandfather. Then they only had my Dad, and he only had me. Your family is sort of the same."

"I don't follow." He leans the rifle against the wall.

"Well, you said you never had any aunts or uncles, so your parents must have both been only children. And they only had you."

"If my mother had lived, they probably would have had more."

"Same with my mother. But I think she was an only child too."

They are silent for a few moments. The hot wind maintains its dirge and moving dust susurrates around the foundation of the house. Joey stretches and yawns.

"Why are you even thinking about all of this?"

"I don't know. It just doesn't seem fair that some families have so many people in them. Like the O'Reilly's. It must be a lot of fun at their house. Or the Kalinsky's."

"Hmmm. Maybe."

"There's something else that isn't fair." Gracie waits for him to ask what that is, but he is silent, so she continues anyway. "It's that in our little families everyone dies before they should. Our families don't have people to spare."

Joey regards her curiously. He is not used to intangible discussions. He stands and picks up the rifle. When he gets to the doorway he turns.

"Are you saying we should make some more people?"

She pretends to ignore him.

"God, it's hot." She wipes her face with the sleeve of her shirt.

"It's ninety."

"How do you know? I don't think it's that hot."

"Listen to the crickets. The faster they chirp, the hotter it is. Gramp always said if you count the chirps in fifteen seconds and add 37, then that's the temperature."

Gracie tosses her head and laughs. "I'm not superstitious. That's funny. Besides, you can't add that fast."

"You think it's funny, do you?" Joey looks at the thermometer hanging by the door. "See? Ninety. Now that's funny too."

"I don't believe you. Let me look!" She trips on the bowl of yellow beans and they scatter across the verandah floor as she pushes past him.

He grabs her by the arms, spins her around against the door, and kisses her open mouth, hard. "You know something else funny? Every time you come close to me your clothes come off."

He pulls up the pink skirt and peels her shirt down over her shoulders, lifts her off her feet, and buries his face in the sweaty separation between her breasts. She reaches behind her head and loosens the tie on her hair and dark waves spill around his head and shoulders. He closes his eyes and pushes into her. But in the darkness the hair is always auburn.

Chapter 37

Winnipeg, 1937

1937. The *Winnipeg Free Press* is a daily reminder of the ravages of the Great Depression, filled with pictures of ditches blown full of fine black dirt, abandoned farmyards with their buildings half buried in drifted topsoil, boxcars carrying legions of men across the country looking for work, trainloads of emergency produce arriving from Ontario, and refugee families in ragged clothing perched on wagons drawn by gaunt horses, headed for anywhere but here. One of the pictures on the front page shows a large billboard sponsored by a Chamber of Commerce somewhere. Men, heads down, are walking past the billboard which reads: Jobless Men Keep Going, We Can't Take Care of our Own.

Once a month a cheque made out to Mhairi Christie arrives in the mail from Denver Atchison, Mac Ward's lawyer. In his twelve years in the Wolf River District Mac was both hard-working and careful. He accumulated not a huge fortune but a respectable collection of assets. Denver Atchison now administers this estate, designed to care for Mhairi and Laidie. It is not a great deal of money, but in these times it is enough to place the Christies in a position to survive the ravages of the Great Depression. When the owner of their rented Hampton Street bungalow is forced to sell off his properties to pay massive debts, they are able to buy the house.

Laidie has a job in the fabric department at Eaton's. She earns only twenty-five dollars a month but on paydays never fails to bring something for three-year-old Blythe from the Woolworth's five and dime on the corner across from where she works. Mhairi has a small clientele from River Heights (for the wealthy still manage to stay wealthy) who buy fabric from Blythe. They do not realize the woman she recommends as a seamstress is her mother.

It is harder for Orville. He works at a small lumberyard for a short time until construction dries up. He drifts from one menial job to another—piece work in a furniture factory, going door-to-door in the more affluent areas of the city looking for handyman work, picking dandelions in Assiniboine Park. It festers in Orville's bitter mind that both Laidie and Mhairi are able to generate more income than he. That, and Mhairi's small monthly stipend, over which he has no control.

Mhairi takes in a boarder in May. Bernice Benning arrives on the recommendation of Mrs. Isabel Green, one of Mhairi's sewing customers, and pays twelve dollars a month for the tiny upstairs bedroom and two meals a day. Bernice brings new meaning to the concept of shyness. Eliciting conversation with her is like trying to pull heavy thread through a fine-eyed needle. She prefers to endure the stifling heat of her little room instead of spending time with the Christies. Except for three-year-old Blythe, that is, who dogs Bernice relentlessly and refuses to be denied conversation. Eventually Bernice decides to allow herself to include Laidie.

The three of them sit in the cubby-hole room under the west roof. It is cooler this evening, and Bernice and Blythe play Mary Mack. The clapping begins slowly.

Miss Mary Mack, Mack, Mack
All dressed in black, black, black
With silver buttons, buttons, buttons
All down her back, back, back.

With each repetition the tempo increases until the clapping pattern reaches the point of impossibility and they dissolve into hysterical laughter. Laidie has never seen Bernice like this.

"Play another game?" Blythe pesters. "Please, please?"

"I think it's bedtime, don't you?"

Blythe manufactures the biggest pout possible. "I want another game."

Bernice cuts in. "You go to bed like sister says, sweetie. Then we can play Mary Mack again tomorrow."

Laidie grabs Blythe before the moment disappears and heads for the stairs.

"Would you come back up after she's in bed?" Bernice is sitting on her bed, feet curled under her like a child.

Laidie returns in ten minutes. She sits for a moment, silent, and studies Bernice. The long dark hair and blue eyes remind her of Gracie Marie.

"I brought us some cookies."

Bernice takes three and sits back on the bed. "Thank you for coming back."

"You're lonesome, aren't you?"

"Yes."

"How old are you?"

"Sixteen. And you?"

"Nineteen." *We could almost be sisters.*

"You're a lot older than Blythe. I thought you were younger. Maybe the same as me."

"Do you have sisters?"

"Yes, Frances and Lillian. Frances is eighteen and Lillian is just twelve. I really miss them. Frances is a hired girl on a farm, but Lillian stays at home and helps my mother."

"Mrs. Green told Mother you're from Stonewall?"

Bernice nods. "My father used to work at the grain elevator but he died three years ago and now my mother doesn't feel good most of the time."

"So why did you come to Winnipeg?"

"We don't have any money." Bernice shifts her feet over the side of the bed and leans to peer out the little square window. "I have to send everything I can to Mama." She is silent, perhaps embarrassed. "My aunt said there were lots of people in Winnipeg who were looking for hired girls. I stayed with her at first but she has three little boys and really didn't have room for me. So here I am."

"Would you like to come downstairs and visit with Mother and Father?"

A curtain of alarm draws itself around Bernice. She pulls her knees up to her chest and shakes her head. The conversation is over.

A month later, Bernice is gone. An envelope with twelve dollars for July's unused room and board is left in the mailbox. There is no explanation, no indication of where she might have gone. Mrs. Isabel Green telephones Mhairi to ask why Bernice has not shown up to do her housework. Laidie writes to Mrs. Benning in Stonewall to find out whether Bernice has returned home, but after three weeks there is still no reply.

"I'm really worried about her, Mama," Laidie says. "She's so shy and innocent. She wouldn't just up and leave like that unless something happened."

Mhairi twists her embroidery thread into a tangle of knots, unaware of the tight jumble of color snarled in her knuckles.

"Maybe, your father…" She cuts the thought off in mid-air. Silence.

Laidie cannot breathe. A long-buried memory rises, putrid, from her subconscious. Bony probing fingers. The smell of peppermint candy barely masking the quickening rasp of bad-tooth breath. The hot shame of her little-girl body betraying her in its fleeting dirty pleasure. Her utter powerlessness.

Mhairi is still twisting the colored strands. She will not look up. Laidie is furious, trembling with her sickening epiphany.

"You knew. Mama, you KNEW. All the time, you knew, and you just let him. How could you not stop him?" Even as she asks the question she remembers sobbing under the bed in terror, listening to her mother's cries. She knows the answer.

Millfield, 1937.

The heat and dust are unrelenting. Gracie Marie lays wet rags along the windowsills and stuffs them into any openings that might allow dust to seep in. At night she hangs dripping wet towels on clotheslines strung up inside the house. The evaporation brings some temporary coolness but blowing dirt seeps in and collects on the towels and by morning they are stiff and filthy. She rinses them in a tub, readying them for another night of service.

Most nights she and Joey sleep naked under wet sheets where by morning the outlines of their bodies are imprinted in dusty smudges. On clear nights like this, when the wind rests for a few hours, they sleep on top of quilts spread on the verandah floor.

Gracie runs her hands over her flat abdomen. Her body is white in the moonlight. Joey snores softly beside her. *I want to be pregnant. I want to know what it feels like to have a baby inside me. Joey's baby. Why doesn't it happen?* Frequency is not the problem; the young McCorries' lust for one another knows no bounds. *Would having a baby turn Joey's lust into love?* Gracie's hand rests on Joey's chest and wanders downward, arousing him.

"My god, Gracie, you are a wild one," he mutters willingly through dissipating sleep. "I used to think you were a good girl. Where do you get this from?"

She rolls on top of him. "Must have been my mother."

Joey walks the fields early in the morning, hopeful. In spite of the incessant heat and wind, moisture from early spring rains holds in the soil long enough for the wheat to fill its kernels. A few small grasshoppers flit in the grass at the edge of the field. Gramp Fred Fletcher mentioned just yesterday that the insects were pressing in from the west. By noon there are enough of the hungry creatures to cause concern. Fred is waiting for Joey when he comes in for dinner.

"Ike Evans says they're eating everything in sight out west of Millfield. Some of the farmers over there are threshing now just to be sure they get something."

"What do you think we should do?"

"It's a little early. There'll be too much moisture in the wheat. But I'd sooner make the damn stuff into cattle feed before I let those chomping little buggers get it."

"What about poison? Dad used something a few years back."

"By the time we got the stuff in, it'd be too late." Fred rubs his whiskers. "We could start cutting tonight, after it cools off."

Gracie brings bread and butter and cucumbers to the table along with a bowl of hard-boiled eggs. "Cut it, Joey. I'll bring you some supper in the field."

Fred nods. "All right, then. We'll start with yours tonight, move to my west forty first thing in the morning."

Gracie awakens to the sound of soft rain. She stretches, turns to drape her legs over Joey, and realizes he has not come in from the field. She rolls onto her stomach, buries her face in the pillow, and listens to the rain. It sounds odd, drops chuffing and scuttling across the roof. She stands and goes to the window, trailing the sheet around her. The sun shines darkly through a living cloud of shining wings. Grasshoppers land on the roof, stumble over each other, fall into the garden, and cover the yard in a writhing mass. She can hear the sounds of millions of little jaws stripping away leaves, stems, anything green and alive.

The tractor putts into the yard. Joey walks toward the house, yellow hoppers flying up in a crazy dance beneath his feet. Gracie opens the door for him along with several of the creatures who ride in on his clothing. One jumps to her shoulder and defecates, a slimy green mass which slides down onto her breast. She does not flinch. Her violet eyes are locked on Joey's. He is crying, silent tears carving clean pathways through the dust on his face. Gracie bats away the hoppers and takes off his shirt and leads him to bed.

The ragged noise of insatiable munching jaws drowns out all other sound.

The heat weighs down like a heavy blanket. On days like this Gracie can almost let herself wish for wind. She goes to the rain barrel at the corner of the house and takes off the lid. The barrel is nearly half full with water left from a rain three weeks ago. She peels off her clothing and climbs into the barrel. The water rises to her shoulders. She doesn't see Tom King pulling into their lane with his big car and doesn't hear him approach. When she rises and turns, he is inches away, leering and already groping at her breasts. She tries to pull away but the barrel traps her. Tom King's loose mouth covers hers and she cannot make a sound. His hands are everywhere, dipping into the water, pinching her buttocks, reaching between her legs. He puts his hands under her arms and pulls her from the water, scraping her knees and shins against the rough rim of the barrel. He presses her against the corner of the house while he tugs at his belt. As strong as Gracie is, she is no match for the corpulent King. She squeezes her eyes shut and steels herself for the inevitable. He leans on top of her. His weight squeezes the air from her lungs.

A loud noise splits the air. Tom King falls to his knees. The back side of the shovel hits him again, this time in the face. Joey McCorrie lifts the shovel again, but Gracie cries out.

"Don't, Joey! You'll kill him!"

"That's what I want to do! I want to kill the bastard!" Joey heaves in huge gulps of air. A bloodied Tom King slouches in the mud by the barrel. Gracie grabs the shovel.

She gives Tom King a sharp poke with the handle. "You get the hell out of here."

King drags himself to his feet and staggers to his car with Gracie, naked and muddy, threatening pursuit.

Joey takes the shovel from Gracie, lifts her and lowers her gently back into the barrel. They do not speak. He cups water in his hands and washes her back and breasts and arms and face. He carries her into the house and eases her onto their bed. His pants fall in a dusty heap on the floor and Gracie pulls him down on top of her still wet body

Chapter 38

Winnipeg, July 1947

Laidie paces. The living room, dimly lit by the streetlight on the boulevard, is quiet except for the squeak in the floor in front of the window. The clock in the dining room chimes four. Fourteen-year-old Blythe is not home. This is not the first time Blythe has rejected her curfew, of course; it is merely the first time she has stayed out this late. The panic-filled thoughts racing about within Laidie's head have no boundaries. Blythe's new friends of the past few months are two or three years older than she, and they are bad news. One of the several boys drives a rattling old blue car with no muffler, usually packed with foul-mouthed teenagers of both sexes. The girls wear tight sweaters and skirts and their mouths are heavy and unnatural with theatrical red lipstick. Unlike Blythe's old friends, they refuse come to the house to get her. Instead, she now runs out at the honk of a horn. Once in a while the muffled conversation of a telephone call summons her to a rendezvous somewhere. So it is in the context of these circumstances that Laidie's fears escalate.

Car accidents, a rape, drunkenness, an arrest—any number of scenarios play themselves out for her. She knows no parents she can call and she cannot bring herself to contact the police or hospitals. Not just yet. There is nothing to do but pace and look out the window, wait for car lights to come down the street, and listen for the sound of approaching voices. Another half-hour passes. A pale halo lifts above the horizon in the east. The back door slams and Blythe bursts into the kitchen, catching her toe on the doormat and cursing.

Laidie confronts her. "Where on earth have you been? It's five in the morning."

"I don't have to tell you where I go. I know how to take care of myself." The thick ugly stench of concentrated cigarette smoke emanates from her disheveled hair and clothing.

"No you don't, that's obvious. This has got to stop, Blythe."

Blythe tosses her head. "Or you're going to what? I don't fucking have to listen to you."

"Yes, you do. I can't put up with this any longer."

"You don't own me. You're just my fucking sister."

The words cut into Laidie, hard and painful. She forces an even voice.

"I love you. That's why I care what you do."

Blythe turns her back on Laidie. "Hah. My own mother doesn't care what I do, why should you?" She storms up the stairs to her room and slams the door.

Two nights later Laidie stands in the doorway, blocking it with her body to intercept Blythe, who has just hung up the phone and is on her way out.

"You're not going out tonight. I told you. This is going to stop."

"And how do you think you're going to stop me? You're not the boss of me. Get out of my way, you bitch."

Laidie doesn't flinch. Blythe plows into her, knocks her off balance, shoving her out of the way.

"Don't bother waiting up," she yells from the sidewalk. Raucous laughter erupts from within the blue car.

Mhairi peers around the corner from the kitchen.

"Is everything all right?" she asks sweetly.

Laidie recovers her balance and follows Blythe outside but the car is already roaring and rattling down the street, burning oil in a stinking blue cloud.

Only when the bulging belly threatens to become evident on her small frame does Blythe thrust the news at Laidie, presenting a trophy of defiance. No softening preamble, no warning. Sarcasm inflates every word.

"I have some news you'll be happy to hear." She watches Laidie's face for the anticipated reaction. "I'm pregnant."

The breath leaves Laidie's body as if she has been tackled by a three-hundred pound football player. She struggles to suck air back into her lungs.

She backs up, feels for the sofa behind her, half sits on the arm. "Blythe, what are you saying?"

"A kid, Laidie. I'm going to have a kid. That's what pregnant means."

"Blythe, oh my God. Oh, my God. What are we going to do?"

"You don't have to do anything, stupid." Blythe goes into the kitchen, opens the refrigerator, and pours herself a glass of milk. She stands with her back to Laidie. "I don't want it. I'm going to give it away."

"Blythe, no. You can't," Laidie whispers. You can't give away your own baby." Tears burn her eyes and she can't swallow. *This isn't real. This can't be real.*

Moments later the blue car pulls up, its occupants swearing and laughing above the noise of the unmuffled exhaust. With exaggerated nonchalance Blythe saunters out and slams the door.

When one door closes, another opens. This is one of Laidie's favorite mantras. She always calls it into service in a positive light. But this door, slamming shut, opens one of a different sort.

When did the beautiful little Blythe of earlier years begin to disappear? What happened? It was just after she turned ten. Just before Orville's death. The bright, helpful, happy child with the pixie-rascal grin and empathy beyond her age, the rescuer of all manner of stray cats and dogs, the skipping champion at school, the piano teacher's favorite. Where did she go?

The truth and circumstances of Blythe's birth occupy a dark corner of Laidie's mind. She has stored the memory there for years, aware of its presence but unwilling to touch it. Now it bursts from its prison and demands to be remembered. It flaunts itself in front of her and she stands back and watches it unfold the layers of the past. A frightened and heartbroken teenager giving birth far from home. Arriving at the Main Street Union Station in Winnipeg two weeks later, Blythe in her arms. Mhairi and Orville waiting to take the baby from her. Aching with the knowledge that she will never see Joey McCorrie again. This memory is the regret that has shaped her life.

Other monstrous shadows reside in a different dark corner of Laidie's psyche, even more deeply interred than the memories of Blythe's birth. Little shining slivers of recall stab and tear at her mind. Shivering outside in the middle of the night. Ringing the doorbell. *Was I locked out? No.* Hiding behind the door. It opens and someone steps outside. *Something in my hand. Something bad.* Laidie pushes the thoughts back into even deeper recesses. *I don't want to go there. I can't make myself go there. I won't.*

Chapter 39

Winnipeg, 1951

Wally Davidson leans back in his old swivel chair and runs long chalky fingers through his hair. He is not a bad-looking man, but one of those insignificant types: a forgettable generic face in combination with an inconspicuous manner. He is mostly invisible. His students are able to identify him because they see him every day, but even some of his colleagues struggle to place him by name and grade.

He looks out the frost-filmed window. A city bus wheezes to a stop across from the school and pauses briefly before pulling away from its miasmic cloud of exhaust. He can barely make out a shadowy form in the swirl of grey. He knows it is Blythe Christie; he has watched her before.

Wally remembers her from his grade five class of several years back. He goes to the cabinet where he keeps his old records and tugs her file from the tightly packed drawer. Her final school picture broadcasts her crooked smile from the top page. A reckless tomboy with scattered freckles across her nose and unruly dark red curls, a clever student, he recollects. She had a bit of a discipline problem; always on the edge of rebellion. Wally is curious. He would like to meet her again. She would be what, now? Eighteen? Nineteen?

As at the end of every school day Wally physically forces himself to don his brown wool coat and scarf. He stretches his toe rubbers over his shoes. He pushes open the outside door a little, peers through the crack as if expecting an ambush. Positioning his feet carefully on the packed icy patches on the steps, he makes his way down to the walkway. He sighs. Wally Davidson hates to go home.

It's not that his home is poor or cold or dirty. Encased in dark bricks, the Assiniboine Avenue house is an imposing old building. Wide windows overlook the street on one side and the river on the other. The interior oak hardwood and dark panelled walls exude privilege and strength. Etta Davidson has been dead for over two months but her presence still overwhelms the house. Formal red velvet furniture, crystal-filled cabinets, flowered kitchen dinnerware, fine white linens. If Wally was uncomfortable in the house with his mother when she was alive, he is even more so now that she is gone. But he is also very lonely.

The next day Wally feigns a bad cough and calls in for a substitute with the most pathetic voice he is able to invent. He drives his car to a reckless half block from Hampton School and waits, slumped down in his seat in case a teacher or student passes by. Not that they would recognize him anyway. Wally finally spies Blythe walking to the bus stop. He drives up beside her and makes an effort at nonchalance.

"Would you like a ride somewhere?"

She recognizes him immediately (he is a little surprised) and accepts.

"Aren't you teaching any more, Mr. Davidson?" She can still be polite when she wants to.

"My mother died a few weeks ago and I took a day off to look after some business. Legal things, you know. To do with her will. She'd been sick for years. It was a blessing." He stops at the intersection. "Where are you going?"

"To the Bay. I have a part time job there." They are silent for several blocks. He steals sideways glances at her, registering her too-bright lipstick and tight black v-neck sweater. There is a worldliness about her, a sort of toughness, which surprises him. He pulls up to the curb at the northeast corner of the Bay.

"I'll be downtown most of the day. I could give you a ride home if the time is right."

She hesitates. "Are you sure? My bus stops right across from here."

"What time are you finished?" he reiterates.

"Three thirty usually, but…"

"I'll pick you up. It won't be out of my way."

There is a flash of that boyish grin from grade five. "If you're sure?"

Wally nods. "Hundred percent."

Blythe is two months pregnant. She tells Wally Davidson the next time he picks her up at the Bay, on a Saturday.

"I thought I better tell you. You know, if I'm going to keep seeing you."

Wally is dumbfounded. This is a bolt from the blue. *How could she have known I might try to take this further?* He fiddles with the radio, zeroes in on CKY. He doesn't speak.

"I guess I shouldn't have said anything." She picks at a snag on her tight red sweater.

"No, no, no, that's all right. I was just digesting that."

"Oh."

"Do you have a boyfriend?"

"Not any more. He disappeared in a hurry when I told him the news."

A light rain is starting to fall. Wally turns on the wipers and checks his speed. He turns the radio up a little, allowing it to fill the voids in the conversation. They reach the intersection of the street where Blythe lives.

"How old are you, Blythe?"

"Eighteen."

"Do your parents know about all this?"

"My father died a few years ago. And no, my mother doesn't know yet. Believe me, she wouldn't care anyway."

Wally pulls up to the curb in front of the Christie house. He taps his fingers on the leather cover of his steering wheel.

"Would you like to go to a movie matinee tomorrow?"

"What's on?"

"I don't know."

"Sure, I guess so."

She steps out into the thin drizzle and walks up the sidewalk to the house. She doesn't look back as he drives away.

Chapter 40

Winnipeg, 1962

Wally is forty-eight, increasingly distant and morose, preoccupied and impatient. No amount of encouragement on Blythe's part can arouse him to speak beyond necessity or to show even a kindly affection. The marriage has up to now been an alliance of differences, like spring weather with its necessary synthesis of sweet smelling warmth and snow squalls, sunshine and grey rain. Until recently he has remained convivial enough. He no longer has any interest in her side of the bed and hasn't for some time, not that this bothers Blythe. But something is strangely different.

"What's the matter, Wally," she ventures, like someone cautiously poking a wasp on a windowsill to see if it's still alive.

She watches him thinking in his painstaking way. He looks out the front window as if focusing on something at a great distance, even though the furthest thing is the house across the street. He picks meticulously at a tiny piece of cuticle on his nail, flicks imaginary motes of dust from his black pants.

Finally he speaks. "You remember I told you about Ian Kinley resigning?"

Blythe thinks for a moment. Kinley. The principal.

He threads his fingers through his sparse sandy hair, now grey on the back of his neck and at his temples. "Kinley didn't give any notice. He just left."

Wally stares back into the distance through the house across the street. "Now we're without a principal for the time being and a pile of extra work is falling on my shoulders until the school board finds a replacement. I'm just tired all the time."

Blythe scrutinizes his face, searching for more. There is nothing. She flares with impatience and her voice is thin and sharp.

"That's it? That's *it*? You don't come home until long after I've gone to bed. And sometimes you don't even *come* to bed. No fucking wonder you're tired."

Wally's lips press together, white and thin and adamant. He is clearly not prepared to discuss this issue any further.

In that moment Blythe can see the working part of the marriage collapsing like gears and springs and bolts disengaging and falling out of a complex machine, the loss of each failed part undermining the structure until it falls silent and stops.

Two days later, a Sunday morning, she finds the note propped against the cold coffeepot. The words are stilted and forced. A template. So much like Walter.

Blythe,

I can no longer live this way. I have decided to go away so I can discover a life for myself that might have some meaning. I realize it was a terrible mistake for me to have married you, and unfair to you as well. You have been a good friend but I have finally come to realize I can't love you in the way you deserve. I hope you will find someone who can make you happy. I will miss you, but I know I will hurt and embarrass you if I stay. I will arrange for the house to be put in your name. I will get in touch with you from Toronto. I am going to be living with Ian Kinley. We have both obtained teaching positions there.

Please forgive me.

Wally

She dreads having to tell Laidie. She will never say, "I told you so," but the implied recriminations will be there, just under the surface.

Should Blythe be stunned? She is not. She puts on a fresh pot of coffee and sits in the kitchen and ruminates about her ten years with Wally.

She moved into the spacious Assiniboine Avenue house after the obligatory honeymoon at Niagara Falls and Wally returned to his fifth grade class, leaving her to unpack their few wedding gifts and plan the promised remodelling of the house.

But first, he had explained, the disposition of his mother's belongings was a priority and had to be done before any renovations could take place.

"Do whatever you want with them," he said. "Throw them in the garbage, give them away, sell them, I don't care. Just get rid of everything."

Blythe remembers what a strange approach that seemed to her at the time. But she set about sorting through the cabinets and closets and trunks where she found everything already organized to perfection: labelled, tagged, arranged, and neatly stowed. It appeared that Mrs. Davidson had been compulsively obsessive about her belongings, so much so that classifying her late mother-in-law's life into cardboard boxes was not a challenging undertaking for Blythe. She took all the clothing to the Salvation Army and called an antique dealer to look at some of the old jewellery and china and crystal, which he bought. Some things she secretly gave to Mhairi and Laidie, like the silver-trimmed green glass salad bowl, the Battenburg lace tablecloth and the shining Royal Doulton ladies in sweeping jewel-coloured dresses. In a brown velvet bag she found an intricately engraved gold pocket watch on a chain. According to the accompanying note from Etta Davidson, it once belonged to Wally's grandmother in England in the mid-1800's. Blythe wound it cautiously with the dainty gold key attached to the chain, and miraculously the watch launched into a faint rhythm of tiny ticks. This she kept for herself.

Wally was more than happy with the purging and never questioned any of the disposals Blythe made. He called the contractors and the renovations and remodelling were quickly completed. This was a heady time for Blythe: selecting materials, designs, colours, and furniture, with money no object. Suddenly the excitement was over and there was nothing to do except keep it all clean. Wally adamantly refused to allow her to get a job. She can still hear his voice. *You're my wife, you don't have to work.* Darren was born five months after the wedding. Blythe entered motherhood with a passion as if to compensate for the throwaway baby of her early teens. Wally, on the other hand, supplied the wherewithal while managing to avoid the involvement.

Darren is now nine. Blythe wonders how he will react to his father's departure. She suspects he will barely notice.

She rereads Walter's exit note with its unspoken but unmistakable facts, folds it in quarters, and slips it into the trash bag in the back porch.

She slides the phone book from its shelf under the phone and looks up the number for the General Hospital School of Nursing. At twenty-eight, Blythe has never experienced independence. That is about to change.

Chapter 41

Millfield, 1950

Spring is late—it's the second week of April already, with so far only one or two days warm enough to begin melting the towering drifts. Last fall's late rains lie frozen and trapped in the thick clay soil beneath the snow. A massive blizzard born in Colorado sweeps across the southern half of Manitoba, adding two feet of heavy wet snow to the landscape. Electricity fails. Cattle go hungry while farmers try to dig out bales of hay. In Millfield the overpowering weight of the snow caves in the roof of the skating rink in the early hours of Easter Sunday morning.

On the Wednesday after Easter, a brilliant blue arch stretches the width of the horizon and the sun blazes across the sky, bucked by a snapping westerly wind. The snow visibly disintegrates, caves in on itself, and drips its water to the ground below where it settles in pools on top of the iced earth. The next day rumbling low clouds roll in like army tanks hell-bent on finishing last fall's business. Torrents fall for three days, eat away at the snowdrifts, and flow over the still-frozen soil. The water spreads over the massive tabletop of prairie, with nowhere to go except into the arteries feeding the great Red River south of Winnipeg. The arteries swell, the temperature rises, more rain falls. When the downpour stops, the sun pounds down on what is left of the snow. The combination of events is a juggernaut of unimaginable proportions.

Wolf River rampages into Millfield for the first time in over twenty-five years. Preparedness is at the bare minimum. Stacks of bags and cars of sand arrive from Bainesville by train. Every capable person works and holding or filling bags, tossing them hand over hand to the area to be diked, piling the little pig-like sacks as fast as they arrive. Wilf Collins paints lines at 6-inch intervals on a poplar pole and lashes it upright to the bridge. The swirling muddy water climbs the marks on the pole as if it were scaling a ladder. It's raining again. The wind shifts to the north.

The farms east of Millfield are not at risk. Their owners work shoulder to shoulder with townspeople, along with hundreds of volunteers from Bainesville, Massinon, and St. Avilla; even people from Winnipeg show up to help. Joey and Gracie strain to hoist sandbags in the bone-chilling cold. The muscles of their backs, shoulders, and arms ache and burn. They lose track of time. The river swallows the lines on the pole. Volunteers work frantically to the last possible minute. They fall back, exhausted, defeated. It is dark when the ugly black water pushes over the bank and breaks through the dike. Tears mix with rain. Wolf River devours streets and avenues, crashes through basement windows, steals away anything not secured. Huge chunks of ice gouge scars into trees and buildings. Debris hangs on branches like witches' laundry.

Joey and Gracie go out to the farm each day to check the livestock and do the necessary chores. They return to Millfield to eat before joining the cleanup volunteers. Millfield's town hall is a repository of piles of sandwiches and cookies, steaming urns of coffee and tea, plates of pickles and cheese—this is the other side of the volunteer effort. The work of recovery is just beginning.

Gracie pushes her hair behind her ear and studies the farm map spread on the kitchen table.

"I think we should summer-fallow the sixty acres down by Tom King's this year."

"Why? I was thinking of putting oats in there."

"We've had pretty good crops off it the past three years." She pencils a comment on the map. "It needs a rest."

"Well, I guess we could plant the oats on the east forty. But I want to keep the west fields for wheat."

"Ike Evans says he's going to plant flax again. It's a good cash crop. Maybe we should try some on last year's summer-fallow."

"We don't have any flax seed."

"Ike does."

Joey capitulates. "Okay. Do you want to talk to him about it?"

She takes their coffee cups to the sink and rinses them. Gracie is clever and business-minded. Since Gramp Fred Fletcher's death two years ago she has taken over the logistics of the operation, which now includes the Fletcher farm.

"Sure. I'll call him at dinnertime." She rubs her neck. The muscles still ache from sandbagging.

"The only thing we need now is some warm weather to get this damn snow off the ground. We need to be on the land in three weeks," Joey says.

Gracie comes around behind him, digs her strong farm-woman fingers into the back of his neck, kneads and rolls, working his muscles into easy slack. He turns around to face her, pulls her to straddle his lap. She is still beautiful, even with faint lines beginning to work their way into the skin around her violet eyes, an odd grey hair sneaking into the curls at the nape of her neck.

"What are your plans for the morning?"

"Bread. I want to get it rising before noon."

"I have something rising before noon."

She laughs and drags him to his feet. "Wouldn't want that to go to waste now, would we?"

Gracie helps Ike Evans unload the bags of flax seed at one end of the hay shed. The lifting exacerbates the pain in her neck and arms. She takes off her work gloves and massages the offending muscles. Ike tosses the last bag on the pile.

"You all right?" He cannot help but compare Gracie to his own wife, Mary Ann, who does not venture into hard labour.

"Sure. I'm just still sore from all the sandbagging last week." She brushes her hair from her face. "Thanks for bringing the flax over, Ike. Sorry Joey couldn't be here to help you."

"No worries. Take it easy, Gracie. See you."

Take it easy. Right. This is just the beginning. She pulls a tarp over the pile of bags and heads to the house to make lunch. The sore neck is worsening.

Once inside she downs three aspirin, puts the kettle on to boil, and gets out meat and bread for sandwiches. While she waits for Joey to show up she goes to the farm map, which she has tacked to the wall by the back door. She scribbles something about flax on the edge of the map and pokes her pencil into the hair behind her ear. She can hear the truck rattling into the yard. Joey comes into the kitchen and throws his jacket over the back of a chair.

"I don't feel great, Gracie. Puked a while ago. I don't think I can eat anything right now."

She studies him. *Why is it that whenever there's something wrong with me, he manages to come up with something worse?* She covers the sandwiches and sets the plate in the refrigerator. She doesn't feel like eating either. Her throat is raw and swollen, and it hurts to swallow. She retrieves the thermometer from the bathroom. They are both running a temperature, one hundred and one degrees.

The flu is going around, says Ivy Fletcher when she brings the mail from town. *It's a bad one, lasts a week or more. You just have to let it run its course.* Joey recovers in a few days, but Gracie's fever refuses to subside. Being Gracie, she insists on getting up to look after meals, update the farm map, and do the laundry. The pain in her neck spreads to her arms and her back. The headache progresses to excruciating intensity and she vomits her breakfast into the toilet. When she hasn't enough strength to lift the teakettle, she surrenders.

"I think I should take you to see the doctor," Joey ventures. *You know Gracie is sick when she can't get out of bed.*

"I just want to be left alone," she says. Gracie has never been one to share suffering. "I just overdid things. I'll be fine in a day or two. Don't forget to clean out the disker. We need to have everything ready to go by next week." She drags the comforter up to her chin. "And you should go over to Gran's for some lunch. I wasn't able to get anything ready." She turns her back to him and faces the window.

It is late afternoon when Joey gets back from the Fletcher place. Ivy sends supper with him—roasted pork and mashed potatoes, canned garden beans and a loaf of fresh bread. He fixes a plate for Gracie and makes a pot of tea.

"You awake, Gracie?"

"Yes."

"Gran sent you some supper."

"I don't think I can eat anything. My throat is so sore I can't swallow."

Joey contemplates the supper and decides to take it in to her anyway, along with a plate for himself. He sits beside the bed. "Will you please try, Gracie? You have to eat something."

"Can you help me, Joey? I need to turn over and I can't make myself move." Her voice is thick, almost slurred. "Every bit of me hurts."

He slips his arm under her shoulders. She feels like a rag doll, limp and soft. He rolls her to face him. "My god, Gracie. What the hell's going on?"

"I just need something to drink, Joey. Do we have any juice?"

He returns with half a glass of apple juice, lifts her upright, and holds the glass to her lips. She takes a small sip and gags when she tries to swallow it. The juice spills down her chin. He lays her back on the pillow and rushes to the telephone.

"Gran, I need you to come over right away. Gracie's a lot worse and I don't know what to do. She can't even move." Ivy is asking diagnostic questions. "Shit, Gran, I don't know. Just get over here." His voice is panic-filled. "Yes, for Christ's sake, I do think you should call the doctor. Hurry, Gran." Joey returns to Gracie. She looks at him, working to focus. Her eyes are neither blue nor violet, but dark flat grey like slate. She struggles to breath as if the air is made of syrup.

Polio, the doctor says. *Quite a few cases around. Most of the time people just think they have the flu. Don't blame yourself. Sometimes it just moves too fast and there isn't anything you can do.*

Chapter 42

Winnipeg, 1964

Mhairi's apathy grows like a carpet of soft dark moss, each year a little larger and deeper, covering and hiding beneath it the scars of her existence. Blythe does not remember her mother ever being talkative, but she is now even less so. With Orville's death over twenty years ago, the need to self-protect, the need for rigid requirements for every facet of life, and the need for mental submission stopped existing. Most women would have blossomed into lives of freedom and self-sufficiency in a similar situation but Mhairi remained passive and docile. Now, as then, she chooses to do nothing about anything. If it weren't for Laidie she would survive on toast and tea and bananas. She spends her time embroidering luncheon cloths and pillowcases and tea towels and knitting mittens and scarves for Blythe, who hasn't lived at home for years. Still, she perseveres with the endless, mindless handwork. Laidie tries to engage her mentally but it is hopeless. The greater part of what was once Mhairi Christie has wandered away. No one knows where she has gone.

Mhairi slips quietly from life one night in early June, simply falling asleep in her chair where Laidie finds her thin wilted body in the morning.

Laidie is grief-stricken in a way most can't know. It is a grief not so much for loss as for the helplessness of the past; for a broken vow. *I'll take care of you, Mama.* As a child she could never have kept that promise and she carries no blame for herself, but it lingers in her mind. Among the ghosts of fear and cowering and submission, she remembers the feel of Mhairi's thin arms around her, comforting and warm even in their own suffering. *I'll take care of you, Mama.* Could she have done more?

At the same time there are other memories nudging at the underbelly of Laidie's subconscious. They are not yet available for retrieval.

Summer is hot and dry. August crickets chirp in the bushes and grass along the sidewalks and a few grasshoppers dine in neighborhood gardens. The air in the house on Hampton Street is thick and heavy, and although it is past noon on Sunday, Laidie lies in bed sticky with sweat, her eyes focused on a fly on the ceiling. In spite of the heat all she wants to do is stay where she is.

The telephone rings and she forces herself to get up and answer it. It is Blythe.

"Would you like to come for dinner?"

Laidie considers this for a short moment.

"I can't today, Blythe. I have some things I have to do."

"You never want to come over," she says. "It's just for dinner, for heaven's sake. You need to get out."

"I don't think I can today, Blythe. Maybe another time."

Blythe pressures for an explanation. "What on earth are you doing that's so important?"

Laidie searches her mind for a plausible excuse. Out of nowhere, it occurs. "I'm going to drive out to Killarney Lake and spend a week or so just relaxing."

Blythe is incredulous. "Laidie, what's got into you? You would go out there all by yourself? Why Killarney? Now I really am worried about you."

"It's nothing. I just feel like going into the country. I'm leaving first thing tomorrow."

Blythe is speechless. Then she thinks about it. Laidie is talking nonsense. She's been a bit odd since Mother died. She's just looking for an excuse not to come over. Tomorrow will arrive and she will still be holed up in the house.

"Okay, Laidie. Let me know if you need any help." This is spoken like a parent's offer to help with the packing of the suitcase when a child is threatening to run away.

"I'll be fine. Don't worry."

But a switch clicked during the conversation and now Laidie is possessed with the idea, however irrational. She is on the road by nine the next morning, after filling her light blue 1956 Chevrolet Bel Air with gas and buying a Manitoba road map at the Texaco station at the corner of Hampton Street and Portage Avenue. A large plastic bag in the back seat bulges with clothing. A lunch of sandwiches made from canned tuna sits on the front seat beside two bottles of Fresca and her purse, which holds two hundred dollars taken from the small metal lock box that belonged to Mhairi.

Laidie has seldom driven outside the city, except to Stonewall to pick up fresh chickens from the chicken farm and vegetables from the market garden there, so when she reaches the western Winnipeg outskirts she feels a small panic. She pulls onto the gravel shoulder and opens one of the Frescas, swallows several gulps, and spreads out the road map. It looks straightforward. She chooses a path she believes will be easy for her to follow. Why Killarney? It is simply the place that came to mind yesterday and she must go where she said she would go.

Laidie pulls over to the side of the road at noon and eats half of the tuna sandwiches. She carries on, comes to Killarney in mid-afternoon, and continues on past the lake, quite some distance actually, until she comes to the sign announcing the next intersection. Millfield 10, arrow pointing to the left. Laidie is the moth; Millfield is the flame. Mhairi and Orville are both gone. Laidie's long ago promise is null and void.

Laidie can see two elevators in the distance and she knows they must mark Millfield's place on the prairie, although she recalls only one from her short time there many years ago. The road she remembers was narrow and roughly gravelled but the highway on which she now travels is smoothly paved with small stones in a tarry base. Nothing looks familiar. *Were there landmarks then? What were they?* She wracks her brain. Nothing. A small bridge with concrete end abutments and metal railings emerges ahead of her. A dusty sign pokes out from the tall grass on the roadside and she slows down. Wolf River. *Is this possible? This isn't much more than a glorified creek.* Laidie presses on, battling the hot muggy air in her car. She rolls the window down but it makes no difference except to fill the car with ear-battering wind.

The elevators are closer now, perhaps two or three miles down the road. Laidie searches from side to side trying to discover something she can recognize. A large stone house about a half-mile distant on the left has a vague familiarity. To her right the railway track is visible on its raised bed, paralleling the road into town. It doesn't look like the railway track that brought the Christies to Millfield so long ago, but it must be, she decides. Then, right ahead, she sees the Millfield Station.

The oxblood red paint of the past is now faded to milky plum. The Millfield sign swings on chains over the old platform, which is battered and crumbling in places but still appears to be in use. Laidie pulls up to the station, and climbs the cracked steps to the platform. The heat of the afternoon feels as it did on that day in 1930 when she stood on those same boards with her parents, waiting for Uncle Mac's friend to come for them. Dust devils swirl in the gravelly parking lot and a flock of iridescent pigeons rises in a noisy disorganized flutter from somewhere behind the station. Laidie squints and peers down the street, which connects with the station at a right angle. A few cars are parked diagonally here and there in front of various stores and a Grey Goose bus is taking on passengers about a block away.

She looks at the platform beneath her feet. A painful and terrible memory pushes up from the greyed boards. *It is fall, early October. Long skeins of Canada geese stretch across the sky, honking their way south. A north-west wind whips the leaves from the trees, which are nearly bare, except for a row of tall willows behind the station. There is a faint smell of stubble smoke in the air. Laidie stands in front of her dark blue suitcase. She is sick and crying. Her father and mother wait apart from her, watching for the train. Their possessions are lined up on the platform waiting to be loaded for the trip to Winnipeg. Laidie has not had a chance to talk to Joey since the last time they met at Wolf River. Orville has allowed no goodbyes.*

The Grey Goose pulls away from its loading zone and the driver presses a long honk on the horn, directed at an errant pedestrian. Laidie looks up from her memory and rearranges her mind. She can see a gravel road leading out of town. *I know we lived three miles east of Millfield. That has to be the right road.* She returns to her car and finishes the last of the Fresca before herding the Chevy over the loose gravel. Nothing looks familiar. *Uncle Mac's house should be near here, and Joey's house just a bit further along. Will I be able to recognize it?* She passes a run-down collection of unpainted buildings and a deserted farmyard where an old bluff of lilacs and caragana stands guard. There are more trees here, oak and poplar and basswood. A little further on and set back a little from the road is a dilapidated unpainted house with a sagging porch and boarded up windows on the second storey. *I know a lot will have changed in thirty-five years, but there must be something I would recognize?*

Ahead is a small wooden bridge with low railings. There is no sign, but Laidie knows it will be Wolf River. Unlike the river beneath the crossing on the highway, this stream is deeper and shadowy. The trees along its grassy banks are tall and thick with foliage and there is no doubt in her mind that this is the same river that meandered through her life for a short time. She crosses the bridge, pulls over to the side of the road and gets out. She takes off her shoes and stockings and winces across the prickly yellow grass to the sloping bank. She eases down to the water where a floating mosaic of leaves and river debris hugs the bank. She sits on the edge and lowers her feet into the water, closes her eyes, and feels the fine cool mud at the bottom.

Time passes, how long she cannot tell. She opens her eyes and looks up and down the river before pulling her feet from its coolness. A huge black leech is attached firmly to her ankle. She calmly squeezes its sucking end, pulls it off, and tosses it back into the water. It is now as it was then. Leeches are a part of life and anyone who swims in the river has to deal with them as a matter of fact. She dips her feet in the water again to rinse off the black mud.

To Laidie the river has not changed at all. Time passed somewhere, but not here.

She picks her way back to the car. A truck is approaching from the east; the first traffic she has seen on this road. It rumbles by in a cloud of fine dust, slows down, and backs up to where she stands.

"Is everything all right?" asks the older woman at the wheel.

"Yes. Well, no. I'm trying to find a place. The McCorries?"

The woman pulls her thick dark brows into a frown and looks at Laidie curiously. "You would have passed it on your way here. It's about two miles back on the north side, the big one with the weathervane on the roof."

There is something vaguely familiar about this woman: stern, self-possessed, and humourless. Laidie shoves her damp feet into her shoes. She can feel the mud that has remained between her toes.

"Oh. Thank you."

The woman in the truck looks at her skeptically. "Do you need anything else?"

"I don't think so. No."

"All right." She shrugs. "If you say so."

The woman drives away and Laidie watches the billow of dust recede down the road. The sun is in the western sky and she realizes it is late afternoon. *What about Killarney? But I really knew all along, didn't I. I never intended to go to Killarney at all.*

Laidie climbs into the car and proceeds to the next turn-off, just a trail leading into a field, where she turns around and heads back west. The big house sits at the end of a lane about as long as city block. The tall weathervane leans its rooster into the sky. She pulls over and stops at the end of the lane.

Will he remember me? Will he forgive me when he finds out what I've done? Laidie squishes her muddy toes against the inside of her shoes. The leech bite on her ankle is bleeding and she wipes it with the hem of her yellow skirt.

She turns into the long treed lane, drives right up to the house, and parks on the gravelly space in front of the porch. The house, grey and paintless, is larger than it appears from the road. The front veranda skews sideways. A broken clothesline slumps in the tall grass, clothespins still attached. The decrepit doghouse by the porch appears to be uninhabited. Beyond the house, a half dozen chickens scratch in the dirt. A light breeze lifts faded pink gingham curtains in an open window. Nothing else moves. There is only the silence of emptiness.

The door inside the porch is unlocked. Laidie pushes it open with her shoulder and goes inside. Nothing is as she remembers from the few times she was in the house with Joey. Dinge coats the window panes above the sinkful of dirty dishes. A pile of oily work clothes sprawls by the door to the bedroom. She steps over them, notes the unmade bed, dust on the floor, and an old television on the dresser. A black and white photograph leans against the mirror. A wedding picture. Laidie squints at the couple. There is no mistake. Joey and Gracie Marie, arms linked, smiling. A silver heart-shaped locket hangs at Gracie Marie's throat.

Blythe dials Laidie's number again. She has been trying to reach her sister since three in the afternoon; it is now seven thirty. She is worried enough to drive over to Laidie's place. The house is locked, the Chevy gone. Yesterday's conversation loops over and over in Blythe's mind. Killarney? Could Laidie possibly have been serious?

She speeds home and leaves her car parked on the street. She dithers frantically. She opens the telephone book and realizes it is only for Winnipeg. Mrs. McPherson next door has relatives and friends in the Portage la Prairie area, so she may also have a rural phone book. Mrs. McPherson does, and Blythe rushes home with the book.

Killarney has several pages of listings and she finds three motels. None of them have registered a Laidie Christie. In the yellow pages at the back she finds another listing, the Killarney Hotel. They are vague and unhelpful. Blythe feels panic welling up in her chest. She calls the Killarney Hospital. Nothing. She paces from room to room, trying to decide what to do. Drive out to Killarney? It would be very late when she arrived there, too late to do anything, really. Wait an hour or two, call all the hotels again in case Laidie checks in later that night? Call the police? What good would they be from here? But there must be police in Killarney? She scans the listings for "police", but there are none. It dawns on her—R.C.M.P. The constable who answers is patient. He records Blythe's scrambled information. She has no idea when Laidie left. She cannot remember her licence plate number, but she was able to give a good description of the car. The constable puts her on hold for a few minutes. They have had no reports of anything unusual involving such a vehicle, he says, and assures her they will let her know if it is found.

Retired school teacher Edina Popham, on her way to Millfield early the next morning, notices a light blue car parked in the ditch close to the Wolf River Bridge. It appears to be the same vehicle she saw there yesterday, she believes, and she gets out to investigate. The car is empty except for crumpled waxed paper wrappings and empty Fresca bottles, a brown leather purse, and a Manitoba road map. The driver's door is ajar. Edina Popham is more aware than most of civic responsibility and she immediately returns home to call the Killarney R.C.M.P. detachment some twenty miles away. But Edina Popham's civic responsibility is tempered with arbitrary discretion, and she decides not to mention seeing the same car the previous day.

Just before noon two constables find Laidie far downstream from the bridge. She sits on the riverbank clinging to a brown plaid car blanket pulled around her shoulders, rocking gently. A mound of shiny river stones surrounds her bare muddy feet. She does not resist when they help her to her feet and lead her to the patrol car.

Blythe catches the Grey Goose bus to Millfield first thing the next morning. She walks the six blocks from the bus depot at the Valley Café to Millfield Hospital. A nurse takes her to Laidie's room. It is just after noon and Laidie's lunch is picked at, scattered across the tray in front of her. She hasn't spoken at all, the nurse says. Childlike, Laidie swings her legs back and forth from where she sits on the hospital bed. She is wearing a dirty yellow skirt and her white blouse gapes open where there should be a button. An uncombed mass of auburn hair frames her face. Blythe collects Laidie's purse and sweater. The nurse has called a volunteer driver to take them to the RCMP detachment to get Laidie's car. The gas tank is empty. Blythe stops at a Co-op service station to fill up. They pull out onto the highway.

"What were you thinking, Laidie? You had me worried to death."

Laidie watches Millfield shrink away in her side view mirror. She is silent.

"I don't get it, Laidie. For fuck's sake, why on Earth would you go to a place like Millfield? A little dump in the boondocks? Laidie, please tell me why."

Laidie rubs her eyes and pushes the passenger seat as far back as it will go.

"I got lost."

Chapter 43

Winnipeg, 1964

Darren Davidson is obsessed with cowboys and horses. He wants to learn to ride; he wants to have a ranch of his own. Blythe smiles helplessly at his wish. He has begged for weeks for a pair of western boots. Blythe believes it will be a passing phase, but by the time Christmas wishes fade into spring and summer brings birthday yearnings, she decides to relent. On a Saturday afternoon in August she takes Darren to the Western Leathers store on Main Street. He tries on several pairs of boots; tan with dark brown inserts on the outside shaft, red with a cream leaf design on the toe (they look like girls', he says), two dark brown pairs, one of them very plain, and a black pair with a metal toe cap and leather that looks like snakeskin across the top of the foot.

The very attentive sales clerk smiles. "I'll bet your dad will like these black ones. What do you think?"

"My Dad went away," says Darren matter-of-factly.

"Is that so, young fella? How old are you?"

"I'm ten," Darren says with an air of importance relating to the double digits of his age.

The clerk is watching Blythe now and he stares intently, smiling. He looks back at the boy.

"So you are taking care of your mother now?"

"We'll take the black ones," Blythe blurts too quickly, even though they are by far the most expensive pair. She writes out a cheque while the man gently wraps each boot in paper and returns them to the box, which he ties with string, making a carrying handle. She hands him the cheque and he studies it closely for a long uncomfortable moment (for Blythe) before sliding it into the till without asking for identification.

"Thank you, Mrs. Davidson," he says. "Here's my card. Don't hesitate to call if there are any problems with the boots."

Small embossed silver stirrups mark the corners of the glossy red business card. Blythe takes the card and glances quickly at the name before tucking it into her purse. She can feel heat spreading over her neck and up to her ears. Eddie Wylie. It's a name she will remember.

She isn't really surprised when he knocks on the door of her house that night. He bends forward in a mock bow.

"I forgot to give you your complimentary leather polish today. Just thought I'd drop it off for you on my way home." He is smiling broadly and Blythe notices his lashes, too long and pretty for a man.

"How did you know my address?"

"You gave me a personalized cheque, remember? I hope you aren't upset with me."

Darren appears behind his mother, clomping noisily in the new black boots.

"Hey, young fella! How's the cowboy?"

Darren grins and kicks at the doormat with his pointed metal toe. Eddie Wylie bends down and studies the boots. "Is that a scratch on your new boot already? Maybe I should put some of this stuff on it for you?"

The question is directed to Blythe. "Why don't you come in, Mr. Wylie?" she surrenders.

He flashes a smile, white teeth blazing. "How did you know *my* name?"

"You gave me your business card, remember?"

She leads the way to the kitchen. While Eddie disengages the boots from the squirming Darren, Blythe spreads newspaper on the table to protect it from the leather polish. Eddie smiles as he rubs the soft paste over the leather, very slowly and thoroughly, into every curve and seam, explaining as he does so how important it is to cover all the surfaces evenly. Darren watches, breathing in the scent of polish and leather.

"It takes about twenty minutes to dry. Then we'll polish it. Okay?" Darren loses interest and disappears into the living room. With the child gone, Blythe is forced to look again at the man in her kitchen. Eddie

Wylie is of medium height, muscular, and tanned. His dark hair curls over his ears and his eyes are as blue as a lake late in the day.

Blythe speaks in measured syllables, controlling her breathing. "Would you like some coffee while we wait?"

"Sure, why not? I'll bet you make good coffee." He leans back on the kitchen chair with his hands clasped behind his head.

Blythe measures the coffee and dumps it into the basket of the percolator. She can feel him watching her the whole time. Heat climbs to her ears again as it had in the leather store. She is finding it hard to believe. *Me. Blythe Davidson. Embarrassed? Shit.* She moves the newspapers to one side and sets the cups on the table while the pot chugs and gurgles.

"What do you take in it?"

"Just black. Same as you, I'm guessing."

"How could you possibly know how I like my coffee?"

Eddie shifts in his chair. That grin again. He shrugs. "Just a feeling, I guess. Am I right?"

Blythe pours two black coffees and Eddie leans forward to breathe in the steam from his cup. "Mmmm. Smells great." A long pause. "How long have you been by yourself?"

Was it really any of his business? "Two years," she says.

"Do you want to talk about it?"

"No." She takes a sip of coffee.

"Okay then. Can I ask what you do?"

"I'm a nurse at the General. I've been there for a year and a half."

"My mother was a nurse. What ward are you on?"

"I'm in intensive care." She knows the words are no more than fillers between them. "It can be pretty challenging."

Eddie smiles as he studies the oak kitchen cabinets and the wide bay window overlooking the back yard. Through the archway to the dining room he can see a well-appointed china cabinet and its reflection in the polished hardwood floor.

Blythe stands. "I think the boots must be ready for polishing."

Eddie glances at his watch. "Has it really been twenty minutes? I guess I'd better get back to the job at hand."

He gives the boots a brisk rubbing with a polishing cloth and sets them on the floor.

"Hey, pal, come and look at your boots," he calls.

Darren drags his feet into the kitchen. He inspects the boots. "Wow! They're even more shiny now! Can I put them on again?"

"Just for a minute, then you're off to bed," Blythe admonished. "It's way past your bedtime."

"Awww…"

"Never mind, buddy. Way you go. I'll be up to say goodnight in a minute."

Eddie stands up. "I guess I'd better be going."

She follows him to the door. "Thank you for your help."

He smiles. "Anything for a customer." He walks to the sidewalk and turns. She is still standing in the open doorway. "Do you think I could drop in again sometime?"

Blythe pretends to think about it. "I guess it would be all right. Just call first to make sure I'm home."

She goes back inside. The polishing cloth has been left behind on the table and she rushes to the door. "Wait! You left this," she calls.

He is about to get into his car and stands with his hand on the door handle. "It's complimentary too," he laughs. "Goodnight, Blythe."

A week passes before Eddie Wylie visits again. Darren is in bed and Blythe is watching the late television news when the doorbell rings.

"Don't you think it's a little late?" She opens the door and he steps inside, leaning against the jamb.

"Sorry I didn't call first."

"Well," she says, looking out into the darkness of the street behind him, "would you like to come in and have a cup of coffee?"

"Are you sure you don't mind?"

She doesn't answer and he follows her into the kitchen. He takes the coffeepot from her and holds her just below the shoulders so she can't move her arms. He kisses her, open-mouthed and soft. She can feel the now-familiar hot surge to her face and a new hungry throbbing lower down when he runs the tip of his tongue around her lips. He carries her to the living room and lowers her gently to the sofa, turns down the volume on the television, and returns to her. Blythe is not able to utter a sound. She pulls him down to her, knowing her body is about to experience an epiphany.

"I can't believe you're going to marry him." Laidie is incredulous. "You've only known him for three months."

"I love him. I deserve some happiness." Blythe is intractable. "He's good to me and he's good to Darren.

"If you love him, waiting a while won't hurt anything. I just think you're rushing things."

"For heaven's sake, Laidie, I've been alone now for over two years. You're not going to change my mind. All the plans are made." She sweeps out of the room.

Laidie throws up her hands in a gesture of helplessness.

They marry a month later. Laidie is the maid of honour and the best man is a friend of Eddie's who works at Polo Park, the racetrack.

Eddie wants to honeymoon in Virginia. He says there are some race-horses he wants to look at while they are there and they will get that out of the way first, he winks. Blythe is in a constant state of arousal in Eddie's presence and laughs in agreement.

The seats in the plane are cramped but that suits them fine. Eddie squeezes Blythe's thigh and runs his hand up to her groin, not caring that the elderly man in the window seat can't help seeing. If anything, Eddie is proud to parade his moves publicly.

"I'm going to the bathroom," Blythe whispers. A minute later, Eddie undoes his seatbelt and slides out of his seat, winking at the elderly man, who quickly averts his gaze to the window. The door to the washroom is unlocked and Blythe is ready for him. He lifts her onto the tiny sink. The roar of the big engines drowns out the clamour of their hasty interlude.

Blythe is still flushed and pleasantly throbbing when they arrive at Washington's National Airport. They retrieve their luggage and Eddie rents a car. They drive straight to a farm near Markton in the north Shenandoah Valley where the horses are stabled.

Eddie examines the animals and talks with the owner for a long time. He comes back to the car, slumps behind the wheel, and stares up at the winding ridge above the valley. His blue eyes are darker than usual.

"What's wrong, Eddie?"

"A lot more fucking money than I figured on." He slaps the steering wheel. "Damn. Damn."

"How much more?" She laughs. "Maybe I could be a shareholder."

"Never mind. We can't afford them." He glowers blackly in the direction of the horse breeder. He is in a bad mood the rest of the day and they return to Washington in silence. They check into a hotel near the airport and Eddie goes straight to bed. Blythe spends a few minutes in the bathroom before returning naked and aroused to slide into bed behind him, but the usually priapic Eddie moves away from her and his position is not negotiable.

The next day Eddie seems to be in a better frame of mind and wants to go back to the mountains. Shenandoah National Park is not far from where they were the day before. He is fascinated, he says, by folk legends of the Shenandoah River and the Blue Ridge Mountains. They pass the Markton junction.

"Were you serious about what you said yesterday? About being a shareholder in the horses?"

Blythe considers. She can afford it, thanks to Walter's guilt-fed generosity. Besides, she had not realized how much these animals mean to her new husband.

"I might be. How much would you need?"

Eddie pulls the car over to the shoulder of the road and backs up to the crossroad. He wheels north to Markton, where Blythe writes a cheque to the horseman. The animals are to be shipped directly to the Polo Park track in Winnipeg. The arrangements are all under control, Eddie promises.

They spend the afternoon on the ridge. The breeze is cool there, far cooler than down below. Below them the historic Shenandoah glistens and curves in its valley and beyond the river, Massanutten Mountain stretches to the hazy south. They park the car at a scenic overlook and descend one of the deep wooded trails. Blue blazes on the trees lead them to a small shaded waterfall cascading over dark green rocks. Mosses and flowers, eternally wet, cling to the water-sprayed cliffs. The marked trail follows the stream but Eddie, almost as if he knows where he is going, battles up through a shadowed tangle of black locust trees to the top of the falls, pulling Blythe behind him. They rest to catch their breath for a few minutes on a rock shelf above the cascade. Blythe can feel the heat of the sun-warmed ground through her slacks. Eddie turns to her and presses her body back and down onto the rock. She can feel the hard warm stone on her back and buttocks as he pulls off her slacks and blouse. She lies naked, cool in the breeze, while Eddie hurriedly strips. He thrusts into her deep and hard and fast and they enter that curious inexorable disconnection where they are unaware that everything or nothing is happening in the world around them. The bruising pain of the rocks cutting into Blythe's back dissolves into a rhythmic current of warm waves radiating from deep inside her as she receives her recompense for her investment in the horses.

On their way back to Washington they stop at Luray Caverns, drawn in by the ubiquitous billboards along the road. They arrive just in time for the departing tour and tag along at the tail end of the crowd. The lights automatically go on ahead of the group and turn off behind them, so they move in a cocoon of light past the towering Giant's Hall, spectacular stalactites and stalagmites (stalactites stick tight, says Blythe, that's how you remember which ones hang down) and Dream Lake, whose deep golden reflections belie its very shallow pool. They enter an area of gigantic formations the size of buses standing on end. Dream Lake is already dark behind them and Eddie pulls Blythe back into the shadows.

Upon their return home, Eddie assumes responsibility for all the finances. Blythe agrees to this, glad to turn the bill paying and money management over to someone else. Besides, she isn't feeling well. She is sick for three full months and Eddie is distant and unsympathetic. This is something we should have talked about first, he says.

Eddie begins taking Darren to the Polo Park racetrack on Portage Avenue that summer. It's Darren's dream come true--a chance to hang out in the stables, stroke the horses, and listen to the stories of the old-timer horsemen who practically live at the track. Once in a while one of the trainers will allow him to ride one of the horses behind the barns. Eddie always drops him off and disappears until the last of the races are finished, but Darren doesn't care. Blythe doesn't know this part of it, but she doesn't mind Darren being at the track. It's good, she thinks, that the two of them are bonding. Besides, she is sick much of the summer and relieved to be left alone.

A fierce blizzard heralds the baby's arrival in March 1964. Although it's not particularly cold, a system from the western states blows in late in the day with heavy wet snow and strong winds, a Colorado Low, says the television weatherman. Eddie curses his way down streets rutted with heavy snow to the Women's Pavilion at the General Hospital where he leaves Blythe, heavily labouring. He doesn't dare stay with her, he says, he might not be able to get home again in the storm. By the time he arrives back at the Assiniboine Avenue house, the telephone is ringing. Darren answers it. Eddie has a son. Michael.

Blythe is shaking and furious. She has kept the details of Eddie's leaving from Laidie, but now it must be told.

"There's nothing left, Laidie. The house, the bank account, the car: he gambled it all away at the fucking race track. He even sold the damned horses to finance his habit."

Laidie hasn't heard Blythe curse for some time. She is holding little Michael on her lap and instinctively puts her hands over his ears.

"Didn't you have any idea what was going on?"

"The horses were just the beginning, Laidie. Damn! I wish I had listened to you."

Laidie pats Blythe's arm and bites back the I-told-you-so. She resists the urge to mention the language.

"I trusted him, I trusted him a hundred percent," Blythe says, her voice rising. "You just bloody wouldn't believe how convincing he could be. I can't even remember now what his fucking reasons were for putting the house in his name. Something to do with taxes, I think he said. Jesus Christ."

She bites at her nails. This is a habit she has never entertained, but the nails are now chewed down to the quick.

"I was so busy being pregnant; I never paid any attention to what he was doing with the business affairs. It was just such a treat not to have to be bothered with all that stuff when I was feeling so god-awful rotten. What a damned idiot I was! He seemed so competent and capable. But the bastard had everything planned, right from the start. When the money was all used up, he just walked out. I came home with the groceries and he was gone. He just cleaned out his clothes from the closet and left. No note, nothing. I called the store where he worked and they told me he hadn't been there for months." She stops for a deep breath. "He must have known that his big spree was over. He got out just before people started phoning and knocking at the door for their damned money. He must have left the city right after he moved out of the house. My house. My house that he mortgaged to finance his gambling. I didn't know until I got the letter from the bank. God only knows how he managed to get away with that."

Laidie is the calm in the storm. She strokes Michael's little fair head. "Was there anything else?"

"I don't have any way of proving it, but I know there were other women, too. Lots of them. Shit." She hesitates. "He had very strong urges. He was, uh, overly passionate, I guess you could say. But he just turned it all off for me after Michael was born. That's why I know he was messing around. He had to be getting it somewhere."

"How did you find out he left town?"

"I swallowed my pride and went out to the track one day last week. Everyone there knows him. He was gone, they said, but no one knew where. Or they just wouldn't say."

"Well, you can't dwell in the past." The comment is a typical Laidie platitude. "The important thing is, what will you do now?"

Blythe is quiet for a long minute, regaining her composure.

"I really want to go back to nursing, Laidie. I would just have to take a couple of refresher courses. I've been doing a lot of thinking about this, but I haven't worked it out yet. How I would manage it, I mean."

Laidie takes a deep breath. "I could take care of both Michael and Darren. I've often thought about how nice it would be for me to see them all the time. And you too." She takes off her glasses and holds them up to the light, looking for smudges. "You know that Mother left me the house and everything, but it was always her intention that I should pass it on to you someday." She returns the glasses to her nose. "I think she would have wanted you to have your inheritance when you really need it. The best way for me to give it to you is to share the house with you now."

"I couldn't let you do that, Laidie."

"I want to. Please."

"I have three weeks before I have to be out of the house. I need some time to get my affairs sorted out." She twists the diamond rings from her finger. "To see what's left, if anything."

"You could move back into your old room." Laidie's nurturing mode has leaped into overdrive. "There would be enough room for Michael there too, for a while. Darren can have the little back bedroom. I'd just have to clean some stuff out of there so he has some space to move."

"I'll have to think about it, Laidie. Moving back here is one thing, but having two boys here, and Michael just a baby…"

"Don't worry, Blythe. I've thought about all this many times before now. Everything will be all right." Laidie stands up. "I'll start cleaning the boxes and things out of the bedrooms this weekend. You can start bringing your things over whenever you're ready."

Blythe nods. There is really no time to think about it. No alternative. It will have to do, for now. But Blythe has no intention of making this a permanent arrangement. She prefers to keep some distance between herself and Laidie.

Darren helps Laidie and Blythe carry boxes from the downstairs bedrooms. "What's inside all these?" he wants to know.

"Mostly Gran and Gramps stuff," Laidie says. "Old books and magazines. Keepsakes and the like."

Blythe inspects the pile of cartons. "Why don't you get rid of some of this?"

Laidie shrugs. "I like to go through it from time to time." She changes the subject. "Can you help me with this mirror? It's not appropriate for a boy's room and I want to move it to my room. It's too heavy for me to manage by myself."

They lift the framed antique from the hangers on the wall and lay it face up on the bed. Blythe looks down into the mirror where her reflection seems to float on top of a deep pool. A light bulb shines up from the bottom of the pool, far below the surface.

"Did I ever tell you about Dream Lake, Laidie?"

"I don't think so. Where is that?"

"In Virginia. It was the same day Eddie made the deal on the race horses, when we were on our honeymoon. We went down in some underground caverns at a place called Luray. I didn't feel comfortable with the idea of going so deep down in the Earth with nothing but rock overhead, but he insisted. He was sort of making fun of me for being nervous. Once we got down there it wasn't all that bad because the caves were really big with high ceilings. And they were lit up, so you could see everything. There was a place that looked like a huge cathedral, with stalactites and stalagmites joined so they looked like pillars. There were even formations that looked like draped curtains, and columns that were named after gods, I can't remember the names. But the thing that stayed in my mind the most about those caverns was the lakes.

"There was one that looked like a shallow little fishpond, about five feet across. Eddie dropped a penny into it and it took a long time to sink to the bottom. The pool was actually eight or ten feet deep, but you couldn't tell. But the other lake was in a cavern with a high ceiling and the water covered the whole floor of the cave. When the guide turned the lights on, the ceiling was reflected in the water. The lake was completely motionless, no ripples or currents at all, and it was so still that it looked as deep as the ceiling was high. The whole cavern was a kind of dark golden colour, with some white streaks on the stalactites that were hanging above. When you looked down into the water, it was like looking down into a deep yellow lake with thin gold towers growing up from its bottom. The guide said it was called Dream Lake because it was an optical illusion. When you looked really closely at the water, you could tell that it was only a few inches deep. You could see the floor of the lake, right there under the surface. It was beautiful. It wasn't like anything I've ever seen in reality, but it was real. It just wasn't what it appeared to be." They each took an end of the mirror and carried it to Laidie's room. "After we passed through the cavern, the guide turned the lights off behind us. I remember thinking, Dream Lake is now just a flat puddle back there in the dark."

Blythe takes the flashy wedding and engagement rings, in their original blue boxes, to the jeweller. She intends to sell them. The jeweller squints through his magnifier. "Cubic zirconia," he smiles. "10 carat setting. You might get $150."

Chapter 44

Winnipeg, 1987

Blythe sits on the balcony of her apartment in the late sunshine of a long June day. Laidie's most personal effects cluster around her in boxes and bags. It is four months since Laidie's funeral but until today, Blythe has found this ultimate task of closure too painful to deal with.

The first box is filled with items from the cedar chest: photograph albums, a few books, a bag of newspaper clippings, old jewellery, and bundles of greeting cards. The newspaper clippings hold little relevance for Blythe and she sets them aside. The few books are literary classics like *Ivanhoe, The Picture of Dorian Gray,* and *A Tale of Two Cities*. The greeting cards encompass every occasion: birthdays, Christmases, thank you cards, invitations, and the like. There is even a small bundle of baby cards the Christies received when Laidie was born.

The ancient photograph albums are filled with black and white pictures mounted on black pages with little adhesive corners. Blythe has no idea of the identity of anyone in the photos. Tucked into the front of one of the albums is a fragile and aged account of Mhairi and Orville Christie's marriage in 1915.

Blythe fingers a small red velvet bag of jewellery (she has never seen this before) before she dumps it out on the table. The pieces are old and tarnished, none seemingly valuable. A tiny brass key tinkles to the floor.

And Blythe immediately remembers the locked birch bark box with the initial "L" on the hinged lid.

The brass key turns easily in the lock.

A small yellowed newspaper clipping from *The Winnipeg Tribune*, dated November 12, 1943, is the first item in the box. There is a ball-point note on the side margin. "This was for you, Blythe." Curious.

Winnipeg Man Found Dead, Police Search for Killer

Police were called yesterday morning to the scene of a murder on Hampton Street. The body of Mr. Orville Christie was discovered in front of his home by his daughter as she left for work. Mr. Christie had been stabbed three times, said Winnipeg Police Corporal Arthur Branson. It is thought that the crime probably took place sometime during the previous night as Mr. Christie had been dead for several hours. Robbery does not appear to have been a motive, as the victim's billfold was untouched in his pocket, said Branson. Family members indicated that Mr. Christie had been out that evening but they heard nothing unusual, and the front door was locked. Police believe Mr. Christie may have been followed and attacked as he returned home. There are no suspects, but the investigation is just beginning, Branson said. Anyone with information which may lead to an arrest is asked to call the Winnipeg Police Department.

Blythe remembers this event well, even though she was only ten at the time. No one ever discussed the murder, and the few times she asked questions about her father's death, Laidie made it clear there would be no answers. It was a locked door.

Blythe sets the clipping aside and continues with the contents of the box. Tucked in close to one side is a small yellowed envelope. Its folds show the wear of handling; of many openings and closings. The brittle paper tears when Blythe opens it and she feels a guilty sense of intrusion into Laidie's privacy. Something heavy wrapped in a brown handkerchief falls to the floor with a clunk. She unfolds the cloth to find a flat, round white stone with a small perfect hole in its centre. A narrow brown leather thong passes through the opening. A tiny handmade folded card of blue paper is tied to one end of the thong. On the inside of the card, an untidy rambling script reads, "Laidie from Joey, Love you forever."

A piece of heavy once-white paper, folded in quarters, is stuck inside the envelope and Blythe eases it out carefully. She stares at the document, trying to make sense of the words undulating before her eyes.

BIRTH CERTIFICATE. This certifies that Blythe Corrie Christie, Sex Female, was born to (Mother) Adelaide Mhairi Christie and (Father) Joey John McCorrie on the first day of May in the year 1932, at Radford Memorial Hospital, Radford, Ontario. The declaration is followed by the unreadable signature of a doctor.

How can this be possible? But the birthdate is correct. That is her name—Blythe Corrie Christie. How can she believe this? It must be a colossal mistake. There must be an explanation. She checks the envelope again. There is nothing else inside.

Wait. A small photograph. A black and white picture of Michael. Blythe has never seen it before. A picture of her own child that she has never seen? Michael, his trademark blond curls falling over his brow in their usual wayward confusion. The crooked smile curling up to his left cheek. The beautiful dark eyes twinkling with mischief. Blythe turns the photo over.

There she sees the same untidy script as on the little card attached to the leather thong.

Joey McCorrie, July, 1931. Millfield, Manitoba Love you forever.

The last trove to be explored is a large yellow plastic bag. Blythe recalls picking it up at the morgue before she went to Laidie's house. She dumps the contents on the table. The old checked bathrobe. One leather slipper. Dentures, eyeglasses, a silver ring. An envelope, postmarked only a week before Laidie's death. Blythe opens it.

A tiny newspaper clipping falls out. It is a very short obituary.

Joey John McCorrie, 1917-1987

Joe McCorrie of the Wolf River District passed away on November 16 at the age of 71. He was predeceased by his wife Gracie Marie and his parents Colin and Saharah McCorrie. Funeral service for Mr. McCorrie will be held at Dunham Funeral Home in Millfield, Wednesday, November 18 at 2:00 PM.

Chapter 45

Winnipeg, 1987

Michael's long blond hair hangs down to his shoulders, hiding an earring that Blythe abhors but tolerates. The two of them sit in the shade on the balcony of the apartment overlooking Portage Avenue. She smiles at him.

We've always been so close to each other. I've never thought of Michael as Eddie's kid. Just mine and Laidie's.

"So what is it you have to tell me, Mom?"

She hesitates, taking in the faded blue jeans and too-big T-shirt and dilapidated sneakers. *You'd never know he was a bright university student. He looks more like a refugee.*

"I want to show you something." She empties the contents of a brown envelope on the table between them. Papers, mostly. Pictures. Something on a leather thong.

"Hey. This looks important."

He picks up the thong with its stone; a smooth white oval with a hole in its centre.

"Cool." He slips the leather circlet over his head. The white stone rests on his chest. "Where'd you get this?"

"It was in one of Laidie's boxes. Along with this." She hands him a folded document.

Michael has never seen a birth certificate like this. His own is just a small plastic wallet card; this is heavy paper, and large. He scans it, nonchalantly at first, then intently, with eyes squinting in disbelief.

"Mom. Where did you get this?"

"Like I said, it was in one of Laidie's boxes."

"Blythe Corrie Christie. That was you."

"That *is* me."

He struggles to absorb the information. "Who the fuck is Joey John McCorrie?"

"He was my father. I never knew."

"And this means that Auntie Laidie was…"

"Yes. She was my mother."

"I don't get it. How could you go all this time and never know? Why wouldn't Auntie Laidie… Holy crap. She was my grandmother?"

Laidie hands him a small snapshot.

"Shit. This looks like me. Even the long hair. Who is this dude?"

"That's Joey John McCorrie. My father. Your grandfather."

"You mean this guy and Auntie Laidie, they… Shit. He doesn't even look as old as I am."

"He wasn't." She passes the newspaper obituary across the table. "He died last November, just a few weeks before Laidie. According to the obituary he was just a year older than she was. So when I was born they would have only been 15 and 16."

"Man. I still don't get it. Why the big secret?"

"Things were a lot different back then, Michael. It would have been a terrible scandal to have an illegitimate baby. I guess my parents…my grandparents…thought it was the only way they could do things."

"Do things? Like what?"

"They pretended to be my parents. That way Laidie could keep me without humiliating the family."

Michael studies the little photograph. He flips it over. Boyish handwriting. *Joey McCorrie July, 1931. Millfield, Manitoba. Love you forever.*

"This was attached to the white stone." She hands him a small blue card with the same script, *Laidie from Joey, Love you forever.*

"It even looks like my writing." Michael spreads the array of information on the table. "Have you told Darren?"

"Not yet. There's more."

"What the fuck more could there be?"

"I got this in the mail yesterday." She passes it to him. "It's a letter from a law firm in Millfield. Joey John McCorrie left everything to Laidie when he died."

"But she's dead too. So what does this mean?"

"Laidie left everything to me and you two boys. So it means that the McCorrie property now goes to us. It'll just take a while for the lawyers to get everything sorted out."

Michael fingers the white stone and the leather thong.

"Can I keep this, Mom?"

"Not right now. Someday."

Chapter 46

Wolf River, 1988

Wolf River Acres was always a good farm. Its land is more than a conglomerate of weathered rock particles and decayed organic matter; it is a living entity. It moves with the myriad life forms within it, and it nurses the foundation of existence. It connects the past to the present, and the present to the future. The black loam, deep and rich and picked clean of stones, has survived the abuses of drought, flooding and humanity, and lies in wait for another season. Windbreaks of tall caragana cross the headlands and a few shallow drainage channels lead from sloughs to ditches. The river meanders its historic channel through the section, and stands of river bottom forest, much of it new generation, line the banks as they did at the turn of the century and before. On the low-lying eastern side of the farm a little meadow spreads like a peaceful green lake within its boundaries of poplar and cottonwood.

Blythe and her two sons wander about, surveying their property.

A few tufts of scrubby faded grass cling tenaciously to life in the gravelly soil by the steps at the back door of the house. Little scabs of yellow paint cling to the weathered board siding and the crooked porch portends collapse with the first gust of wind. An old doghouse, its doorway clogged with weeds, sags against the south wall of the house. Near the decayed remains of a woodpile, a ruined clothesline disappears into the tall grass and rotted clothespins cling to the tangled wire like gangly broken insects. The barn, still square and straight, is the best building on the place. Its loft seems to have eyes set deep in its upper shadows to oversee the yard, the grain bins, the slumping chicken shed, and the bleak grey house with its sagging weathervane. A decrepit fence outlines the boundaries of the yard, its decaying posts leaning and veering like a parade of drunks trying to walk a straight line.

The house is another story; a trip backwards in time. Since Joe McCorrie's death last November it has been locked; nearly seven months now. Humid fusty air, almost visible with its weight, rolls out the opened door. Inside is a disaster of poverty, of things undone and uncleaned. Faded vestiges of long ago comfort and warmth hint from the peeling wallpaper and sun-rotted curtains. But unlike the land, the house is not capable of regeneration. Any life it may have once extracted from its dwellers is extinct.

Trash litters the kitchen, which is large enough to park a truck in with room to spare. All downstairs rooms open off this once-centre of farm life: two bedrooms, a darkly curtained living room, a small wash-up room by the back door. Blythe picks her way through piles of paper and tin cans and dirty farm boots. Loose linoleum tiles crack and shift beneath her feet and dust lifts its motes into the light from the open door. In what must have been the master bedroom, clothing and papers lie everywhere. The dresser lazes under a dusty litter of books and small bottles and containers. Blythe wipes a grey layer from a small dusty photograph. It appears to be a wedding picture. She keeps it. Next to the largest bedroom another door hangs open leading to a dark wood stairway. She hesitates and decides to climb the narrow steps. Only one of the three bedrooms upstairs looks as if it has ever been used, the other two hold only a few boxes and some broken furniture. Mouse droppings are everywhere. Downstairs, Darren and Michael check the cupboards and pantry as if half expecting to find food. They descend to the small cinder block basement where dim light filters in through a narrow foundation window. Rows of dust-laden jars of preserves stand in tidy rows on wooden shelves. Hand-printed labels still adhere to the jars. The dates are all 1949.

Blythe comes downstairs. "Well? Have we seen enough?"

On their way out the back door she stops to examine a large faded piece of paper tacked to the wall. Under the age-yellowed surface, a notated map of the farm struggles to be seen. Close to one edge of the map Blythe can make out the words, *Flax this yr. summer-fallow*. Just above the map she notices a small framed charcoal sketch of two wolves with yellow eyes. There is something familiar about it; something she can't quite pin down. She removes the picture and shoves it into her purse along with the wedding photo.

"There's nothing here that we need that can't be fixed," says Darren. "The barn's in pretty good shape. The fences'll have to be rebuilt from scratch but I think we can handle that."

"We can just bulldoze the other old buildings," says Michael. "It'll be perfect."

"It's too bad about the house," their mother muses. "There must be a lot of history there."

Summer, 1989. Wolf River Stables is up and running. A tall cedar house faces the road, its wide windows mirroring the fields, and a large white mobile home nestles a little behind it close to a grove of oak trees. A new doghouse accommodates Hampton, the hyper-crazy Border collie. The barn is clean and repaired and painted, and straight white fences march around the property. A newly-dug well dips into the wide aquifer beneath the land and a humming windmill keeps water troughs full for the horses. The farmer who rented and cared for the land for the past fifteen years has renewed his lease and at the same time agreed to relinquish a quarter section back to the new owners to be used for pasture and a training track. Several spirited horses cavort in the fenced field. The little meadow down by the cottonwoods is busy producing a field of sweet hay.

Blythe sits on the deck of her mobile home. She watches Darren and Michael come from the barn to the house they share. She is in awe of the perfect confluence of events that has placed her family here. In this place, upon this piece of land, everything is clear and relieved of weight. This point in time and space is a magnet, at last pulling together the shimmering sad bits and pieces of the past into a final reality. Eventually, what is left must be the truth, dark and shiny and astonishing.

She goes indoors to make tea.

Epilogue

1989

The first day of October settles in with wind and cold rain by evening. Blythe puts her supper dishes in the dishwasher and starts the cycle. One of her favorite movies is on TV tonight, again. She cuddles into the comfort of one of Mhairi's old crocheted afghans and tunes in the channel. Five minutes until show time.

The knock at the door is muffled by driving rain. It comes again, louder and sharper. Blythe throws off the afghan and shuffles to the door. An elderly woman in a sagging black jacket stands on the doorstep under a huge red umbrella.

"Are you Blythe?"

"Yes, I am. And you are…?"

"I am Edina Popham. I've been wanting to come and visit with you ever since you moved in."

Blythe looks past Edina Popham into the inclement night. A small dark car sits on the lane. *You picked quite a night, old lady.* She holds the door open and takes the red umbrella.

"Well. Come in then, Mrs. Popham."

"It's Miss Popham."

"All right. Miss Popham." Blythe takes the black jacket, sopping in spite of the umbrella, and hangs it on the coat tree. "Have a seat. Can I get you a cup of tea?"

"That would be lovely." The old woman settles herself into the chair opposite Blythe. She gets right to the point. "I suppose you must be curious about your families?"

Blythe sees the TV movie in her peripheral vision. "I don't follow."

"I knew them all. All the tragedies. Everything that happened to bring you and your boys to Wolf River."

Blythe brings the teapot and two china cups into the living room on a wooden tray, along with cream and sugar and teaspoons and a plate of oatmeal cookies. She pours the tea and passes the first cup to the elderly woman. Blythe turns off the television. Edina Popham pulls her dark brows together and takes a deep breath.

"I was the schoolteacher at Wolf River School. Your mother Laidie was only fourteen when the Christies moved here from Ontario. A lovely girl. Everybody loved her. Joey McCorrie most of all. The two of them didn't think I knew, of course, but seeing them together at school every day, I could tell. It was the second summer the Christies were here, the two of them couldn't be separated. Poor Laidie, she had to go to all kinds of trouble to get out of their house. Her father Orville was a cruel man and had to control everyone completely. Her mother, her name was Mary, I think, was afraid to stand up to him. They were your grandparents. Mary hid her bruises most of the time, but everyone knew Orville was beating her. I wondered about Laidie, but it didn't seem as if she was being abused.

"I knew Laidie was going to have a baby the day she came back to school the second fall they were here. Probably even before she knew herself. I don't know, there was just something different about her. She seemed older and was certainly wiser. She and Gracie Marie Martens spent hours whispering and talking and giggling when they weren't working. I've often wondered whether she told Gracie Marie what was going on. I could see that Gracie wanted Joey too, but that was a well-kept secret on Gracie's part.

"Everything came to a head right after Thanksgiving. Laidie missed a week of school—that was unheard of for her. She showed up one day just as classes were done for the day to pick up her belongings. I could tell she had been crying. Her face was red and swollen and I could see bruises on her arms. But she wouldn't talk to me. She just grabbed her books and rushed outside with Gracie Marie. The next week I got a letter from her mother asking me to mail transfer papers for a school in Winnipeg. I was probably the only person who knew where she went. That's the last anyone saw of her."

Edina pauses for a refill of tea and helps herself to another oatmeal cookie. She tucks a loose salt-and-pepper strand into the braided roll at the back of her neck.

"But that wasn't the end of things for Joey McCorrie. He was devastated. He came around the school trying to find out where Laidie was, but I couldn't tell him, of course. Oh, I wanted to. It was all I could do to keep it to myself. I think he knew that I knew where she was. He never spoke to me again. And he never knew about the baby.

"And that was when the Depression was starting. Everyone worked so hard and for what? Nothing. Your great-grandfather Ford McCorrie died of a heart attack and the next year Gracie Marie's father froze to death in a blizzard. That was when Colin and Joey had Gracie come to be a live-in housekeeper. That same year Colin came down with dust pneumonia and he died too." Edina Popham's voice is suddenly husky. "Colin…" She pauses for a moment. "It was just one tragedy after another after another. Joey and Gracie Marie got married the next spring—they were living together by then anyway. Gracie loved Joey as much as Joey loved Laidie. Joey didn't realize it, but he could never have managed without Gracie. She was the fuel in the fire, smart, and worked her fingers to the bone. It was so sad when she died. Polio, right when the 1950's outbreaks were starting. She was only sick for a week or so. Joey had her buried with her parents. There was a lot of talk about that at the time. Everyone thought Gracie should have been buried in the McCorrie plot, but I think that somewhere in Joey's mind he still had the thought that he was saving that place for Laidie.

"That was the beginning of the end for Joey. A long, drawn-out end. Maybe he really did love Gracie and just didn't know it, because after she died he just stopped trying and let everything go to wrack and ruin."

Edina adjusts her bifocals and takes another cookie. There is one more thing.

"You know, I saw you when you came to Millfield that time to get Laidie. What was that, close to twenty-five years ago? I knew it was Laidie as soon as I saw her out on that road; that beautiful dark red hair. I don't think she recognized me. I gave her directions to the McCorrie house, but I guess when she got there Joey wasn't home. The next thing I heard, the police brought her up from the river the next day. I made a big mistake. I should have told her who I was; I should have talked to her. I have never been able to get that out of my mind. I could have helped both of them. They could have been together.

"I thought long and hard before I sent her the newspaper clipping about his death. I just thought she deserved to know, after all those years."

Blythe swallows hard on the lump invading her throat.

"What happened to him?"

"Heart attack, they said. The mail man found him in the barn, went looking for him when his mail wasn't picked up from his mailbox for over a week."

"How did you know where to send the clipping?"

"Believe it or not, I still had the address that Laidie's mother gave me to forward the school transfer papers to. It was the same as an address in the Winnipeg telephone book for an A Christie. Imagine. After all those years, the same address."

"I want to show you something." Blythe slides a small birch bark box from the shelf beside the TV set. "This is all I have to connect to those years." She spreads the contents on the coffee table. There are three sketches: one of Mhairi, from Mac Ward's belongings, one of a young girl with violet-colored eyes (that's Gracie Marie, Edina Popham says), and a larger framed sketch of a pair of wolves, these with brilliant yellow eyes. In the bottom of each sketch are the flowing initials, LC. A birch bark bracelet, penciled on the inside with "Love you forever." A faded snapshot of a teenage boy. On a leather thong, a round white stone with a hole in its centre.

The rain has stopped. Edina Popham stands up and collects her red umbrella.

"Yes," she says. "I knew them all."

Bibliography

Anderson, Allan Remembering *the Farm* pub MacMillan of Canada 1978

Cartwright and District History Committee, *Memories Along the Badger Revisited* pub Friesen Printers, 1985

Gray, James H. *The Winter Years* pub MacMillan of Canada 1966

Marriott, Anne The Wind Our Enemy, 1939

Proctor, Madeline L. Bonnie Doon Fire, *Woodlands Echoes* pub Derksen Printers Ltd. 1960

Langrell, Opal, and Committee, Tween *Meadow and Meridian* pub Interlake Graphics 1985

Salt Lake Telegram, Salt Lake City, UT 21 Jul 1903
Isla WY Crushed by Hay Rake, Jul 1903

Stark, Peter The Cold Hard Facts of Freezing to Death, *Outside Magazine* January 1997

Wikipedia.com, Canadian Wheat Board

livinghistoryfarm.org

torontothenandnow.blogspot.ca

rootsweb.ancestry.com